my
throat
an open
grave

my
throat
an open
grave

TORI BOVALINO

PAGE STREET YA

PAGE STREET YA

First published in 2024 by
Page Street Publishing Co.
27 Congress Street, Suite 1511
Salem, MA 01970
www.pagestreetpublishing.com

The passage from Rainier Maria Rilke's poem "Orpheus, Eurydice, Hermes,"
as translated by Franz Wright, first appeared in *The Unknown Rilke:
Expanded Edition* (Oberlin College Press, copyright © 1990 by Oberlin
College), and is reprinted by permission of Oberlin College Press.

Distributed by Macmillan, sales in Canada by The Canadian Manda Group.

28   27   26   25   24   1   2   3   4   5

ISBN-13: 978-1-64567-930-1
ISBN-10: 1-64567-930-6
Library of Congress Control Number: 2023936744

Cover and book design by Rosie Stewart for Page Street Publishing Co.
Cover illustration © Tristan Elwell

Printed and bound in the United States

For the girls who can never quite be good enough.

CONTENT WARNINGS

Blood, gore, death, animal death (deer),
animal gore (deer), body horror, suicidal ideation

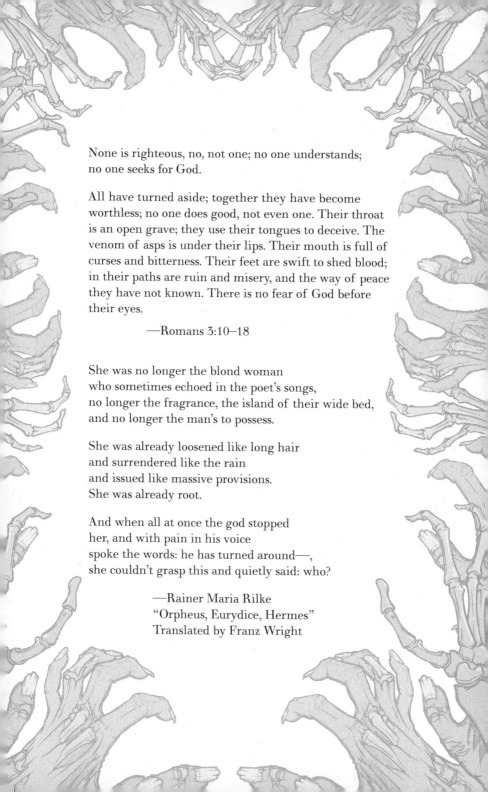

None is righteous, no, not one; no one understands;
no one seeks for God.

All have turned aside; together they have become
worthless; no one does good, not even one. Their throat
is an open grave; they use their tongues to deceive. The
venom of asps is under their lips. Their mouth is full of
curses and bitterness. Their feet are swift to shed blood;
in their paths are ruin and misery, and the way of peace
they have not known. There is no fear of God before
their eyes.

     —Romans 3:10–18

She was no longer the blond woman
who sometimes echoed in the poet's songs,
no longer the fragrance, the island of their wide bed,
and no longer the man's to possess.

She was already loosened like long hair
and surrendered like the rain
and issued like massive provisions.
She was already root.

And when all at once the god stopped
her, and with pain in his voice
spoke the words: he has turned around—,
she couldn't grasp this and quietly said: who?

     —Rainer Maria Rilke
     "Orpheus, Eurydice, Hermes"
     Translated by Franz Wright

One

When I think of purity, I don't think of the water that runs in the river past our backyard, or the water in the baptism font at the front of the church, where my mother and father and their mothers and fathers were baptized, all the way back; where I was baptized too. I don't think of the clean white sheets on my bed or the innocent face Owen has when he's drifting off to sleep. When I think of purity, I think of the bathtub; of cramming myself all the way in, all the way to the bottom, of squinching my eyes shut and opening my mouth and letting the water run in to clean me from the inside out. I think of screaming—but even more often, I think of inhaling. Letting go.

I haven't let myself think about it too much, not since last year, when the slope was too slippery and I was in danger of falling. Now, the last breath of summer is hot on my cheek through the window of my history class, and there's a fly buzzing against the glass, and for the first time in a while, I again find myself thinking of drowning.

The thought is interrupted by a paper slipped under my arm, onto my desk. I peek down. It's from Jess, the only one who I'm back on regular terms with again. Few others were so keen to take me back in after last year, when I was pulled out for home-schooling; but it didn't take my parents long to give up on the institution of homeschooling entirely and throw me back in among the other kids my age.

River? the note reads. I glance up at the clock. It's a quarter after two, with only fifteen minutes left in the school day. But there's work to do at home, dishes to wash, and endless piles of laundry to sort through, and Mom's shift starts at 4:30 so I need to get home to take care of Owen. But even so, I nod, just enough so she can see. An hour won't change the world—nor will it set me back too much.

A new school year. A new start. A new chance to prove that I'm normal, whole, acceptable to be friends with.

When the bell rings, I drape my bag over my back and wait for Jess to put her notes and folders into her backpack. Even though it's only September, even though more kids here drop out than go to college, Jess has her heart set on New York. She's the only one in history class still taking notes, the scratching of her pen on her paper, the backing track to Mr. Cary's droning voice recounting the Battle of Gettysburg for the fifteenth time.

I don't comment on her notes like some of the other kids do.

If she wants to get out of here, escape Carver County and wash the Appalachian dirt from her skin until it burns, leave this nook of Pennsylvania behind until she forgets all of our names, I can't blame her.

Unlike the rest of us, she has a way out. A plan.

I follow Jess to her locker. I don't have anything to put in mine—I gave up taking notes and bringing my books around during the first week of school, right around the time Pete Majors overdosed and the teachers stopped looking us too closely in the eye. We're seventeen. Basically adults. Should be able to get our own lives together, if we want.

She switches out her books and grabs a jacket, rambling about how she's going to homecoming in the next town over with one of the boys from their football team. Jess and I have been friends since we were babies, just about—our moms have always worked at the diner, sticking us in a booth in the back to be quiet when they had the same shift, and dropping us at one another's houses when they worked opposite shifts. Jess's face, her brown eyes and dark skin and curly black hair, are all as familiar to me as my own.

"Are you going to homecoming? Here, or at MV, or Uniontown?" Jess asks.

I shrug. "Probably not. Don't know anyone," I say.

"I can get you a date," Jess says, shooting me a sneaky look under her eyelashes. We don't talk publicly about how I dropped off the calendar, stopped going to football games and driving to the next town over with her and a couple of other kids to see the movies. How I vanished for the entirety of last summer and our junior year, only to reappear like everything was normal on the first day back. It wasn't like I shut out everyone—Jess *did* see me, after all, even when I didn't want her to, but nobody else has. She knows I'm testy about that.

"I'm okay," I say, feigning a smile. "You know how shifts are. It's impossible for me to get a weekend off."

Jess shrugs, possibly because it's a lie and she can see right through it. Right through *me*. I've been working at the gas station in our town since I turned fifteen, and though I'm sure Hank would cover a shift if I wanted him to, I don't want to ask.

I go with her to her rusted out pickup truck, listening half-heartedly as she describes her homecoming dress and scrolls through pictures of it on her phone. She's talking to this guy, and I think he's nice enough—she's brought him by the gas station for slurpies on a few of my shifts—but my stomach is still tangled up in knots. I want to warn her, to tell her, to grip her face in my hands and press my thumbs into her cheekbones and scream until I can't breathe anymore.

But I don't. I get into the passenger seat, and when Jess goes through the drive-through at McDonald's she gets herself a Sprite and me a Coke and a large fry for us to split, and I try to find words to say to her as she drives the quick five-minute trek to the park by the river. There, we settle on a log and drink our pops and watch the Youghiogheny rush by.

There's a peace here, on the river, with the sound of it drowning out everything else. It's like we sang in music class, when we were little: *Take me to the water, take me to the water, take me to the water, to be baptized.*

Intrusive thoughts always seem to find me here: I wonder what Jess would do if I slipped off the log, down the muddy slope, and slunk away into the rushing river.

"Where would you go if you left Winston?" Jess asks. It's a game we play, a twist of make-believe.

"New Orleans," I say this time. That's the trick—a different place every time. We pretend there's the option of escape from this town.

Jess snorts. "Why?"

I nod to the woods, spreading out endlessly across the river from us. "Different set of ghosts, I guess."

That makes Jess choke on her Sprite. "You shouldn't say things like that."

I shrug, but she's smiling now, and I feel the corner of my mouth turn up even as the lump in my throat grows harder. "What's *he* going to do? Eat me?"

It's a front. It's easier to pretend to *not* believe than to acknowledge there might be yet another deity out there that doesn't care. And Jess of all people, who knows me better than I know myself, snorts. "He could, you know. They all could. Who knows what they're capable of."

"The Lord of the Wood?"

"Of course. And everything else in there."

I take a long draw of my Coke and shove a fry in my mouth to hide anything else my expression tries to do. Jess isn't good with silence, isn't good at feeling like she's wrong. But also—she knows me. She knows I believe in him with my entire crumpled, little heart, no matter how much I deny it. You can't disbelieve something that patently exists.

"Cassie Lewis says she's seen him. Recently."

"Mmm." So have I, but I don't go around gossiping about it. Fundamentally, it doesn't matter if the Lord is real or not: All he does is lurk in the woods and steal kids when it suits his needs. But that hasn't happened in years, not since Maria.

"Surrounded by wraiths. Just across the river when she was up here, parking with Trent McCoy."

"Did they . . . ?" I ask, caught by something else in that statement, my throat feeling even worse, more constricted.

"What? Cassie? No. Never." She takes another sip, the ice rattling in her cup. "But the LoW," she says, slipping into the nickname we used to use for him when we were kids. "Don't laugh at me, but . . . I think he's coming back. Coming closer. Choosing his next target. People have seen him lately."

"Like who?"

"The night before Pete Majors had the fentanyl incident, they say he saw them too. Covered in blood, chewing on a deer heart in a clearing off the access path near the Grady's."

This time, I nearly choke. "You've got to be kidding me."

"Well, it's not like we can ask him. And I believe what he said—he told me himself, at the party right before . . ." She swallows hard, then takes another sip. But I know what she means. He wasn't the first person in our in our class to die, and he probably, terribly, won't be the last.

"How was he sure it was the LoW?" I ask.

"Glowing eyes," Jess says. I stare into the river, watching the water rush over the rocks. About fifteen minutes away, the Yough turns into a popular white water tract, split into three sections. Jess and I have done it before, gone through the Middle Yough in bright yellow ducky boats, sunning ourselves on the hot vinyl with the oars resting over our hips on the lulls where there was no white water. I wish we could do that again, careless, our fingers trailing through the water as we hold on to one another's boats with our other hands, as we talk about nothing.

"It's been years since Maria was taken," Jess says, swirling the ice in her Sprite. It crunches, over-loud, a human noise amidst all the nature. "Maybe he's hungry again."

It's a fear that I can't bear to examine. Not knowing what I know—not being who I am. Jess and I were at an impressionable age when the last baby was taken, when the last girl went missing;

we were nearly teenagers, right at the time when the warnings about the Lord grew louder and more frequent. The memory comes of that hot, sticky night that bled into an even hotter morning, summer in full bloom—I woke up to find Grammy sitting at the kitchen table with one of her paperback mystery novels, bleary, earlier than usual. *Where's Mom?* I'd asked, and she just shook her head, lips pressed tight, folding down the corner to mark her page. *Nowhere you want to be,* she'd told me. When she kissed my forehead, she said, *You watch yourself, Leah. Don't let yourself fall. Keep steady—he'll know if you aren't. He'll know, and he'll catch you, and once you're caught, there's no turning back. Keep up your prayers. Pray for that girl, and that baby, and pray for yourself.*

I try, desperately, to sound mocking and lighthearted. "Have you seen the LoW?" I ask her. "You live near the woods."

She snorts, but her fingers go instinctively to the dainty gold cross she wears around her neck like a charm of protection. "*Everyone* lives near the woods." She's right, but unlike Jess, I don't spend my free time gazing through the trees, searching for ghosts. I have other things to worry about.

Perhaps if she says yes . . . if she's seen those eyes . . . maybe I would've told her of the shadow in the woods, lurking at the edge of the tree line. But even thinking of it makes my palms sweat, my stomach clench.

"No," Jess says finally. "I've never seen him. You really don't believe in him? Even with all the evidence? All the things he's done?"

I shake my head because, for the moment, my throat is too tight for words. Somehow, this is what we always end up on, no matter how little time has passed since the last time we deconstructed his existence: the Lord of the Wood, who we've been taught to fear. When I was a little girl, Grammy and Mom spoke of him in hushed whispers and threats of warning.

I didn't believe her then, not really. Not until I was on the edge of thirteen, a girl at risk—but not the girl he chose.

In Winston, we're taught to go to church every Sunday, to pray for our own souls, to do what is right and good and holy. And in Winston, we know that if we do not obey, there are worse things than death: The Lord of the Wood will catch us if we stray. His shadow is there in the spaces between the trees; his terrible amber eyes watch us all from just across the river, waiting for us to slip.

It's the threat hanging over all of us. He likes girls from our village, likes the ones who are wicked. Likes to lure them in by taking kids, stealing away the ones we can't live without. Perhaps, I usually think, when I talk of this with Jess . . . perhaps I should be more afraid.

"Do you ever wonder," Jess asks, very quietly, "about Maria?"

I swallow hard. Maria Sinclair, the last girl he led astray. I remember her, mostly in flashes: her pin-straight dark hair in two thick braids; the bright white smile of her school picture that her aunt from out of town insisted on hanging around, on missing posters; Maria from down the street, wheeling her bike up the drive, nodding to Jess and me sunbathing in the front yard.

Jess knew her better. I barely knew her at all, and then she was gone, and everyone knew the absence of her better than anything.

"No," I say.

Jess is unconvinced. She looks off into nothing, past the river, into the murky shadows of the wood, and I cannot have this conversation.

Stalling, I check my phone and find that it's nearly four. "I should go," I say. "Owen duty."

Jess wrinkles her nose, but she gets up. I don't have a car, and I live slightly too far away to walk. If I don't have Jess to drive me, I usually take my bike, and I left it at home this morning. It was raining, so Mom dropped me off.

"I'm so glad I'm an only child," she says.

"Jealous."

We don't resume our conversation about the Lord of the Wood when we're on the winding road that passes through town, then follows the river to my house. I almost tell her I believe in him too, drop the posturing and spill it all. But I don't. I don't tell her that I think I've seen the LoW myself, with his glowing amber eyes peeking through the trees. Many times, probably, in the shadow of the wood near my house in the briefest span of twilight, or in the curve of the road that follows the forest when we take the turns too fast, or even in my dreams.

I don't fear him, either. The Lord of the Wood, his servants and his wraiths, whatever ghosts people think live in the woods on the other side of the river—I don't care about them. I don't have the time. And maybe that marks me as an adult, a permanent resident of Winston, born here and destined to die here. Maybe the LoW appears to everyone—and maybe, it's only the ones who care about seeing him who can't hack it here, the ones who leave.

If I don't believe in him, he can't be real. If I don't believe in him, I might be safe. If I don't believe in him—

Outside my house, Jess hesitates, hands on the wheel, eyes on the road, like we're not pulled over. "I think of them all the time," she says finally.

"Who?"

"The girls."

There's a pause, a beat, and I—I almost ask. Her hand moves, going to that cross again, and she worries her lip with her teeth. My hands are clenched into fists, knuckles white, nails digging into the meat of my palms. I don't know why she keeps bringing this up—I don't know why she can't let it go.

"I think of him," I say, and it's the first honest thing I've said all afternoon.

Jess laughs, the sound short and hollow. "I thought you didn't believe in him."

But when I reach out, her hand is there ready to catch mine, and she squeezes so tight I feel my knuckles creak.

Of course I believe in him. And whatever she feels—I feel it too. A looming dread, a crackle of static in the air, like we're all waiting for the storm to descend.

Mom's not happy when I come in and ditch my backpack near the front door. She's pacing back and forth with Owen fussing in her arms, never fully frowning when she holds him, never fully able to be angry. She's been wanting Owen ever since I was little. A whole slew of kids that never came. She always wanted a big family, but instead, she just got the two of us.

"I'll put him down, but I've got to go," Mom snaps, barely looking at me. It's 4:15, sure, but the diner is five minutes down the road, and I don't remember the last time I went somewhere after school.

"That's fine," I say. "I'll feed him in a bit."

"You should've called if you were running late."

"I'm sorry," I say, going to the kitchen and searching for formula. There's not much left in the tin, but it's not like I can go out and get more—the small store in town is a thirty-minute walk, and I'm not putting Owen in a stroller and dragging him down the winding, sidewalk-less road. I'm too paranoid for that.

If anything happens to Owen on my watch, Mom will kill me. "We're low on formula," I call to her.

"Right, because I don't have eyes," she says. "I hope your brother grows up to be just as smart as you."

I wince, but let it go. It's not worth pushing, not worth fighting. Mom brushes past me in her blue skirt and white uniform blouse. I watch her back as she disappears down the hallway to Owen's room. While she struggles to get him to sleep, I gather up the discarded bottles from the living room and kitchen and wash them one by one. She leaves Owen's door cracked when she comes back out.

"I'll be home late," she says quietly. "Need to stay to close."

"No worries."

"Make sure he sleeps."

"I will."

"And eats."

"Of course."

"And don't you dare go out or have anyone over," she says, pulling on her shoes. "I don't have time to clean up after you, Leah."

"Right."

With that, she's out the door, and I hear her noisy, old Toyota start up in the drive. I stare straight ahead at the window over the sink, the window that faces out over the river, out at the wood. I take deep breaths. I listen. After I feel like my heart is no longer self-destructing, I get started on the dishes.

Two

My brother Owen is nine months old. He was born in December, the night before the shortest day of the year, coming into the world with a full head of hair and ice-blue eyes and a voice he hasn't stopped using since. An hour after I get home, when I've finished the dishes and I'm halfway through folding onesies and burping cloths and matching up tiny socks, he shouts from his room.

I swallow hard. But unlike a grown person, this call cannot be denied.

I go in and peer into his crib. He's squalling, his little face red and wrinkled, his hands mashed into fists that he waves into the air. I take a deep breath—I don't know what to do with him, how to hold him, how to calm him, even though he's alone with me just as much as he is with Mom, and far more than he is with Dad. But I grit my teeth, gather my nerves, and reach into the crib. He's heavy, heavy and squirmy and hot. He does not go easily against my shoulder, but instead scratches at my face and pounds on my shoulder with his tiny hands and nails.

"I know, I know," I murmur against his sweaty head. "I wouldn't wake up either, if I didn't have to."

He does not listen to me, nor understand. He just yells and yells and yells.

I do everything I can think of: stroke his hair and change his diaper, feed him half a bottle, rock him in the chair in the corner of the living room, even though I get queasy with the press of his warm skin against mine. But nothing happens. It's as if he knows I'm not Mom, knows I have no idea about any of this. Sometimes, in the dark of the night, when I'm in my room next to his and he's screaming like this, I wonder if he hates me even though he's not old enough to feel anything like hatred. I wonder if he'll grow up scowling at me, if he'll speak to me like Mom does, with derision and cruelty, as soon as he learns how to walk.

"I'm trying," I say to no one.

Soon enough, I can't take it. I put him in his Pack 'n Play in the corner of the room where he sits and screams and yells. Mom has taken him to the doctor so many times, even though we don't have the insurance to pay for visits like that—but if the baby needs something, Mom makes whatever sacrifices she needs to. I guess that's what it is to be a good mother.

But there's nothing wrong with him. Maybe he just hates me,

hates us, hates the fact that we brought him into this world and kept him.

I try and read a book, an old, cozy mystery from the collec tion Grammy left me when she died, but it's impossible. I even try to go through some of my English book, or watch a cooking show, but nothing can drown him out. I go to the kitchen and fix another bottle.

When I look up, I swear I catch a flash of amber across the river, just from the edge of the trees. It's probably a deer, or a fox, or even a charm hanging from a tree. It's probably not him, the Lord of the Wood, the name they whisper in town with even more reverence and fear than the name of God.

It's defiance alone that keeps me at the window, staring out with a glare that I hope would frighten even a deity away. He's taken from Winston many times before, but I can't find it within myself to care. The Lord has never hurt nor helped me, so I don't have the time to spare worrying about him.

If he's not real, he can't—

The particle board underside of the counter gives when I dig my nails in, stopping the thought in its tracks. I wish I had some name, some religion that I believed could save me. I wish I could look to the stars and whisper the name of my own personal god and be whisked away somewhere new, somewhere that didn't hurt so much.

But I can't, and it doesn't matter if the LoW exists if he only lurks in the forest and lives on in bad memories and folklore, and in the *real* world, Owen is still crying. He takes his bottle as reluctantly as he does anything else, and by the time the sky turns red with the light of the dying sun, he is fussily closing his eyes in that sleepy way that signals bedtime.

I bathe him and dress him, touching him always but as little as possible. I dress him in a brown sleep sack with little bear ears, even though one ear is hanging by a thread. When he's cuter, it's easier to handle him.

He starts crying again in earnest the second I lay him down. But now, I can deal with it—we have a routine, one full hour of the day when I can understand him, when he can't hate me with his scrunched face and tiny punching fists. I open the window to let in the cool air and settle in front of the little electric keyboard piano.

This room used to be mine, before I moved into the one next to it, barely bigger than a closet. There was no space for my keyboard, so it lived here, and I was practicing very quietly one night when Owen was three months old, and he just went quiet behind me—then, I realized how easily he fell asleep, with the sound of me playing. After that, it became a ritual, the only thing I could conclusively get to work—but only in the hours when night is falling, only in the dim haze of twilight.

I turn the volume down and begin to play. Immediately, Owen quiets, his cries turning to small squeaks, then eventually, to silence.

I run through scales, through arpeggios, through a nocturne that I knew fully once. I started playing piano when I was in kindergarten, back when Dad had a job at the mill before it shut down for good. Before he took the trucking job that kept him from home for weeks on end, with only a scant word between assignments.

I play even when I'm sure Owen's asleep. I used to sing, too, before Owen was born. Look up chords to any song I heard on the radio, figure it all out, play like it was the only thing that could get me out of Winston. And maybe it could—I was good. But I don't sing anymore. I'm too tired.

These hours, when Owen is finally asleep and I can let go of the feeling that he hates me, when we can coexist, are my favorites. I can play piano, the muscle memory coming back with every chord, until it's all a wash of music. Until everything else fades away.

Sometimes, I play until Mom comes home and she catches me here and scolds me. She thinks I'll wake the baby up. But truthfully, I think my playing is the only thing that keeps him sleeping most nights.

Not tonight. My heart feels odd and heavy. I think again about what I talked about with Jess at the riverside. She'd said Cassie Lewis was out with Trent McCoy, just as casually as it was nothing, and I'd let it slip by as if it *was* nothing. But I remember when I was the one out with Trent.

It started with a flirtation over winter break a few years back, going to his basketball games with his jersey number written on my cheek in black face paint. That was all it should've been—a flirtation, and maybe a kiss at a party. It shouldn't have extended to the river, to his car. When I close my eyes, I can recall how his leather seats smelled of peppermint.

I don't want to remember any more. Anything else is jagged, too much, a reminder that Trent cast me off just like everyone else. I was just a girl whom he could waste his time on before moving on to the next.

I leave off playing piano. There's no point—Owen is asleep. My work is done.

Like one of the Lord of the Wood's wraiths, I haunt the house. Unlike the wraiths, I'm productive, switching out laundry and vacuuming floors, cleaning the bathroom until it's up to Mom's standards. Only then do I let myself curl up on the couch and half-heartedly look through my history homework. But shock of all shocks, even that can't hold my attention. I lie back on the couch, staring up at the water-stained ceiling, thinking of nothing. Of everything.

Jess asked if I wanted to go to homecoming. Maybe I do— but I can't afford a dress and I have nothing nice enough and no one to go with. I don't *have* to go with anyone either, but if Jess is taking a date, then . . . well, I've sworn off dating, so there is no *then*. It's nice to pretend, though. To imagine it. Dressing up, going out, Jess's arm linked in mine. Laughing, like we used to.

I don't realize I've fallen asleep until I jolt awake, heart pounding. I must've been having some nightmare that I don't remember—but no. There's a crackling noise coming from down the hall, from where the bedrooms are. If I focus, it sounds like fire.

I leap up and tear down the hall. My mouth is full of bile, my heart pounding in my throat, and I can't stop hearing the crackling, smelling smoke in the air. I burst through Owen's door—

And nothing is wrong. There's no fire. The crackling has stopped. At least, that's what I think until I turn on the light and peer over the edge of the crib, and then I'm screaming before I even know what's happening.

There's a bundle of sticks in the place where Owen slept only an hour ago. They're tied together with white ribbon, laying in the middle of the baby mattress. There's a scattering of petals over them, red and white, unfamiliar.

Hideously, in a moment that I cannot take back nor deny, the first thing I feel is a terrible rush of relief. Like his whole life has been a dream.

But that is an irrational reaction, one that I would regret if I wasn't so deeply rotten—and I don't know if I'll ever forgive myself for that. I don't know if I'll ever feel as guilty about the relief as I should.

When I press my hand to the place where Owen slept, it's still warm. That detail is enough to call me back: because Owen is not here and he was only minutes ago, and I spring into action. Owen *has* to be here.

The Lord.

I turn the mattress over, look everywhere in the room, under the bed and down the hall but I know the truth: *He's gone, he's gone, he's gone.*

The Lord has come.

He takes babies from our homes in Winston, leaving behind a changeling of sticks or ice. And though I haven't put any trust in God since I was fifteen, I whisper prayer after prayer under my breath as I tear our tiny home apart. It's a lesson in futility—even if I didn't believe in the Lord of the Wood, I'd know that—but I have to do it. I have to do *something*.

There's no sign of Owen in the house, so I take my flash-light and search the perimeter outside. His window is wide open, wider than how I left it, but that only deepens the fear in my stomach.

Above his window, on the siding of our house, there's a dark handprint marring the white. I lean close enough to see the out-line of where it drips, to note that it is still wet. I can't tell if it's blood or juice or paint—but in the growing darkness, it is red-tinged black.

Distantly, past the river, in the woods, I hear the high-pitched sound of a woman's laugh.

A few feet from Owen's open window, a bit of brown fabric is caught on the grass. I stoop down and turn it over and over in my hands. It's the bear ear from his onesie, the thread torn as if it was left here to taunt me.

Owen is gone.

Three

When Mom comes home, I'm still out in the field between our house and the river, scouring the grass for any sign of him, hoping desperately I'm wrong. But there's a bloody handprint above Owen's open window, still wet, and I know that I can't be.

"Leah?" she shouts from the drive, barely illuminated by the dim bulb of the porch light. "What are you doing?"

I look at her, and the words flee from my mouth. Oddly, for a flash of a moment, I'm sure she's going to think that *I* did this.

But Mom grew up here. She's the one who told me the stories of the Lord of the Wood in the first place. Other towns might have scares and spooks and ghosts that haunt the bridges and long stretches of empty road, but here in Winston, we have the Lord. Always have, always will.

Some say he's a faerie that snatches babies from their cribs to crunch their bones. Others think he's a ghost, too—maybe a father who lost a child, or maybe an immortal murderer, hunkered in the wood. And of course there are the holdovers from the panic that don't think there's just one Lord of the Wood, but a whole slew of them, a cult out there primed for devil worship.

It doesn't matter what or who he is, or how he and his followers have come to be. What matters is that he takes. Every few years, just when there's a lull of peace, just when people get too comfortable, he comes back again and takes one of our own.

This time, he's opened his terrible claws and slipped through the window and taken what is *mine*.

When Mom gets close enough to see me, to see the wind whipping the sheer curtains in Owen's open window and the bloody handprint on the dirty siding of our house, her face twists into a mask of rage.

She doesn't say anything, not in words. The cry that comes from her mouth is visceral, horrible, as she throws herself toward the window. She leans in, her body half-enveloped in shadows, tangled in the curtains.

Mom turns to me, and I cannot look at her. I only wince when she gets close and grabs me, when her nails dig into my cheek. "*You*," she hisses, her breathing unsteady and raw with despair. "You *fucking* let him go, Leah. How could you do this? To your brother? To *me*?"

"I didn't know," I insist. "I didn't hear—I didn't see—"

She pulls away, jerking my chin hard. She doesn't feel like my mother anymore—in her eyes is something unknowable, a dark pit of grief that I cannot comprehend. I want so badly, in this moment, to be someone else.

"You'll pay for this," she says.

Please, I want to beg, grab her hands, fall to my knees, and bury my face in her skirt like I used to when I was a scared child. *Don't blame me. Don't make me do this. Don't make this burden mine.*

"Mom—" I plead, grasping at her hand. She pulls it away, quick and final, and for just a moment, I see her for who she was before Owen was born.

"You knew the risks," she says, looking out toward the dark, snaking river and the wood beyond. I wonder if he's watching us, the Lord who takes without warning, who ruins us all in the end. "You know what I've gotta do," she says, her voice even softer.

I nod, vicious tears clawing at my throat. I refuse to cry. I will not be weak, standing before her, understanding the weight of what she's about to sacrifice.

"Please don't," I say, but my voice carries no weight. "I can find him. I can fix this."

I wish I could see the part of her that was a girl, growing up in the shadow of this town, before she let it decide to own her. Consecrated in the waters of the church in the watchful gaze of the Lord of the Wood's domain, in this place where the forest takes more than it ever gives back.

"Of course you'll fix it. You'll have no choice," she says. "But you'll have to do it right."

Mom is up the rest of the night, making calls. I roll into fetal position in my threadbare nightgown on my twin bed, staring out at the moon through the window.

Mom said I should bathe and pray, offering my sins up. She knows what's going to happen tomorrow when dawn breaks, and I guess I do too. Not the details, not yet; but the general idea of it has been scolded into me since I was old enough to know what rules I was never permitted to break.

If the Lord of the Wood keeps Owen, his soul is lost to us. He'll die out there. They'll sacrifice him, or eat him, or keep him among their cult—whatever they do, we're not getting Owen back.

But I lost him, and I have some odd sense of power here. As long as I act quickly, according to the rules of Winston, I can go appeal to the Lord of the Wood. Get him to grant us mercy, if that's possible.

Except, I don't know if it *is* possible—no one does. Every girl who's been sent to bargain has never been seen again.

I remember her. The last girl. The last time the terrible maw of the wood opened; the last time the jaws of the Lord gnashed down on a girl that was *ours*.

The only time I was old enough to remember, it was with Maria Sinclair and her baby. It was a hot summer night, hotter than this one, and she'd gone to bed with the baby next to her after drinking a bit too much whiskey. When she woke, she found she was clutching a half-melted hunk of ice to her breast. Something about the story never struck me right—perhaps it was because Jess knew Maria from dance, and Jess swore Maria wasn't that type of girl; perhaps it was because Maria always seemed too *nice* to catch the eye of someone like the Lord.

After Maria was gone for a year, the rest of the Sinclairs left town.

I wasn't old enough, that time, to go to the church when dawn broke. Just shy of thirteen, I wasn't allowed to see the truth of it. I don't know what waits for me, what they'll say or do, or how they'll send me away.

What I do know is that Maria Sinclair and her baby were never seen again. Sometimes, when I go to a party with Jess at the Grady's or the Tate's or the Pingo's, when the night is dark and the fire is crackling down to embers, someone claims that they've seen her ghost.

Then, I used to half believe it, but now I hope they're wrong. I hope that when they sent Maria over the river and into the wood to claim her baby from the Lord, she took the first trail she found and ran somewhere far, far away, reinvented herself as many miles from the reaches of Winston as she could get. I hope she didn't die in those woods, because if she did, there's a good chance that I'm going to die too.

They say he's the devil. They say he's hideous, the Lord of the Wood, with gnarled skin like the root of trees and the eyes of a wolf, ready to open his jaws and swallow a young girl whole. Or sometimes, they say he's the most beautiful person ever seen, with a full head of curls colored like the leaves when fall comes roaring over the mountains.

My door opens, and I shut my eyes and tuck my hands into fists under my chin like I've been sleeping this whole time.

Across the tiny room, I hear Mom breathing. Her breath hitches, just a bit. She crosses the room and I hold my breath. Her fingertips trail over my forehead, pushing aside the baby hairs stuck to my skin with sweat.

She doesn't do this anymore—she's not tender with me, not now that there's Owen around. Once, I was her baby too.

She didn't just lose Owen to the Lord of the Wood. I'm responsible for him—he was taken under my watch. If I don't come back, she's losing me too. Her daughter, her firstborn.

She loved me once, just as much as she loves Owen now. I have to believe that.

Mom takes her hand back and draws a shaky breath. I barely

hear her leave, shutting the door behind her. I don't open my eyes.

If I don't come back with Owen, she will never forgive me. It would better if I didn't come back at all.

four

Mom wakes me just before dawn. "It's time," she says, pushing a bundle of fabric at me. I unroll it, revealing a thin, white, cap-sleeve sundress. It must be Mom's from when she was younger, because it's certainly not mine. I don't own any white dresses—and last year, I grew out of the one from my confirmation.

Without another word, she leaves me to get myself up.

The dress is pretty and delicate with dainty eyelet flowers along the trim. I put it on and go to the bathroom to check how it looks. The dress makes me look pale and tired, but it reminds me of a similar dress from a musical that Jess and I use to watch clips from when we were younger, thinking we were rebellious. It's tight on my chest and too short on my thighs, almost indecent. But if it was actually indecent, my mother would not have given it to me to wear.

I brush my teeth and pull my hair into two French braids. No makeup, no jewelry. I consider my silver cross, the twin to Jess's, but I leave it hanging on its pin. The girl in the mirror looks much younger than I feel.

"We've got to go," Mom says, hesitating in the doorway. Her blond hair hangs loose around her shoulders. She wears a modest blue dress and dirty, white knock-off Keds from Walmart. She takes in the dress and frowns—but she doesn't say anything. I wonder, for just a second, if that should worry me.

There's no use asking her to comfort me or hug me. Asking gives her the option to refuse, and I will not let her break my heart by turning away.

Instead, I keep my words to myself, suffocating in my throat, as I follow her out to the front porch. Dew clings to the grass, shining like teardrops as the sun slowly begins to ascend. There are little red wildflowers poking up through the grass, through the cracks in the concrete—I don't remember seeing them yesterday, and I don't see them in any of our neighbors' yards. Just ours. It's like a scattering of blood drops over the grass. I suck a breath through my teeth, pushing away all thoughts of gore.

If Grammy was here, she'd grip my shoulders, kiss my forehead, and tell me I was blessed, and the blessed will be forgiven.

Mom doesn't tell me I'll be forgiven.

"Where are we going?" I ask.

"To church," she says.

I swallow hard. "Should I call Dad?" I ask as I open the car door, the thought occurring to me as a formality.

She just shoots me a look and gets in the car. *He won't want to talk to you*, it says. And why would he? I've ruined every-thing—I've lost his son.

The ride to church is short, less than ten minutes. In Winston, everything is within ten minutes of the church. It's in the center of town, just up a little hill. Next to it is a graveyard where my grandparents and great-grandparents and great-great-grandparents are buried, all the Joneses as far back as they go. If you go through the graveyard, down the little hill on the back, the river separates the land from the forest. When I was younger, I used to sneak out of the social part of youth group with Jess and Trent McCoy and Blaire Grady and a couple of others, and we'd skip stones and gossip. Once, Blaire slipped on one of the mossy stones in the bank and fell right into the river. She would've washed away if Trent didn't grab her, pulling her out of the water soaked through and bleeding as if she'd been born again.

Mom pulls into the gravel lot. It's full of cars, which terrifies me. I think again of Maria Sinclair, of what happened to her.

The god we worship called for Abraham to kill his only son, sacrifice him on the altar as a show of devotion. What if Abraham had not heard when God urged him to stay his hand?

How can everyone be so sure Maria Sinclair is dead, if they did not witness her death themselves?

But Owen is gone, and it's my fault, and I'm not going to convince Mom out of whatever punishment she and all of Winston have already chosen for me.

I slip out of the car and follow Mom to the church. I've always thought the church looks just how country churches are meant to look: white clapboard outside with a steeple, and wooden pews with a long aisle going all the way up to the altar.

There are those little red flowers again, scattered in a trail leading up to the church steps, petals crushed by passersby into the boards of the steps as if they'd grown through the wood overnight. I want to pick one of them, to crush a petal between my fingers, to see if it's real—but I don't. I keep my chin up, and I follow Mom.

Mom pushes the doors open. Half of Winston is here, filling the church. I squint against the light streaming through the window over the altar, illuminating the dust motes that dance through the air. Pastor Samuel stands at the front of the church, a Bible in his hands, a grave expression on his face. He's dressed in a flannel and jeans. It looks incongruous to see him here like that, without his robes or nice clothes. A bastardization.

More of those petals are scattered down the aisle, like the flower girl has come and gone and I'm processing like a bride. The little blooms cling to the edges of the pews, the pulpit, the cross, accusatory and shocking with their bright red color.

Near the front, Jess stands with her parents. She mouths

something to me, but I don't know what it is. I've never been good at reading lips.

Mom pushes me forward. I stumble, nearly falling to my knees.

It's so quiet inside I can hear the sound of cars as they rumble down the highway that passes through the other side of town. Every eye is on me, judgmental and terrible. For a hysterical moment, I imagine someone is going to throw rotten fruit at me, like they do in the bad movies, or bathe me in pig's blood like Carrie, but I clamp my jaw on the bubble of uneasy laughter before it can escape.

"Stop there," Mom mutters when I'm halfway down the aisle. Though it's early, the muggy September heat is pressing in on me, compounding with my anxiety. I anxiously wipe a bead of sweat from my collarbone.

"Leah Scarlett Jones," Pastor Samuel starts, letting my name hang in the air, and though he has none of his Sunday best on, his voice booms in the church like he's preaching fire and brimstone. I swallow hard. I've never been singled out like this, so thoroughly, so publicly. I feel oddly ashamed in my too-short white dress but there's nowhere to hide. I try to look around at the faces so I don't have to look at Pastor Samuel. My eyes light on Mr. Benton, who manages the grocery store—he's leering at me, his eyes trained on my chest. I look away.

"Your transgressions have led to a breach in the community," Pastor Samuel says. "Between the hours of nine and midnight, by your own account, you allowed a demonic presence into your home and sacrificed your brother to the devil."

I look at Jess, then at Trent standing in the pew behind her, both of their eyes wide with shock. "But that's not what—" I start, but Mom's hand lands heavy on my shoulder. She squeezes, her nails digging in again.

"In repentance, you will be cleansed with the spirit and sent on a pilgrimage to rescue that innocent baby and bring him back again."

I'd rather face anything other than this. Anything other than the looming wood and the Lord who lurks there.

"Is there a witness?" Pastor Samuel asks.

Silence hangs heavy in the air. I swallow hard, scanning the people again. Nearly all of them have known me since I was a baby, have watched me grow up here. I wait for one of them to speak for me.

Just as Jess's mouth opens, as she turns her head, my mother steps up before me.

"I'm the witness," she says, her voice flat and emotionless. She pulls the bundle of sticks out of a bag she carries, holding it as tenderly as she would hold Owen. Red petals fall from the bundle, joining those already scattered on the floor. Someone in the crowd gasps, and though we're far from Catholic, old Esther Fallow crosses herself.

"What did you see?" Pastor Samuel asks.

Mom doesn't look at me, but I stare at her like I can see beneath her skin, understand the layers beneath her flat expression, know for sure how she could betray me like I'm not even her daughter.

"I left Leah alone with the baby. When I came home, the baby was gone and my home was marked with the hand of the devil."

Any sympathetic gazes are gone. Jess isn't looking at me anymore. I wish she'd turn her head, that her gentle brown eyes would focus on me, that she'd come and grab me and we'd run from this place.

"And do you think it's Leah's fault the Lord of the Wood visited your house and stole your baby away?"

There it is—the question, as blunt as could be. Still, Mom doesn't look at me. *Do it*, I plead silently, full of old vitriol. *Look me in the eye.* Her free hand is balled into a fist at her side, the veins standing out in sharp relief.

"Yes," Mom says.

I wish, more than anything, that I could hate her. That I didn't want her to love me so, so desperately.

Pastor Samuel nods. He expected this—after all, it was Mom that made the call, Mom who got this motley assembly together. "The devils from the wood have made their exchange and left their sign." He kicks at one of the little drifts of petals, scattering them, crushing the delicate flesh into the carpet.

He reaches for a bowl and comes down the aisle toward me.

When he's close enough that I can see every strand of gray shooting through his dark hair, he stops. He's tall, towering over me in my white dress like a terrible communion. I can't see what's in the bowl but it smells like hot iron.

He dips his hand in the bowl, flat palmed, and presses it to my chest. "You're tasked with the salvation of the baby boy you destroyed," Pastor Samuel says, "or you'll face death at the hands of the wood."

When he pulls his hand back, my chest feels sticky and wet. I look down, barely choking back my hysteria when I see what he's done: My chest is marked with a handprint of blood, from nearly my collarbones over the swell of my breasts, bleeding over the top of the dress and onto my skin.

"To the river," he says, and when he stalks past me down the aisle, the others shift to follow.

The procession is just as silent as we trudge across the grass, through the graveyard, down the hill. I cannot look at my mother, or anyone else, for that matter. No one speaks to me. I follow behind Pastor Samuel, my eyes glued to his back, as my heart thunders in my chest.

He stops at the river, right by the place Blaire fell in all those years ago. I wonder if she remembers—I think she's behind me now, but I can't be sure.

"Leah Jones," Pastor Samuel says. He holds his hand out to me. It's caked in blood.

I step forward. He takes my hands in his and slowly, slowly, he steps into the river, pulling me to follow.

We haven't had that much rain so the river isn't rushing like usual. The water is frigid as I step in and my shoes sink into the mud. I let out an involuntary hiss, but Pastor Samuel doesn't even react.

I wonder how many times he's done this. He's only in his mid-thirties, maybe early forties—but he's been the pastor of Winston for as long as I can remember. I wonder, if he went somewhere else he would come back craving blood.

He stops in the middle, where the water is nearly up to my chest and just around his waist. His gaze is terrible as he looks down over me, hungry and wanton. Goosebumps rise on my skin. I want to let go of his hands, to use them to cover myself as the white fabric of my dress goes muddy and see-through.

I think—terribly, irrepressibly—he's *enjoying* this.

"Once you get to the other side," Pastor Samuel says, just to me, "he'll come for you."

"And then what?"

Pastor Samuel doesn't answer me. Louder, so everyone else can hear, he says, "On this day, I cleanse you of your sins. Leah Scarlett Jones, you have been tasked with repentance. Here is your sentence: You must find the Lord of the Wood to recover what you have lost. Do not squander your only chance at redemption."

I have so many questions rising from my chest, but no time at all to ask them. Pastor Samuel puts his hands on my shoulders and pushes me down, until my knees buckle and the water closes in over my head.

I only just remember to hold my breath. For the briefest of moments, I consider what would happen if I opened my mouth and let the water in.

five

When I surface, it's like the whole world has changed. Like hours have passed. Paster Samuel is gone, and there are no others left on the bank. I glance over my shoulder, but it's all as it should be—just empty.

Ahead, the wood beckons. I half swim, half trudge forward through the mud and rocks at the bottom of the river, fighting the current. I drag myself out onto the bank, my dress soiled and soaked, the blood a fading pink stain on my chest. But it's there, which means I'm not dreaming. I didn't make it up.

The town did not stand behind me, not now and not ever. My mother has forsaken me unless I bring her son back. And all that waits for me in the wood . . . well, I don't think I'll find my salvation there.

But Owen is gone, and it's all my fault.

I raise my face to the sky and let the sun warm my skin. And then, chin high, I face my fate. One step at a time, dripping blood and river water, I make my way into the wood.

At first, the forest is no different than it has ever been. I stumble from the riverbank to one of the hunting trails. Unlike most of us in Winston, people from Carver County and beyond aren't so afraid to go into the woods. There are hunters in neighboring towns, and hikers who come to the beauty spots along the Yough on the weekend, but they don't really come into our town. And as far as I know, they don't care about the Lord of the Wood.

It's not really cold, but I'm dripping wet, and it is chilly under the canopy out of the reach of the sun. I wish I would've brought a sweatshirt, or a pack, or anything more practical than just this flimsy dress and my now-soggy shoes. The last time Jess and I did anything remotely nature-y she spent the whole time worrying about ticks and poison ivy. If I encounter either of those, let alone any creatures or the Lord himself, I'm basically screwed.

Plus, I don't have food. Or water.

My stomach churns and I stop to gaze up at the leaves spreading out above me. I can't go back, but without supplies, I'm not sure how far I can really go.

Pastor Samuel said the Lord would be waiting for me on the other side. I hesitate, still within sight of the river, and look around. Nothing is moving besides the usual creatures: birds, a couple of squirrels, maybe a grinny in a nearby bush just off the trail. But there's nothing to indicate the Lord is coming for me, no bellow of his great hunting horn, no crackle of leaves or breaking of sticks. I do another turn in case I missed something the first time, but there's no one here but me.

I chew on my thumbnail, ignoring the taste of river water on my hands.

Do I just . . . wait?

There is no guidebook to this. I was not taught the protocol in school, not even in the years when I was paying attention. And besides Maria Sinclair, I was too young to remember any other babies taken or girls sent to the wood—I only know the stories of them, the absences they left behind. I don't know what my punishment—my pilgrimage—is meant to look like.

But I also don't know if they can see me from town. Perhaps whatever weird ritual Pastor Samuel performed on me created a veil between worlds, one that they can see through and I cannot.

Maybe, they're all there on the banks, laughing at me.

That thought spurs me into action faster than anything else, which probably doesn't say anything too nice about my character.

I walk. There's a little patch of white flowers, twins to the red ones that grew in the church. The trail spreads out before me, arcing gently uphill. I've never been in this part of the woods, obviously, but I *have* been in the woods before, in the nearby parks and further stretches. There, it's more civilized, tamer, where they don't worry about the things that take. I'm not too freaked out by the scuttling of creatures and the wind through the trees, but I am probably too aware for the good of my nerves. I keep expecting him to appear on the path ahead of me, come to claim me.

But he doesn't.

With no other clues, I follow the little patches of white flowers into the depths of the wood. I walk until my shoes are nearly dry, even though they leave aching blisters on my feet. I walk even as the trail narrows and branches snag on my skirt. I walk until my belly is impossible to ignore with its aching and grumbling, and then I turn in another slow circle and take stock.

Perhaps I went the wrong direction? I'm not sure there *is* such a thing. He's the Lord of the Wood. According to Blaire's campfire stories, he's meant to be omnipresent, all-knowing. If I'm in his wood and he hasn't found me yet, he's probably just toying with me.

Or busy eating Owen's bones.

The thought chases away any hunger I have, leaving only nausea behind. I sway and only manage to keep myself upright by gripping a nearby tree.

Forward. If I want to find Owen, prove myself to my mother and the town, and head back quickly, then I need to keep pressing forward. If the Lord of the Wood will not come for me, I must come for him.

So I walk.

The smell hits me first.

It's meaty and raw and putrid, a slow creeping change from the fresh scent of chlorophyll and dirt. I press a hand over my nose and stop on the trail, but there's nothing ahead of me that I can see through the trees.

It must be nearly noon, since the sun is high above me, and I've only stopped to rest twice. I pause again on the trail for another slow circle. Perhaps this smell of rot is the Lord's signature? It's earthy and terrible, and he's supposed to be . . . well, earthy and terrible, so it all checks out. Though I can't be certain the patches of flowers are related to the Lord, it makes sense that he has other signs, other omens. Perhaps this is one of them.

I press forward, tripping on a root and stumbling into a clearing that I didn't see from the trail. It's not a big clearing, with sunlight only dappled through the leaves, and the gore at the other side is sudden and far too close.

Across the grass, about ten paces away, the bodies of two deer are fuzzy and bloated with rot. The closest has its eyes open, tongue lolled through its barely open mouth. Its antlers are locked with that of the other deer, entwined like lovers in death—death that they probably wrought on themselves by fighting, getting stuck, and falling.

But that's not the worst of it. Someone has slashed the closer deer's stomach open, so the guts and viscera and clotted blood spill out into the clearing. Bloated flies circle the torn flesh, and even from this distance I can see the white, rice-like wiggling maggots slipping through the guts.

I turn over my shoulder and retch. There's nothing in my stomach but acid, but it all crawls up from inside of me.

When I'm done, I wipe my mouth and lean against a tree. I . . . don't know what to do. Ahead of me, the deer are between me and the rest of the trail. I'll have to go closer, skirt the edges of the small clearing, go around them. I need to move forward, but I can't look away from those twisted, locked antlers.

Perhaps the deer hold some sort of answer.

I grit my teeth and face the corpses. Rustle up what I know about the Lord of the Wood. Honestly, it's not much. I know that we fear him, that some say he's our own version of the devil, come to keep the town of Winston in line and on God's path.

But there are others, like Kara Meritt, the artist who lives above the bookstore, who says the Lord is there to keep the natural world in balance. And old Esther Fallow, who believes he's the devil, goes on and on about his propensity for animal sacrifice.

I edge closer to the deer. I didn't have money on Esther Fallow being correct in this situation, but the evidence in front of me says otherwise. Maybe she's right. Maybe the Lord of the Wood does make unholy sacrifices; maybe he has cursed the town; maybe he's already eaten Owen and he's sharpening his weapons to come for me.

No girl has come home before. Perhaps the deer are a sign: I should run, and I should do it *now*.

But there's Owen, and duty, and the memory of Mom's disappointment. I can imagine her now, at home, running through prayer after prayer in her head, waiting for us to come home.

When I'm only a foot or so away, I stoop down, one hand pressed over my nose and mouth to try to keep the stench away. I don't know what to look for, what marks a sacrifice, but I force myself to look, to examine the viscera.

"What are you doing?"

The voice comes from behind me, startling me so thoroughly that I nearly pitch forward into the deer guts. I jump back to my feet and whip around to find a boy. He's standing at the edge of the clearing, staring.

"I—"

But there are no answers. There are no words. Only shock as I stare at him. He's about my age, with medium brown skin and dark, curly hair. There's a light dusting of freckles across his nose. Despite the sticky heat, he wears a button-down shirt rolled up to his elbows and trousers. I have to do a double take because he's actually wearing suspenders, and I have never actually seen suspenders on anyone under retirement age.

He nods to the deer. "What did you do to them?"

"I—I found it like this. Them. Found them like this." I

gesture to the deer behind me with both hands, holding my palms open to show I don't have the weapon necessary for this kind of destruction. It hits me that maybe this whole thing has gone awry, and now some kid from Uniontown thinks I'm a hideous animal murderer on the loose.

He raises an eyebrow. "Why are you so deep in the wood? Are you lost?"

I swallow hard. Technically, no. But also, technically yes. My brain catches on the fact that I'm deep in the woods—he knows it too. "Why are you out here? Are *you* lost?"

He stares at me evenly. Goosebumps raise on the skin of my arms.

In a voice I don't quite recognize, a small voice that I barely believe comes from my mouth, I say quietly, "I'm here to seek the Lord of the Wood."

The boy's eyebrows knit together. He examines me, my short dress and muddy shoes, the red handprint on my chest—but not like he's leering.

I wait. If he didn't know what I was talking about, he would've broken the silence.

Finally, he sighs. The boy nods once, making a decision. "I'll take you to him," he says. "But it's still a bit of a walk."

Relief surges through me. "I can do that," I say, crossing the clearing toward the boy. I'm glad to leave the deer behind, glad that I don't have to investigate it further. Drawing closer, I can see that his eyes are two different colors: one the dark, deep brown of rich soil; one hazel, like shifting autumn leaves.

"Are you . . ." I'm not sure how to finish the sentence. It's not like I can call the Lord's following a cult, not with a member of it standing before me. I don't really even know what he *is*. "Are you one of his followers?" I ask, sticking to language Pastor Samuel would use. If they were right about the Lord of the Wood's existence, perhaps they were right about his people, too.

The boy nods once. He turns and sets off into the woods, not following any trail in particular, but skirting through the underbrush. I notice, with some glee, that he's also following the haphazard little patches of white flowers—or, at least, they're still on our trail. I follow him closely, trying my best to replicate his footsteps.

We continue in silence for a while. I should probably consider the intelligence of this, of following a strange boy through the woods simply because he claims to be a member of the cult I'm looking for, but I'm starting to think of his intervention as a rescue. If he hadn't found me, who knows how long I'd be wandering through the woods, searching for some mystical wood god.

Usually I'm good at silence, but as the afternoon drags on, as the branches snap underfoot and my dress continues to snag on thorns that cut my legs, I find it weighing on me. Finally, I speak.

"What is your name?" I ask.

The boy doesn't look at me. He only presses forward, and

enough time has passed that I think he's not going to answer when he says, "Tristan."

"Tristan," I repeat. "I'm Leah."

Nothing. He says nothing. I stare at his back, the earthy cream shirt broken up by the dark cut of his suspenders.

"I'm here to find a baby? He disappeared yesterday?"

"Mmph."

I gather up my courage. *Mmph* is not an answer. "Would you know anything about that?"

Tristan sighs, his shoulders dipping. "You'll get your answers soon enough," he says wearily.

I bite my lip, nearly tripping over an errant tree root. He's right—he's taking me to the Lord, which is a favor enough. I shouldn't press him when he's doing me a kindness. Perhaps he loves the cult, but hates the baby-taking aspect. Perhaps he was taken himself as a baby, raised here, and finds the current practice abhorrent.

Or perhaps he's lying about all of it and luring me deeper and deeper into the woods to kill me. Maybe that's the truth of the girls that went in pursuing what the Lord took: maybe we were what he wanted all along.

Six

We walk until I feel the stickiness of blood where my shoes rub against my heels, until my gnawing hunger is impossible to ignore, until the sky above us bleeds with a sunset and I want to crush every little white flower in sight. In the woods, it grows darker and darker.

I wonder if time or space is distorted. Surely, there's not this much wilderness—surely, we should've come across something or someone by now. But we walk and walk and walk, longer than I've gone in one spell before, and I'm about to ask Tristan for a rest when I notice a thinning in the trees ahead.

"Is that . . . ?"

"That's where we're going," he says. That's all. He's not very forthcoming.

"We're much farther than I imagined," I admit. I thought it

would be easy, when Pastor Samuel gave me my instructions and pushed me under the water. I thought the Lord would just be there, waiting on the other side.

"Sometimes it's easier," Tristan says, which explains nothing.

As we draw closer, I smell woodsmoke and the rich scent of cooking meat. My mouth waters and my stomach grumbles loud enough that I'm sure Tristan can hear it. If he does, he gives no indication.

The sounds grow louder, too: laughter, and gentle voices, and the sound of a guitar being strummed somewhere. The clang of pots and dishes.

"Tristan," I whisper, gripped with an odd terror. All I know is Winston. All I know is that these people took my brother—and I'm scared.

I'm *petrified*.

He looks back, his expression softening when he sees my face. Tristan holds out a hand to me.

"No one here is going to hurt you," he says.

I don't know if I believe him. After everything I've been through, today and before, with all the hurt I'm holding locked in my chest, I don't know if I can. If I deserve to be safe.

They took Owen. Maria Sinclair came into these woods, with the Lord's followers, and never came back, not to mention all the girls that came before. Girls like me. Maybe they were promised safety too.

But I *want* to believe him. I want safety, even if it's here, in the unknown. Even though none of them came back.

I take his hand.

We break through the trees, into the clearing. It's not quite vast, but it is roomy, a maze of cabins and fortified tents and cooking fires, scattered groups of people, a few animals. A white wolf-like dog gnaws on a desiccated football at the campfire closest to us. It looks up when Tristan enters the clearing, the only thing that seems to notice us. The wolf's yellow eyes are wide and luminescent and it sniffs the air twice, whiskers twitching, before it goes back to the football.

An old woman comes out of the cabin behind the dog and frowns at Tristan. "What's that you've got?" she says, like he's brought back a pile of sticks or a strange plant instead of a girl.

"A supplicant," Tristan says.

Supplicant. *My supplicant, even the daughter of my dispersed, shall bring my offering.* The half-verse rings in my head, aching like the sound of the church bells behind Pastor Samuel's voice.

But is he wrong? I've come here to take back Owen, but I don't have any power in this realm. In truth, I've come here to beg.

The old church rule, the one Mom always said as she dug into her purse as the offering plate went around, the one Grammy taught me with pennies after Sunday school, calls for a tenth of all worldly goods to go to God. Fear prickles under my skin—the Lord of the Wood will not settle for ten percent, not of anything

I own. I wonder what percentage it would take of me to make me into something else.

The old woman takes me in with steady, brown eyes. She's white, paler than me, dusted with freckles. Her hair is clinging to its ginger color, overtaken by gray, coiled with frizzy curls.

"When is the audience?"

Tristan shrugs, bending to stroke the dog. It rolls over onto its back, offering its furry belly. I'm disconcerted by the wolf-like creature, almost as much as I'm disconcerted by the others who have left their work behind, who now watch us in a loose semicircle.

"Tonight."

I swallow hard. I don't like how he talks about me like I'm not right here.

"Where is he?" I ask, my voice catching in my throat. I clear it and push on. "Is he here now? Can I get this over with?"

Tristan stands and the dog moves too, sitting next to him like a familiar. "Official business is only carried out under twilight," he says, and nothing more. Before I can ask anything further, Tristan turns on his heel and slices a path through the camp. The dog treads obediently at his heel. I watch, dumbstruck, as they disappear.

"Come, girl," the old woman says. "Let's wash that blood off."

Her name is Ruth, she tells me as she shucks my white dress unceremoniously over my head, and she calls herself the Keeper. I don't know what that means, and she makes no move to explain, even when I ask.

I tolerate her rough fingers as she drags me to a heavy basin full of water. She scrubs at my skin until it's pink and raw, until every trace of Pastor Samuel's hands and the dirt of Winston and the wood is gone from me. Until I'm new.

My hair is a different story, and Ruth is less gentle than even my mother when she scrubs and detangles the long, brown mess of curls.

"I'm capable of washing myself," I say.

Ruth harumphs.

Since I'm not trusted with my own hygiene, I take the time to examine my surroundings in the rare moments my eyes aren't burning with soapy water. It's a cozy little cabin, cool enough despite the late summer heat outside. It's one room, with a bed pushed into the corner under the window. Austerely clean, too; the only decoration is dried herbs hanging above the big cast-iron stove in the kitchen section of the room. The basin I sit in is next to the great gaping hole of a fireplace, and the remnants of ash smell like cherry wood.

It's comfortable and unfussy. Maybe it could belong in my little town, the home of some aunt or grandmother who doesn't care for televisions or technology, who wants to retire in the peace of the woods.

But that's a dangerous line of thought. I spare a glance at Ruth as she picks up my hand and scrubs at the dirt under my fingernails. She is not an aunt, or a grandmother. She is no kin of mine. She belongs to the very group that stole Owen away, that brought this treachery onto me.

"It's not long from twilight, is it?" I ask, swallowing my fear. The cabin has started to take on a bit of a dim cast as the light through the window begins to wane.

She tugs me by the elbows and I stand, the water trickling back into the basin as it streams off of me. I want to feel ashamed of my nakedness in front of her, but it feels like being ashamed in front of a nurse. Everything about her demeanor says that she is above my shame. Trying to cover my nakedness would be more offensive and odder than standing here bare.

"Not long now." She turns away to grab a heavy towel from a nearby shelf. I dry myself and step out of the basin, waiting for instructions.

Ruth and Tristan have not been forthcoming. Though I hate it, though I crave answers and need to know what news they have of Owen, I need to wait. Patience.

In the Lord of the Wood's domain, I am not the one making a schedule. Based on the length of my day, the distance of our trek, I'm not even sure the rules of the world I know apply here. Between all the walking, both alone and with Tristan, and Ruth's preparations, the period of time has definitely been longer than a day. I don't know how to explain it other than to say that time feels weird, stretched and uncertain, and I feel lost within it like I'm caught in a tidal wave.

Ruth hands me gray undershorts and a dress of thin white muslin. I pull it over my head and do up the tiny buttons at my wrists, but leave the ones at my throat open. It is gauzy, thin and insubstantial, and I worry that it might be partially transparent, but I have no mirror to check.

She leaves me standing helpless in the middle of the room and peers out one of the windows. The shadows have lengthened, the corners black with darkness. I bite my lip and clench my fists, digging my nails into my palms.

"It's time, girl," she says.

I swallow my fear, my worry. I'm here for Owen: to claim him, to recover him, to bring him home. My palms are clammy at the thought of it. I think of his skin against mine, hot with sweat, his writhing limbs and squalling cry. I want to be sick.

You'll pay for this, Mom said. With only the Lord's mercy looming ahead, I'm terrified to discover the cost.

I follow her out the door of the cabin. It's the dimmer end of twilight. Fireflies light in the forest behind us, glittering through the trees. A loose group of people stand outside, holding torches and lanterns. They're wearing rough-spun fabric, dresses like my thin muslin in muted shades of cream and brown, trousers and shirts like Tristan's, looking like citizens of an old-time mining town. I try not to catch anyone's eye. I'm afraid that if I look, I'll find the same hatred that I did in the church this morning, in those that have known me all my life: horror, anger, betrayal.

To my surprise, Ruth grabs my hand. "It'll be okay," she says, but all I can think about is the girls who didn't come back.

I follow the mob of people, gradually accumulating more, as we make our way through the little village. Cooking fires are abandoned. A curious gray cat comes up and winds through my legs, nearly tripping me, before disappearing through an open door. It all reminds me of a horror movie Jess and I watched two summers back, one about a group of men on a camping trip and a ritualistic cult. I swallow hard, pushing away images of blood and torture and sacrifice.

I cannot break. Cannot hyperventilate. I take my eyes off the ground and hold my head high, looking ahead. The group of people block my view, but we're all ambling toward the far end of the community, where the cabins and tents open to a rough circle of cleared ground. A great bonfire burns in the middle, the heat from it radiant in the cooling night.

But when the people part in front of me, when I look past the bonfire, I see that the space is not cleared at all. In the center of it is a great throne, wrought from branches and thorns. I cannot see where the roots begin and end, cannot make out where one plant becomes another. They form a great, horned chair that reminds me uncomfortably of the entwined antlers of the deer from earlier.

He's supposed to be terrible, the Lord. The scariest thing I've ever seen, or the most beautiful, with antlers cresting from his temples and thick bark growing on the backs of his hands. He's supposed to have the slit pupils of a cat suspended in lucent yellow irises, or appear too tall and elongated, like he'd been stretched. He's supposed to be a sight to behold, and everyone who has seen him looks off into the middle distance when asked to relay what he looks like, then just shakes their head.

On the throne, his cheekbones glimmering with some sort of highlight or magic, sits the only person here I recognize. It takes me a second to put it together: the throne, the wolf seated by his side, the boy himself.

He is not awful, not terrible, and it occurs to me like a punch to the stomach—despite hearing every story Winston has ever told of him, every half-caught breath and terrified whisper, I don't actually know *anything* about the Lord, his person, his beliefs, or his domain. Because this—this is a surprise that leaves me reeling, hands in fists, nails digging into my palms.

Tristan.

Tristan is the Lord of the Wood.

Seven

I curse under my breath, feeling like a fool. Of course he's the Lord of the Wood—who else would've come to get me? That's who I was sent for, who I was offered to as sacrifice. I should've known the second he stepped into the clearing.

Of course everyone in Winston would have it wrong or exaggerate the truth—it's his unbelonging that makes him terrible. To someone like Esther Fallow, who cringes back from even the creeping shadow of the forest at sundown, this boy and his wolf are worse than the devil. That's what we're meant to fear, isn't it? Not the things that *look* evil, but the ones that look just as sweet and nice as honey, the sins that come back to bite you like a viper lying in wait. It's so easy to trust a beautiful thing, to let yourself go deeper and deeper until you take a breath and realize the oxygen has been all sucked out and you're suffocating.

"You didn't tell me," I say, the ferocity of my voice surprising even me. "You didn't tell me who you were."

He gazes at me evenly, unphased. He's changed into a nicer shirt, embroidered with flowers and vines. Rings glitter on his fingers, metal and onyx and ruby and opal, and a circlet is visible in his hair, gleaming through his dark curls. Earlier, I thought him to be my age, maybe a year older. But now, sitting on his throne with his wolf at his side, he looks impossible to place. Eternal. Old as the wood itself, young as the newest drop of dew on the morning grass. The firelight flickers between us, reflecting in his mismatched eyes. Standing here, appealing for his mercy, I have the same feeling of embarrassment that I had more than once standing before Trent in some of our not-so-great moments.

"You didn't ask me."

I laugh, shocked by the unfairness of it all. "I did!"

"You asked if I was a follower," he says, his expression remaining closed and unreadable. And he's right—I did. I hate myself for not recognizing the signs, not being suspicious enough. Perhaps if I'd just spared one second of thought, I would've seen the obvious.

That's what's wrong with you, Leah, I hear my mom's voice in the back of my head, from one of our many screaming matches. *You never* think. *You just* do, *damn the consequences.*

That's my problem: I always trust the beautiful thing without stopping first to check its teeth.

I swallow hard. My impulsive, passionate heart will not save me now. I have to think. Have to process.

Fighting with the Lord of the Wood is not going to get me anywhere. Though the stories were wrong about his appearance, they might be right about something else. Some of the tales talk about his trickiness, how he can catch you in a snare and steal even your shadow right from underneath you.

I take a shaky breath. "It doesn't matter now. I'm here to get back something you stole."

"I do not steal. I only take what is offered to me."

I bite my lip, my teeth slipping easily into the groove I left earlier. "Owen is mine. No one gave him to you."

Tristan's eyebrow slips upward. He does not speak for a moment, though I fear what he will say next. Finally, he says, "So, you accept responsibility for the child?"

"He's my brother," I say, the words sounding hollow. The people behind me are silent as the grave. I wish someone would speak for me, would help, but they're all strangers—and I'm certain they're on Tristan's side anyway. Even if some of them are probably from Winston, long-since corrupted in this soil.

No one spoke for me this morning when I was surrounded by people who have known me all my life. Of course no one will speak for me now.

I did not see Owen among them. I don't hear his squalling cry. Anxiety gnaws at my stomach. I don't even know for certain he's still here.

For all I know, he could be dead. But if Owen is dead, so am I. I cannot go back to Winston without him.

"In order to get the boy back," Tristan says, his voice carrying across the space between us with weighted authority, "you must make me a trade."

I swallow hard. "A trade? What kind of trade?"

Tristan watches me evenly. It's like we're playing at some game, but I have no idea of the rules. In town, sometimes they say the Lord is one of the fair folk, a fae. But I don't know anything about that, about them. I can't understand the truth of him, even as he sits before me with his heavy throne and great wolf, but I don't know if that makes my situation better or worse.

I should be afraid of him. In the pit of my stomach, I know it; the truth is there in the hair on the back of my neck, standing on end. But I cannot, because—*because*—

I cannot, because of the thing I won't allow myself to recall. Not now. Not here. The girls he took never came back, but what's to say they never got out? And even being here, even knowing that there's risk—at least it's real. Tangible. At least I see it in front of me.

"Something that costs you. I will make a trade for the boy, if it's fitting."

"I . . ." I think of the piggy bank under my bed, collecting dust. It has a few hundred dollars in it that I was hoping to eventually use for a car, but I don't think that's the kind of thing Tristan wants from me. If the stories from Winston are to be believed, he wants something more . . . visceral. "A limb?" I say, offering my hand. It will hurt, but so does everything else.

"What good is a limb when I have a whole boy?"

I wince. Hopefully that means Owen has not yet been eaten.

"Surely there's something you can give me," Tristan says, his voice softer this time. His tone stirs a memory in me, one of sitting in Owen's room on a frigid winter night. Mom was working late so it was just him and me, miserable as always. He was probably six months old at that point, screaming his head off until I played a song for him. But I remember the bitter cold, the frost creeping across the window. I remember looking up, and seeing a shadowed figure in the field for only a moment before it disappeared.

"A song," I say, the words tearing out of me before I can stop them. I look at him, hoping my expression is fierce and terrible, stubborn as the sunshine in midwinter. "I'll write a song for you."

A titter of whispers sounds in the crowd behind me. Tristan considers this. His gaze slips past me, over my shoulder, and I have the strangest feeling that we've lived this scene before. I ignore the gnawing dread in my stomach, the heat of the fire between us. I force myself to look at him, to take everything in from the copper circlet that gleams in his messy curls to the shining metal-capped toes of his heavy laced boots.

I could run. I think if I turned right now and darted into the darkness of the woods, away from the Lord—not to Winston, either, just away—I think I would make it. They wouldn't come after me, and I'd just be another missing girl, and Owen just another victim. And for a flickering half second, the darker part of me considers it.

Finally, he dips his head. The Lord of the Wood has made his decision.

"Come here, Leah."

I don't run. I force my feet to move and step carefully around the fire. A knot explodes within it, sending a spray of embers into the space between us. If I get out of this clearing, away from the fire, and look up into the night sky, I'm sure it would be breathtaking. The constellations laid out as clear as the embers floating on the wind.

I stop at the foot of his throne. This close, I can see more clearly the dusting of gold on his cheekbones, and the rings he wears on all of his fingers. His shirt is unbuttoned at the throat, and I watch his Adam's apple bob as he swallows.

"It is no small thing," he says, softer now that we're right next to each other, "to make a trade with me."

I cannot find it in myself to be afraid. Not knowing what I know, not asking what I have.

There was potential in me, once. A whole lot of it. I was good enough to bring tears to Grammy's eyes, good enough to win contests the next town over. Mom said I spoiled everything, squandered it, smashed my talent into dust and scattered it into the wind. Dad stopped saying anything at all. And I believe them. I'm destined for Winston, for a forever-life in this awful town where everyone sees me as a black hole of all the things I never became.

I cannot let temptation and heat and my own misdirection turn my desires into smoke all over again. I can't run and leave Owen here. I can't neglect this, my duty, the one thing I can do to make it right.

"What is at stake?" I ask. Not for Owen. For *me*.

"If you fail, you will remain here, in my realm," the Lord says—and it's something like relief, when he does. Maybe that's the truth of the other girls: Maybe they all failed in their quests, and are here, safe and whole in the wood. Maybe Maria is behind me now with all the other daughters Winston forgot.

If I fail, I won't be able to go back to Winston anyway. "I'll take that deal," I say, perhaps too quickly.

If I was a good girl, the kind of girl that Winston wanted, staying here would be a fate worse than death. If I was good, I would *not* take that deal.

If I was the type of girl Winston loved, I'd be able to look at Tristan without my breath catching in my throat for all the wrong reasons.

"Wouldn't you like to think on it a little longer? I can give you until dawn."

There's no point in that. I shake my head. I came here for Owen, and I'm not leaving here without him.

"Very well." Tristan shifts, drawing a thin knife from a sheath in his belt. "You will have one moon cycle and no longer to complete your task and make your trade. In that time, you are free to reside here as a guest in my own dwelling. Are these terms to your liking?"

"Yes," I say, the word barely escaping my lips. A month. I can do that—can't I? I glance up, through the trees, at the new moon and its darkness. By the time the moon is new again, all of this will be over.

He holds the knife up, the silver of it glimmering just as brightly as his rings in the light of the fire. He stands up, so close that the toes of his boots frame either side of my feet. "We must make a blood oath, then, to seal our agreement. Give me your hand."

I do as he asks and watch as he nicks the pad of my thumb. He does it to his own, too, and dark blood wells up against our skin. I only watch, an observer in my own life rather than a participant, as he unites our hands and our blood.

The hair on the back of my neck rises. Tristan's wolf sniffs at the hem of my dress.

Tristan's hand jerks mine, pulling me closer, close enough that I can see the hairs curling on the nape of his neck. "Do you fear me?" he whispers.

Behind us, the gathering has grown louder. No one much cares about me, now that I've made my deal.

I look up at him, indignant. I was told the Lord of the Wood was fearsome and terrible, but even with his great wolf, he's still just a boy.

All of our lives, we've been taught to fear him. Told that he takes whatever he can, that his cult relies on preying on what we have to offer. I've lived my life in the shadow of his territory, waiting for something to happen. The truth is this: I don't fear him, because unlike everything else I've been taught to believe in, he follows through. They warned me about the Lord, and in some way, I always knew he was coming. He is not some unknown force, some omniscient and omnipresent being meant to judge and punish. He is not an empty threat. He is real. He is flesh. His punishment, whatever it may be, is not something I have to wait for in earnest fear: It is coming. It is here.

He can hurt me, but at least I know that. At least I see him in front of me. At least, when the time comes, I will be able to see the fatal blow coming.

"No," I declare.

There's a vicious relief in it, to face up against the worst thing that could happen, and to the culmination of my worst decisions staring back. There's only so long you can walk the edge before you teeter over and fall; here we are, crashing together into the unknown that waits on the other side.

His smile is half-surprised, like he wasn't expecting me to deny it. He releases my hand and raises his own to his mouth. When he licks away the blood on his thumb, his gaze does not leave mine.

"I hope you know what you're doing, Leah Jones," he says, and there's sadness in his smile and the way he says my name. I don't ask how he knows my last name. He's the Lord of the Wood. For all I can tell, he knows everything.

I think, taking in his gaze, that he certainly knows the worst of me.

I hope I know what I'm doing too.

Eight

After my agreement is sealed, I stumble back into the crowd. Ruth is at my side before I can go looking for her, and she offers me a bowl of thick stew and homemade bread. I eat it, surprised by the ferocity of my hunger.

"Are you tired?" she asks once I have finished sopping up the last of the stew with my bread.

"Yeah, actually." I look around, taking in the others at their campfires, the furtive glances and hushed whispers. "Where did all of these people come from?" I ask. If I'm going to be here for a full month, I might as well figure out who I'm spending it with.

Ruth shrugs. "All over," she says, which isn't very helpful.

"Where are *you* from?" I ask.

"A little farther south," she says, but that's not really an answer either. "Tired enough to go? I can show you to your room."

It's a dismissal if I've ever heard one, but she's right. I am tired. It feels like it's been an eternity since Pastor Samuel pressed his blood-soaked hand to my chest and sent me into the wood, but it was only this morning.

"Please," I say.

Ruth doesn't go back to her little cabin. Instead, she leads us off to the side of the fire, toward the wood. We break through the trees and follow a little snaking path. I don't know how she can follow it in the heavy dark without a light, but she doesn't even seem to notice.

Eventually, we come to another house: a fortress of stone and wood, built up against a sheer wall of rock. I take in the stone walls, creeping with ivy, and the heavy wooden door. Candlelight flickers through the window, warm and inviting.

"What is this place?" I ask.

"It's called the Hollow," she says, pushing open the door. "Tristan lives here."

I don't love the idea of staying with him, but no one else is offering space for me. Ruth's small cottage doesn't have the room, even if she'd offered to keep me.

I swallow down my unease, following her in. It's homey and simple, and everything looks handmade. We walk through a sparse foyer and past doorways, through which I can see a sitting room with a roaring fire, a kitchen, and a room with a great many books piled on an oak desk. She guides the way up the stairs. The decoratively carved banister is silk under my hands.

Here, there is a single hall lined with doors. She leads me to the farthest one. "That one's Tristan's," she says, gesturing all the way to the other side, "but it's best you don't disturb him."

I nod. It's probably best if I keep as far from him as possible. He took my trade easily enough, but I can't trust that he doesn't have tricks to put me off my quest.

Ruth shows me to my room and leaves me there. I hesitate, wondering if she'll spare me some wisdom, or a warning, as the old women always seem to in the stories I've been told. In Winston, it's always the old women trying to offer me advice, catching my hand and holding it, imparting wisdom cloaked in metaphor, like how there's something to be said about cows and milk and relativity to purchase.

But Ruth doesn't say anything at all, and I can't push down the thready, breathless panic at the thought of being here alone—and later, alone, *with* Tristan. When she's halfway out the door, I say, "Ruth."

She stops. Waits.

"Tristan. Is he . . . he won't hurt me, will he?"

At this, her face softens. "No," she says. "That's not the kind of person he is."

I chew on my lip, tasting the blood. I don't know if I can trust her, if I can take her word for it—but coming from her, from someone who has fed me and dressed me, it means *something*. And there's no qualification to follow it, no other warning. Perhaps that's what makes me bold.

"The other girls. The ones from Winston. What happened to them?"

There's no change in her face, no raising or lowering of her guard. "The Lord never harmed them," she says, as if that answers anything at all.

"Are they here?" I ask, wondering if Maria was behind me at the fire, if I could find her.

Ruth looks at me for a long moment, like she's considering me, reading me to the bone. "None wished to stay," she says finally.

Then, she turns, and she goes. Downstairs, the heavy door opens and closes, and through the window I watch her trek back off toward the clearing.

Alone. I'm alone.

I look around. I refuse to think of Ruth and her non-answer, or how it makes my mouth dry and my heart trip. *Wishing not to stay* is not the same as *leaving*, so I can't say for certain that they're gone. But it seems more likely that they're not here— so they must've gone somewhere else. For all I know, Maria Sinclair took her baby from this place, from the town that thought nothing of casting her out, and she ran. Maybe they all did.

I want to believe that. And until I see proof to the contrary, for my own sanity, I should.

The furniture is plain and simple, like everything else here. A wooden bed covered with a thick blue and white quilt, a writing desk against the window, a heavily carved armoire on the far wall, a basin of water on the vanity in the corner of the room. I swallow hard. I didn't think to ask about bathrooms, or plumbing, or anything obvious to me but not necessarily required here.

The water in the basin is warm. Though I'm freshly bathed, thanks to Ruth, I dip my hands in and splash the water on my face anyway. The mirror over the vanity reflects my image back to me, only just distorted enough to be disconcerting. My brown hair is a mare, tendrils curling away in all directions in sweat. Jess always jokes that she can tell my stress levels from the untidiness of my hair alone. Now, worried and alone, I am a sight.

And I still really don't know anything about Owen's whereabouts. Earlier, bargaining with the Lord of the Wood, it felt like I'd won something. I'm not so sure that I have anymore.

A month is a long time here. For all I know, I could be bargaining for a bag of my brother's bones.

I meet my own eyes in the mirror, this strange girl who grows stranger before me. I force myself to look.

Sinner. Distrustful. Forsaken. All of these words, they encompass who I am. What I've done. I grip the edge of the basin, staring down into the water within.

Perhaps I have never been due a reckoning, an escape. I am just as evil as my mother says, just as bad a daughter as anyone anywhere could have.

I blow out the candle on the vanity, letting the darkness swallow the room. Letting it swallow me whole.

Nine

When I wake, there's barely a second to remember where I am before my eyes light on the face hovering inches above mine. I shriek, swatting out, making contact with the person standing above me.

"Ow!"

"What are you doing!" I shout, barely making it a question.

"*I'm* being nice!"

It takes me a second to collect myself, to slow my breathing. My visitor stands over by the armoire in a rough-spun shirt and trousers with thick, heavy boots—the same kind of thing Tristan wears. Between us, the trunk from the end of my bed has been dragged over to my bedside, with a breakfast of bread and eggs and apple slices laid out on it.

"I'm Fletcher," my visitor says, rubbing the arm I must've accidentally smacked. "They/them pronouns. Not sure how common it is to be out in your neck of the woods."

I stare at them, letting the words make sense. "Oh," I say. They're right. It's not common to be out as anything other than cis or straight in Winston—I've never met a non-binary person in town, at least not someone who is out in town, at least not someone who is out—but I *have* been on the internet before. "Um, thank you for breakfast. Sorry I hit you?"

Fletcher shrugs. They have fine features and blond hair cropped close against their scalp. "Sorry I scared you."

I nod, taking the quiet to let my heart slow down. It takes only a few seconds for the memories of yesterday to come rushing back, for the gore of the deer and the heat of the fire and the rush of fear when I made my oath.

"Did Tristan send you?" I ask.

"Kind of. He asked me to make sure you were okay this morning. I live here, cook for the household, keep up the gardens outside. That kind of thing."

I didn't notice any gardens around the Hollow last night, but to be fair, I wasn't looking at much in my exhausted, terrified state.

It strikes me that Tristan asked Fletcher to make sure I was okay—which is not something that aligns with what I know of the Lord, or the stories of his cruelty. It puts me on edge a bit, realizing again I actually don't know anything about him.

Fletcher gestures to the plate. "Please, eat. I can keep you company, if you want."

I nod, sliding down to sit cross-legged on the floor, and swipe butter over the bread. It's good: The butter must have honey and salt in it, and the bread is sweet and soft. Fresh this morning, if I know anything.

I'm not a morning person, so it takes an embarrassing amount of time before I realize I can ask Fletcher questions too. Perhaps they'll be more forthcoming than Ruth.

"Are you one of the Lord's followers?" I ask, even though the question went badly last time. But I don't know where else to start.

"I'm a part of this community, if that's what you mean," Fletcher says easily.

I can't very well ask if it's a cult. If it is, they'll say it isn't. And if it isn't . . . well, believing in a cult is better than believing in anything else at play here.

"Were you born into it?" I ask.

Fletcher shakes their head. "No. None are born here, and those that are raised here are encouraged to go out into the world. Decide if they want to stay here for good."

I chew on my bread, considering this. I don't know if I believe them—but then again, if the "community" needs to steal babies, it would make sense if no one was born here. Maybe Fletcher's answer is more of a misdirection than a lie.

"And what is this place, then?"

Fletcher raises an eyebrow. "What do you mean?" they ask, like they're tempting me. I'm not brave enough for tricks and wordplay.

I push my plate away, half-eaten. "Y'all have been terrorizing my town for as long as memory goes back. Stealing kids. Hurting people. One of you stole my brother, and you can't tell me I'm not here for nothing, because Tristan already basically confirmed it." Anxiety knots in my stomach, but the worst Fletcher can do is tell me nothing.

"I walked through the woods for hours yesterday. Much longer than a day, I think, but there's no way I'm that far from Winston."

"Maybe you got turned around. Walked in circles."

"Maybe," I say, "but I was following Tristan for a while, too, and I don't know why he'd lead me in circles."

"Maybe we don't like your folk knowing where we live," Fletcher says, and I don't think I'm imagining the bite in their words.

I wince. It's true—no one in Winston has anything good to say about the Lord and his followers, and I certainly don't either.

"Can you prove we did anything to hurt you or your town? That Tristan did?"

"He stole my brother," I snap, probably too harsh. "That's been proven, has it not?"

Fletcher just watches me evenly until I look away, down at

my hands.

"We all come here to find something," Fletcher says, unprompted.

"Right," I say. It checks out. After all, I'm only here to find Owen, and then I'll be out of here as soon as possible. Once this month is up, once he's safely and unhappily back in my arms, I'm off.

"Some of us require a bit more looking." Fletcher moves from their position against the wall and stands over me. "Are you done eating?"

I nod, pushing the plate away—then stop, holding my silverware. If Fletcher goes, I'll be alone, and I don't know if I'm quite ready to be by myself yet. I don't know what I'm supposed to be doing here. I don't have anything to write a song with, and I'm not sure if it's an unfair advantage to ask Tristan for help.

"Should I . . . be doing something? Other than my task?" I ask, hating how meek and uncertain I sound. I was so much better at being brash and assertive when I was a child. I wore my stubbornness with pride. Now I wonder if it's all worn away, my nerve carried off like river sediment in the Yough before I'm even fully grown.

"Explore. Make yourself comfortable." Fletcher nods to the window. "No one here hates you, Leah. Not like you think they do. Not like they might where you're from."

"How do you know that they hate me in Winston?"

They scoff. "You're here, aren't you?"

Before I can defend myself, Fletcher is gone, taking any trace of my breakfast with them. Alone again, I go to the window and look out. I can barely see the lightening in the trees ahead where the clearing is.

I have a month, but perhaps I can get this over with ahead of time. I can't fight the unease shifting around just under my skin, keeping me prickly and nervous. I'll get myself dressed, find Ruth, see if she can help me get everything I need to write my song. And then I'll get it finished and get out of here. Maybe it'll even take less than a week, if that's allowed. Owen and I can go home, and I can put all of this behind me.

Steeling my nerves, I go through the armoire and drawers until I find underthings and another dress in soft blue cotton. I put them on and abandon my worn-in tennis shoes for a pair of boots I find in the bottom of the trunk.

Eerily, everything fits. It's like Tristan knew I was coming.

I scrape my messy tangle of hair into a bun and leave my bedroom behind. It's weird leaving the house without my phone, a wallet, or house keys. I feel naked without any of the trappings of my everyday life. When I shut the front door, I test it out just in case, but it remains unlocked and opens easily.

Outside, I hesitate. There are things I need to do, people I need to talk to—but. Outside the house, back in the open, knowing that I'm in the Lord's domain, it's impossible to find the bravery or certainty or frustrated exhaustion I cloaked myself in last night.

There's a scraping sound coming from the other side of the house. It must be Fletcher, tending the garden. I stomp through the mud in my heavy boots, seeking them out, because they might actually know where Tristan is or what the other girls offered to him, or what happened to them. I just need to push a little harder, get what I need. *Someone* here will tell me the truth.

But it isn't Fletcher digging on the side of the house. It's Tristan, his hands caked in mud as he moves stones around the edge of a small pond. His wolf lays in the shadow of the house, its eyes tracing after Tristan's every move. He's not wearing that copper circlet anymore. Here, he looks like a boy, and not . . . well, not whatever he is.

"Hi," I say, before I can think better of it.

Tristan looks up at me. I think he was aware of my presence before, could hear me moving through the half-cleared dirt pathway.

"Hi," he says, making no move to stop his work.

I nod to the wolf. "What's your dog's name?"

"Whit," Tristan says. He reaches forward to scratch the wolf's great head. Whit's eyes close and his black nose twitches. "I possibly wasn't the most creative in my younger years, but he doesn't seem to mind."

I snort. The wolf's eyes open and he gazes at me. It takes me a second to realize Tristan is looking, too. Their eyes weigh me down.

I'm not here to talk about wolves. "I want to see Owen," I say.

Tristan's expression changes in an instant, locks down. I knot my fingers in the soft cotton skirt of my dress. That look makes me feel small, and I hate it.

"I can't do that," he says.

"Tristan—"

"Not yet," he snaps, cutting me off. I chew on my lip. There's the taste of blood nearly immediately—I worried it too much last night and my teeth slip into the healing wounds.

"How do you expect me to trust you if I can't see him?" I ask.

Tristan stands, rising to his full height. This close, he towers over me. I step back, desperate for space.

"No one said you had to trust me," Tristan says magnanimously. "We made a bargain. Not a vow."

I look away, off into the wood. The sheer wall of rock that backs the Hollow runs for another hundred yards, then peters out into a hill. I could probably walk up the whole thing, sit on the edge, look down on Tristan and his estate. I could make it small, frameable within my hands. A matter of perspective.

Tristan sighs unexpectedly. "He's safe, Leah," he says. I don't realize I'm crying until he offers me a handkerchief from his pocket. I grimace, wiping the tears with my hand instead. He sighs again and shoves the handkerchief away.

"I cannot take you to him today. It is not my right. But I can show you something else."

"Why should I believe you?" I ask, since trust is certainly off the table.

"It will help you with your task."

I look back at him, his brown skin and black curls and mismatched eyes. He's beautiful. I think, if he walked through the gas station on my shift, or down the halls of my high school, my heart would thud faster every time he passed. I'd think there was something otherworldly about him. Maybe I'd have full conversations with Jess about his long eyelashes and full lips. He'd be beautiful in my town, in my world, but he's even more beautiful here in the green of the wood, where the dappled sunlight makes traceries of gold on his skin. And I cannot let that burn me, cannot let that distract me.

I don't have to trust him—but he didn't lead me astray in the woods yesterday, and I don't think it's in his interest to lead me astray just yet.

"Okay," I agree. "Show me."

Ten

Yet again, I find myself following Tristan through the woods. He's slower this time, so I'm at his side rather than staring at his back, but he still knows the way and I don't. If he turned and left me, I would be truly lost.

"I'm sorry I snapped at you," Tristan says finally, when the silence between us is thick and heavy. "I only meant that it's easiest for everyone if you focus on the task at hand."

I nod. "I'll be sure to do that."

Tristan's mouth thins into a line. It's not the response he wanted. Well, too bad—I don't want to be here, and it seems he doesn't want me to be here either.

I keep my eyes on the path, avoiding stones and roots. The trail isn't as clear here as it was on the way from Winston.

Tristan stops and I barely notice in time to avoid stumbling into him. He's looking at a tree, brow furrowed. I glance over too, taking in the dark spots on the leaves, the patches of rot on the trunk.

"What is that?" I ask.

He shrugs. Tristan goes to the tree and puts both hands on the bark, gazing up at its height. The wind stirs, rustling the leaves. He runs one hand farther up the trunk and I watch the movement of his fingers on the bark, perhaps too intently. He still wears one ring, a simple gold one, now edged with dirt from his earlier work. He moves closer, close enough that his body is nearly pressed against the tree.

Above us, the dark spots on the leaves begin to fade. He rests his forehead against the bark and I watch, mystified, as the rot recedes from the trunk. His fingers twist, coaxing, and from the ground beneath his feet, vines twist from nothing at a dizzying speed, wrapping around the tree, covering the places the rot once was like bandages. Flowers bloom, white against the green and brown.

I stare, open-mouthed.

Tristan backs away, eying his handiwork. "It's okay now," he says, running his fingers along one of the fresh green vines. "I try to keep our part of the forest healthy. Whole."

I should be afraid. I should hold tight to what my mother told me about the Lord, fear him and his power. I should not speak a word to him again, let alone trust him.

I clench my hands into fists. "You're not human," I say. Perhaps it's obvious.

He eyes me warily. "No, I'm not."

"What are you?"

A bird calls up ahead, and he gazes into the sky. Whit did not come with us, choosing instead to find a shady patch against the house. I suddenly wish he was here, if nothing else than to serve as a witness.

"I don't know," Tristan says finally. He bends down to pick a few of the flowers from the vine, and sticks them in the pocket of his shirt. "I don't know if there's a word for what I am."

"But how do you *know* that?" I ask, biting back the frustration.

He shrugs, standing back up, setting off down the path once more like he can leave this conversation behind with his handiwork. "How do you know you're human? How do you know what it means to be one of your ilk? You were once told that you were human, that you were mortal. I was told that I was not. I know that I am different because I am—I don't know the name or the classification for those differences, as perhaps I never had to name myself, never had to defend what I am. I am the Lord of the Wood, like my brother before me and our mother before him, and I know what I can do, and what I cannot. But to know what I am? That's not something for me to declare."

I was not expecting such a speech from him. We stare at each other, the air full of a smell like ozone mixed with chlorophyll. I can't place the scent, but I don't think I should be able to. Perhaps it's the smell of Tristan's magic.

I can't worry about the details, or stumble over every question. I'm not here to find answers, or assimilate with the Lord's cult, or find out who he is, or learn anything at all. I'm here to finish my quest and get Owen and go home.

It doesn't matter who he is. Where we are. The rules of this place do not concern me.

That's what I tell myself.

"Okay," I say, inclining my head just enough, like I would after Pastor Samuel gives me the communion wafer and says a blessing over my head. Supplication.

"Okay," Tristan says. He takes a deep breath and runs his hand through his curls, looking off into the distance. The set of his shoulders is tense—he's not accustomed to explaining himself. I wonder if it's a kind of lowering, to come down to my level. I'm just a girl, and not a very valuable one at that.

"Come on," Tristan says, stalking off ahead. "The surprise is waiting."

I bite my tongue from saying more and follow him, picking a careful path through the woods. I steal a look up at him, just to be sure he's still going ahead, not looking back at me.

Tristan doesn't owe me anything. He didn't simply give Owen back, even though he'd been stolen—that involved a barter, a sacrifice. Even to *get here*, I needed to sacrifice. I don't believe he'll give me anything easily that is outside the realm of common hospitality. Not answers, not Owen, not help. I should keep that in mind.

It doesn't matter, I tell myself. I don't need his answers, and I don't need his help. I don't need to know any more than I already do. It *doesn't matter*.

I'm so deep in my own thoughts that it takes me a moment to realize that Tristan is humming to himself. Well, half humming—some of the bits are lyrics in a reedy baritone, and he switches back and forth absentmindedly.

I don't recognize the tune, but I like it. It's ... warm. Mournful. It's like the hymn Grammy would sing to me on Black Friday, as we boiled Easter eggs for dying on Saturday morning and fried up fish for dinner before the church service. It reminds me of her wrinkled hands, certain as can be as she flipped the golden brown fish, not caring if the hot oil splattered her. The name comes to me the more I probe at the memory: "The Old Rugged Cross." I'm certain that's not what Tristan's singing, but it's similar enough.

I listen a bit longer, until I can mimic the tune. When I hum along with him, he stops abruptly and looks back.

"Didn't think your kin remembered that song," Tristan says.

"We don't."

Tristan makes a face, his lips pressed together, but then he seems to think better of whatever line of thought he's going down. He shrugs and slows his pace slightly so we're walking together, side by side, instead of me following behind.

"You offered up a song so readily," Tristan says.

"You wouldn't settle for a limb."

He snorts. "If you really want to give me one, I'll take it. But you'll still owe me a song."

I glance over to find him looking askance at me. His eyelashes are so long, framing his mismatched eyes, casting shadows over his cheeks. The light is thin from the overcast sky. It seems like twilight light, old and gray, but it's far too early for that.

"What limb would you choose?" I ask, trying to keep my tone as light as possible.

He shrugs. "I imagine Whit would quite enjoy your radius. An arm would do."

"Hmm." I stick my hands in my dress pockets—and pause. There's something in there. I pull it out and hold it, flat in my palm. A small cloth bag, see-through, with seeds inside.

Tristan's brow furrows. "I think that's Ruth's."

"Well *I* didn't take it so—"

"I wasn't accusing you of taking it," he says. He plucks it out of my hand and squints at it, probing the seeds. "That's who the clothes are from. Ruth, from when she was younger."

I bite my lip again, wincing at the pain of the wound I can't stop worrying. It wasn't really that I thought he was accusing me . . . it's just that, in Winston, that would be the easiest assumption for my parents to make. That I'd taken something, inadvertently or otherwise. I can be forgetful sometimes. Leave things in pockets, come home from work with the gas station's bathroom key still in my hand, leave the back door unlocked after I go to take the trash out. Jess tells me that it's okay, that we all do these little things, but my mother hates it more than anything. Says I'm irresponsible and immature, that I don't know the value of things; I'm too naive to remember anything useful.

She once got Pastor Samuel to give me a whole talk about responsibility one evening when I was fifteen. It was right when Dad started working away, right when it shifted from the three of us to the two, when my responsibilities grew and grew and grew. I remember the stern look on his face, the sweat forming on his upper lip as he talked to me about the importance of heeding my mother. He quoted some scripture that I've now forgotten—I remember thinking it wasn't a particularly good verse—but it made Mom happy, so I tried to look respectful and kind and good, and kept my head down.

But the seeds. Tristan puts the packet back in my hand. "She won't care," he says. "They're not important. Keep it."

I nod, ducking my head to hide my reddening cheeks. I don't even know why the rush of embarrassment hits.

"Here we are," Tristan says, surprising me. I glance around. It's just woodland still, nothing else to see. But he's stumbling over a rockfall, and his curly head disappears just past it. I hurry to follow him and stop in my tracks, nearly sliding down the mossy rock in my surprise.

On the other side, in the middle of the wood, nestled into a thick patch of ivy and bramble, Tristan leans against a piano.

A *piano*.

We have a few pianos at school. One in the music room, one on the stage of the ramshackle auditorium. And a third one, tucked into an old cleaning closet that some of the band students use for a practice room. It's not soundproofed, so sometimes if you go back there after lunch you can hear the squawking of a clarinet or the blare of a trumpet as they run through music. The old choir teacher, Miss Chambers, gave me the key to it back when I was a freshman, when she heard I was interested in playing. She didn't even take it away when she went on to a different school district with a bigger budget, who didn't call the choir rude names during the quiet parts of their in-school concerts.

It was my refuge on the days when Jess was out sick, or when Mom had to drop me off at school early before work. I'd sit at that piano and run scales and try to play chords from popular songs on the radio, and run through the different pieces that Miss Chambers kept stored in the bench. When I came back after being out for junior year, it was devastating to find the janitors had taken the closet back, piled supplies on and around the old piano until it was unplayable, and the loss ached in me like I'd had a limb torn away. It was out of tune, but it was *mine*.

Not really—of course it was the school's—but it was my thing, my little piece of contentment. So much better than my dinky keyboard that didn't have enough keys.

Now, there's a whole other piano, sitting right there in the misty forest with Tristan beaming in front of it like he's presenting me with some sort of prize.

I can't find the words in me to speak.

"Where did you get that?" I ask finally when sense returns. It looks old—and possibly out of tune, since it's been standing here in the damp wood long enough to have ivy twining around the legs—and beyond that, I can't imagine Tristan walking into some sort of instrument store or secondhand shop and putting down the money for this. I can't imagine anyone bringing it here.

The light in his eyes dims. "I didn't get it," he says. "It's always been here, or it was meant to be here, or it appeared because it had to. What matters that it *is*."

More cryptic answers, but I don't push. I pick my way through the ivy to the piano. It's gorgeous, red-mahogany wood and smooth, ivory keys. I slip past Tristan and lower myself onto the seat. When I play the piano, it isn't out of tune at all. The tone is gorgeous and sweet, flowing over the forest like river water. I play a snippet from a Hans Zimmer score that I obsessed over a few years ago to check if any keys stick, if any sound is dead or out of tune.

When I look up, Tristan is leaning on the piano, elbows on the leaf-scattered wood, watching me intently.

I swallow hard, pulling my hands back and knotting my fingers in my lap. "It's beautiful. Thank you."

"It's yours, for as long as you want it. I hope it will be of use to you."

"It will," I say. I don't know how else to phrase my gratitude—or if I should trust this gift in the first place. I don't know Tristan's magic. Perhaps the piano will just disappear when I really need it. The thought makes my stomach turn.

I don't know how to not ruin good things. I don't know how to keep them—how to make myself worth the *having*.

As if he can physically see my guard going up, Tristan nods and steps back. "I'll leave you to your work," he says. "You should be able to find your way back on your own. Just keep a clear image of the Hollow in your mind, and the forest will not let you go astray."

Before I can respond, he's on his way, cutting a line through the trees with a confidence that makes me uneasy.

Eleven

No matter how I try, how many exercises I play, the notes do not come easily. I stay at the piano until the twilight wood begins to grow darker and I can no longer ignore the chill in the air. My thoughts keep turning, willingly or otherwise, to the girls who came before me. Tristan hasn't been cruel in the slightest, not like he should've been, not like the stories said he would be. *No one* here has been cruel. But Ruth said the other girls chose not to stay.

If this is how it is, if this is what the wood is like . . . I don't know why they'd go back to Winston. But perhaps, as usual, that points to a failing in my character. *They* could bear the weight of expectations, and even the heavier despair of disappointment.

Or maybe they didn't. Maybe all the girls came out of the wood and realized there's something more than Winston out there, left this town and Carver County without a word and never looked back. It wouldn't be hard—and the thought is more tempting to me than it should be.

It's too cold when the sun is nearly gone, and only then do I leave, trying to keep the Hollow in my mind, like Tristan told me to. Soon—much sooner than it felt this morning—I can see the edge of the cliff and the incline down. When I reach the house, the windows are warm with light. Whatever Fletcher is cooking inside smells good.

I knock the mud off my boots on the front stoop and leave them unlaced by the front door. In my socks, I follow the scent permeating the house. It's good and rich, gravy and butter and bread, and my hunt leads me through a sitting room and an office, to the back of the house. There, I find a big wooden table with eight chairs in front of a crackling fire.

I hesitate. Only one place is set. But upon closer inspection, there's a note there, next to the pewter cup of water:

Eat.

-T

The note could be for Fletcher, but I doubt it. The chair creaks when I lower myself down and tuck my knees under the table. My mouth waters at the sight of the food even as an odd gnawing loneliness tugs at my stomach.

It isn't that I want company, for Tristan or Fletcher or Ruth or one of the others out there who I haven't met to join me. But the loneliness tugs at me all the same.

I tell myself it doesn't matter. I won't have help in my quest—I should get used to loneliness.

My hands are folded out of muscle memory, the short three lines of grace tripping off my tongue, and I'm halfway through the blessing when I realize there's no *reason* for it—Mom isn't here watching me, judging me, and no one will know. I hesitate, the words *we are fed* lingering on my tongue, but what's the point of stopping?

My feelings about religion and my own faith are too tangled with disappointment and scar tissue to look at them with any nuance. It's certainly not something I can handle right now.

" . . . Give us Lord our daily bread. Amen." I finish it, more out of duty, out of habit, than anything else. Anxiously, I check over my shoulder—I don't know how I'd feel if Tristan heard me praying. What he'd think. What I'd want him to say.

The plate in front of me is piled with potatoes and parsnips, roasted chicken and gravy, with a crusty slice of bread to one side. I eat until the loneliness is buried and my stomach feels heavy and warm. Then, I pick my way back through the house, upstairs, to my rooms. It's too hot with the raging fire in the fireplace, so I open the window a few inches to let the cool air in.

There are a few books in the cubbies of the desk and a cloth-bound notebook. I was never much a reader though: that was Jess. When we were younger, we used to read fantasy series together, her racing ahead of me and waiting impatiently for me to finish book after book. Then, Emily Cart was our other best friend, and we thought she was so cool because she wasn't born in Winston. But she was only there for two or three years until her parents decided the town was too weird, too religious, too superstitious, and they whisked her away to a new town.

I flick through the books. They're old: *Alice in Wonderland* and *Tales of the Brothers Grimm* and *Wuthering Heights*, all yellowed and cracking at the spines. I read a page of each and discard them into the corner.

It's almost dark out, and a light rain has started. It patters on the roof. I consider going to find Tristan for entertainment, but I think better of it. Even going for a bath seems like too much effort.

Everything feels like too much effort. I stare at my reflection in the window, letting the heaviness of my limbs weigh me down.

Mom says I'm lazy, and I know Dad thinks it too. Grammy didn't agree, since I would do anything she asked of me—but she was also nice to me. Jess had a running argument that I "didn't apply myself" in school, like she was just parroting Mr. Gumpton, our guidance counselor. But maybe I am lazy, and terrible, and full of all the wrong things, all of this mess crowding inside of me, strangling out any ground that goodness would otherwise have.

I don't know if I believe that. In truth, I spend a lot of time inside my own head—so much that I think I'm distracted, so overwhelmed with my own little world that I forget there are other things going on outside of it. So in love with romantic notions of what is and isn't that I get carried away. And that's what got me, this concept that everything would turn out okay, that I was some heroine in a story of Winston, when that was not at all the case. I'm just as destined for that cursed soil as my mother, and her mother before her.

I'm so deep in my own thoughts that I barely notice the muddy fingers gripping my windowsill until the second hand appears.

My throat locks—I can't scream. I skitter back, knocking my chair to the ground. I can't see the shape outside the window, not fully, not with the glow of candlelight in the room.

"*Leah.*" The voice is rugged and rough, terrible. I have the urge to grab the window and slam it down on those fingers, but that requires going closer to the window, to the *thing*.

A pale face appears in the gap. Eyes black as coals.

Someone—some*thing* has come for me. I cannot move, panic flooding every other sense. The scream catches in my throat, a breathless lump that chokes me.

Finally, my body reacts. I grab for the fireplace poker and launch at the window, at the *thing*. I lash out, smash the glass, stab at the hands until they're gone and there's a heavy thud on the ground under my window.

The poker drips with black, brackish blood. I don't know what damage I've done to the creature, but I suspect it was a lot.

Hesitantly, I lean out the window and check the ground below. There's nothing there—whatever was at my window, trying to get in, has already run off.

"Leah?"

I turn, hand to my heart as if I can press it in, command it to stop thudding quite so hard.

Tristan blinks at me, perplexed. His shirt is halfway unbuttoned like I caught him in the middle of undressing, his suspenders off his shoulders and hanging down by his hips. Like me, he doesn't wear shoes, and his socks are heavy and woolen and he looks so devastatingly human, even though I know better. Even though he *told* me differently.

I realize how *I* look, then. Perhaps less human, wild-eyed, hair askew, standing in front of the shattered window with a bloody poker in my hands.

"There was something at my window," I stammer.

One dark eyebrow rises. "What kind of something?"

I swallow hard. But really, besides that pale face and dark eyes, those muddy fingers with dirt crusted under the nails, I don't know. For all I know, I've just stabbed Fletcher.

"Um. Pale? Skinny fingers? Knew my name, too."

Tristan makes a low noise in his throat. He's across the room in four quick strides and leans over me to take in the wreckage. His sleeves are rolled to his elbows, and his arms are corded with muscle. I imagine he does a lot of manual labor to get those kinds of muscles—and then I know I'm looking too much, and I curse myself for it.

At least the adrenaline has mostly wound down.

He examines the dirt on the windowsill. "It was probably just a ghost," he says.

"*Just a ghost?*" I repeat, aghast.

His eyes shift to me. I realize how close he is to me in front of the window, his body radiating heat on my arm closest to him as the rest of me is hit with the chill of the air from outside. I step back, settling closer to the fire. Almost close enough to burn.

Tristan busies himself with the shattered glass, cleaning it away with the spine of one of the books. "They're . . . kind of ghosts. Omens. They don't really bother me anymore, but I don't have much in my past that could be used to bother me."

I don't like how his eyes catch me when he says that. Like he knows I have something to answer for, some atonement. A shudder runs down my spine, and I remember the shape of his mouth when he called me his supplicant.

"What do you mean, kind of ghosts?"

Tristan shrugs. He goes to the big trunk at the end of my bed, the one Fletcher set as a table this morning, and pulls a heavy blanket from inside. He drapes this over the curtain rod to keep out the cold—and block out the sight.

I don't know if I like it. If something climbs up now, I can imagine it, slithering under that curtain. Hovering over me in my sleep with great black eyes.

"You can answer me," I snap, too harsh. But I'm so tired of him, his secrecy and his half-explanations.

I'm tired of being here, where I don't know anyone or understand anything. Maybe they hated me in Winston, but at least I understood that. At least I knew I was lazy and terrible and that the whispers when I passed by in the lunchroom were about me. But even the awfulness was predictable. I woke up to my mother's disappointment, dealt with Owen's inexplicable hatred, forced myself through the school day, buried myself in responsibilities and shifts at the gas station, and tried to cleanse myself in prayer every Sunday, tried to become someone else. I held it all in, let it out in the times when I ducked my head under the water and screamed and screamed and screamed.

My point is, it was awful, but it was a terribleness that I understood. Here, even the mundane is a mystery, and I hate it. I hate not knowing my place, not understanding the rules.

In Winston, even if I broke the rules, at least I knew them first.

Tristan takes a step toward me. "Why are you so desperate to know everything?"

I bare my teeth like a cornered animal. "Why are you so insistent on keeping me in the dark?"

Tristan takes another step closer. He's just a few inches taller than me, but even so, he's intimidating. Perhaps it's because he's the Lord of this wood and everything in it, and right now, that includes me. Perhaps it's because there *is* something unknowable and inhuman and his mismatched eyes and that scares me—or perhaps because it *should,* and it doesn't.

My mom always told me that if I kept moving closer and closer to the fire, I would wake up one day and find myself burned. She said that little girls, *good* little girls, shouldn't crave sin like I do.

But if defiance is a sin, then I'm already gone. Destined to burn forever and ever. I try to make myself seem bigger, more intimidating, as I face Tristan down.

"Anything I deign not to tell you," he says softly, "is for your own safety."

"But—"

"You are not one of us, Leah. You know that as well as I do. Many of our secrets have no explanation."

I cross my arms over my chest, leaning into the bitter familiarity of defiance. "I don't accept that," I say. "Something was just trying to get in my *window,* Tristan—maybe you don't care about me knowing things, but how am I supposed to feel safe here?"

I don't know what I expect—perhaps for him to roll his eyes, turn on his heel, tell me I don't know what's good for me. He'd be right—I don't.

But he doesn't. If anything, his gaze softens. "I want you to be able to sleep at night," he says.

And that . . . something about the way he says it, the gentleness, catches me off guard. Now I'm the one flushed and looking away. "You don't have to tell me I don't belong here. I already know."

It's not the point, and we both know it. A deflection. Protection from knowing too much, from leaning too far.

Tristan says, "There are things in these woods that are echoes—be they of pain, of memory, of anger and sadness. But they're here, and most of us have come to terms with them. You might've noticed there is no time here, not really. There are only the echoes of what has happened or what is to come. That's the truth. The ghosts in this realm cannot hurt you. They do not exist. They are only reminders."

I glance up, away from the shattered glass, to find him watching me.

"And you?" I ask. "Are you a memory, then?"

His hand reaches out, hovers between us, before he links it with mine. "No," he says, looking at our twined hands. I cannot move, pinned under his gaze. "I am flesh and blood, and I am to be your reckoning."

His mouth quirks up, the edge of a smile flirting on his full lips. I know my eyebrows are drawn together, that I'm pouting up at him, but I can't stop.

"But tomorrow," Tristan says, "I will grant you one request: We will go see Owen, if only to prove to you that I'm telling the truth. I've done him no harm."

"Oh." The moisture evaporates from my mouth. I can't hide the flicker of panic in my face before Tristan sees it.

"You won't need your song now, of course," he says quickly, like that's what I was panicking about. I nod, trying to cover, because it's impossible to explain to him that, though I'm confused and stressed and lost, these have been the first hours of my life since Owen was born that I could think of anything else.

That I *like* not worrying about Owen, even though I came to save him.

"Thank you," I say anyway, because I have to. I nod toward the window. "And thank you for helping me."

"Of course," Tristan says, fading even farther back toward the door. The mirth is gone, like something in him switched off. His shoulders fall slightly, and he's just a boy—not the Lord, not my protector. He runs a hand through his hair, and he looks at anything but me. For the first time, I'm struck by the idea that he might not always be such a domineering figure.

Perhaps I've misread him—aligned the trappings of the Lord, the mystery of the figure Winston has always feared, with the boy in front of me. I don't know how to reconcile the two of them, the god and the flesh.

"If you need me or anything from me, please ask. Fletcher is here too, if it's too much for you to trust me. You shouldn't—I'm sorry I haven't been the most hospitable."

As if I need more reason to owe him.

I shake my head, waiting for him to leave so I can collapse in on myself. "It's fine. Thank you."

Tristan nods. He goes out, leaving me to my own devices. When I'm sure he's gone, I dart back to the window and lift up the heavy blanket. There's no reflection now, of course, with the glass shattered, so it's easy to look out and see the dark of the forest laid out below.

There, in the shadow of one of the tall, thick trees, I see the girl, half in shadow. Pale skin, almost luminescent in the moon-light, a nightgown of plain white cotton, dark hair. There are spots of blood on her nightgown, probably where they've dripped from her head, where I hit her with the poker.

A ghost. *My* ghost, if Tristan is to believed—not literally, but I feel the aching sadness rolling off of her even from this distance.

I didn't know ghosts could bleed.

I stare at her. She stares back. I'm not sure how long we stay like that until, in the space between one blink and the next, she disappears.

Twelve

Fletcher doesn't wake me in the morning, but there's a breakfast tray waiting for me all the same. I can only pick at it. The lead in my stomach doesn't allow for much of an appetite.

Tristan is taking me to see Owen today. Owen, who I came here for. Owen, who I promised to save, who I would sacrifice anything for if pushed hard enough. Apparently.

I leave the breakfast and peek out of my room. There's a small bathroom a few doors down, fitted with something like modern plumbing. I run the water in the bath while I pee and discard my nightgown into a heap in the corner of the floor. There's a sturdy shelving unit full of rough towels, and I grab one.

Though I did nothing to the water, it smells like lavender and rosemary. I lower myself into the steaming bath, all the way down, until the water closes over my head.

When we were in eighth grade, a nuclear physicist came to talk to us about reactors. It was for a state-funded program, trying to get more of us into STEM. Didn't really work—most of us tend to stay around Winston, and it's not like there are many STEM jobs going there—but the whole school filed into the dilapidated auditorium and were not-so-nicely forced into silence for the entirety of his talk. Jess sat on one side of me, Trent on the other, and we went back and forth playing games of tic-tac-toe on the back of the chair in front of us.

But that's not the point. The main thing I remember about that talk is this: Nuclear reactors are submerged in water, and the water prevents radiation from escaping. And if a major nuclear event was happening, he suggested we all run for the closest lake and swim for the bottom.

I'm not sure how much I believe all that—I'm not a science person—but I get that water is a buffer. It has a smothering effect. And down here, it's like I can think whatever I want, scream and shout and put my brain through the worst and most terrible thoughts, and it doesn't escape besides a few bubbles to the surface. No one ever heard me, when I was under water: not Mom or Dad or Grammy, not Jess, not even God.

It's safe. It's peaceful. It's like a quiet home for all of the worst parts of me.

I come up for air, and let myself sink back down. In Tristan's deep bathtub, with the sunlight shining through the far window glimmering on the water and my closed eyelids, it feels okay.

I don't want to see Owen. I'm only going because it's expected of me, because I have to.

I don't want to save Owen.

My life was better without him.

I miss who I was in the time before he existed.

I let all of it rush out, play across my mind in a shout. My thoughts haven't felt this clear or sharp in months and I think it has something to do with the fact that these are the first couple of nights I've slept clear through since Owen was born.

I'd be damned if these thoughts got out, if there was actual confirmation to my mom and everyone else that I was just as rotten inside as they thought I was. I imagine a knife, slicing me open from collarbone to pelvis, hands splitting me open to expose the evil black sludge of corruption within me. Everything inside of me is bad, sinful, awful: That's what Pastor Samuel told me last year, at one of those awful dinners Mom hosted where the three of us sat around the table and the two of them talked over me until their barbed words worked their way under my skin and I could take no more. The dinners always ended in shouting from me, and sharp, derisive words from them.

Mom always hoped I could be saved. Healed. That something would make me into a good girl, a daughter she could be proud of.

I surface. Wipe the damp strands of hair from my face. Hug

my knees to my chest. With the water streaming down my face, it's hard to tell if I am crying or not.

When Tristan comes for me, I'm finishing my second braid. The other hangs wet and heavy over my shoulder, dripping onto my sage green button-down dress. I remind myself that I'll have to venture into the village and thank Ruth for her clothes when we're back—they're all soft and well-made, comfortable in the changing season of the forest.

Tristan meets my eye in the mirror and perches on the edge of my bed. He doesn't say anything in greeting. I watch his reflection as his gaze shifts over to my broken window, with the blanket covering it tied to one side to let the light in. He presses his lips together in an expression I can't read.

"I suppose you don't have plastic wrap and duct tape," I say, tying off my braid and wringing the water out of the end.

"Hmm?"

"For the window." I pull on my wool socks and grab a notebook, in case some sort of inspiration strikes for my song. I need *something* to come to me—so far, all I can think to write about is how relieved I am to sleep without Owen crying, and I don't think that makes a convincing argument for Tristan to give him back.

"I'll fix it within the next few days," Tristan says absently. "What is *duck tape?*"

"Duct. Sticky. Fixes things."

"Mmph." He looks me up and down, from my wool-covered feet to my wet hair. "Ready?"

"As I'll ever be." I follow him downstairs and lace my boots by the front door. Outside, the air smells like fresh dirt and rain.

"Did the ghost bother you any more?" Tristan asks. His tone is light, casual, despite the topic of discussion.

I shake my head, and he doesn't push. We walk through the woods in a silence that no longer feels hostile. I don't know what shifted—maybe it was last night, in my room, with his face shadowed by firelight—but I don't think he hates me. I don't even think he wants to keep me very much. It's just a process, and if I think of it like that, perhaps it makes everything else easier. At the very least, it allows me to look at Tristan (it's easier to only use his name and not acknowledge that he's the Lord of the Wood) as something other than my enemy.

He seems lost in his own thoughts as we walk. He slips into humming again, the same tune as yesterday or one very similar. I try my best to commit the notes of it to memory.

I don't know how long we walk through the woods, the sunlight dappled green through the leaves, the only sound Tristan's humming and the crunch of our boots through the underbrush. The trail is narrow, and his hand brushes mine often enough that we stop apologizing for it.

Eventually, I can smell the smoke of a woodfire, and soon after, there's a little cottage through the trees. It's the kind that I always imagined when I read fairy tales: gray stone and wood, worn in, surrounded by a garden of wildflowers that looks equal parts tidy and unkempt. There's a man outside, wearing clothes similar to Tristan's—old fashioned, well-made, ones I wouldn't expect to find in the mall. He's chopping wood mechanically, getting through one piece and pushing it aside for the next in smooth, repetitive motions.

Tristan stops, and I pause next to him. There's no sound of crying coming from the cottage. Only birdsong, and the babbling of a creek in the distance.

"Are you going to say something?" I ask. "Introduce me to them? Tell that man why we're here?"

Tristan shakes his head. "They can't see us right now."

I frown, moving forward. We're well within the man's eye-line, and I'm sure he's taken with his work but it's not like we're hiding behind trees or anything.

"I mean, they actually can't see us," Tristan says to my back. "We're in a different eddy in the river of time."

I look over my shoulder at him, uncertain. "I don't know what you're talking about." Sometimes, he's unnervingly cryptic.

Tristan's mouth thins to a line. He goes up to the man, *right* up to him, and puts his hand on the piece of wood just as the man raises the axe over his shoulder. He's going to get his *hand chopped off,* and I shriek and cover my eyes before I see the whole grisly thing—

But the axe whistles down, and there's a noise as it cuts through the wood. No sound of flesh or bone, no shout from Tristan.

The birds sound the same. The creek babbles on.

I look straight ahead. Tristan is still there, his hand now in midair as the man knocks aside the cut wood and loads up another piece.

It takes a moment for my heart to stop racing. For my breathing to return to normal.

"I wouldn't put you in a position worse than the one you're already in," Tristan says to me. I don't understand his meaning, but it doesn't matter.

"That wasn't very nice," I tell him.

"Sometimes it's easier to do a demonstration. Time—it's all a bit hard to explain, is it not?"

Perhaps that's allowable. I slowly make my way through the last few feet of underbrush into the clearing and join Tristan as he leans against the wall and looks through the window.

Inside, it's warm and cozy, with a pot bubbling on the stove. We can see the main living area, with a kitchen and dining table and a cozy area for sitting. There, a woman sits in a rocking chair. Owen sleeps on her chest, his hand curled into a fist under his cheek. Drool drips from his parted lips. I think she's singing to him as she's rocking him, but I can't tell for certain.

And I—

I—

I am not prepared for the utter gut punch of feeling that rips through me at the sight of him. When I was younger, I used to think all babies look the same, but I know him as well as I know my own reflection. Owen, *my* Owen, in this unfamiliar place, sleeping soundly. There are wood toys scattered on the floor, much nicer than the ones we were ever able to afford, and he's wrapped in a blanket that looks handmade and I cannot fathom the adoration in the woman's face as she sings to him, rocks him, loves him.

I'm moving before I can think any better of it, staggering back through the woods and away, away, away. I can't look at this, can't accept it—to do so would be to confront the utter relief I've felt over the last few days, the weight of the burden lifted off of me. To do so would be terrible, hideous, perilous and I am—

I am weak, and I am terrible, and corrupted and rotten, all of the things Mom said I was, all the things they tell us not to be over and over again. I stagger forward until I trip on a rock and lurch to my knees, and I dig my fingers into the soil, past the bracken of underbrush, and I sob.

The best thing I have ever seen, the most relief I've ever felt, has come from seeing Owen in someone else's arms. Someone else's responsibility. Someone else's family.

There's a hand on my back, and then someone is pulling my shoulders, dragging me out of the dirt. I sprawl across a lap, strong arms wrapped around me, and I tangle my fingers in his shirt.

It's Tristan's stomach I'm crying into, Tristan's lap I'm sprawled across, Tristan's arms holding me tight, voice comforting me, hands in my hair, but I don't care. I *cannot* care.

Part of my brain is latched onto this, incapable of understanding how he can be so easily softened into someone willing to give me comfort when no one else I'd always loved would. It's a dangerous line of thought, one I can't risk myself falling into.

But the greater part of my brain is on Owen—Owen who I love, Owen who I hate, Owen who I lost.

"I'm sorry," he says, over and over again. "I'm so sorry. If I'd known how hard it would be to see him—"

But that makes me cry worse, because it was not hard at all. It's the imagining him coming back that's hard. Imagining carrying him through the woods, all the way to Winston.

His voice is unsteady when he says, "I only take what is given, Leah. I only get what is offered to me, and I cannot—"

I know. I know, I know, I know.

I sit up, shoulders still shaking with the grief of it all. Tuck my knees to my chest. Tristan watches me steadily, face twisted with despair, and I want so badly to be held again. I wipe the tears, probably streaking mud all over my face.

"I'm the one who asked you to take him," I say, my words barely a whisper in my tear-rough throat. "I'm the one who offered him to you."

Thirteen

Twice, I offered Owen to the Lord of the Wood, though I
didn't know that was what I was doing. But it was, and I had,
and it's my fault that he's here, just like everything else.

The second time I offered Owen, the time that stuck, was
during a bitterly cold night in the dead of winter. Owen was just
over two weeks old and the year was ticking down by the minute.
Mom was out, working the New Year's Eve party shift. Jess came
by for a few hours with a pilfered fifth of Fireball that only she
drank (I refused to, because I had resolved to be *responsible* this
time) before she left for a party across town hosted by another
classmate.

I wasn't invited. And even if I had been, I had to take care of
Owen.

I remember the awful exhaustion of his first week of life.
How I had transformed all at once into the unfamiliar creature

that gazed back at me from the mirror, eyes dark with bags, un-showered, terrible. In Owen's first days, I had to do everything possible to help Mom. She insisted on going back to work as soon as she could, and despite the fact that it was utterly terrible—we needed the money. She knew it, I knew it, and though it was absolute agony, she did what she had to do. What she was strong enough to do.

Jess left at ten after a call to her mom, proving that we were in the same place, not at any parties, just hanging out at my house with Owen screaming in the background. I sat on the front steps without a coat on, the chill hideous and awful as the frost crept through my jeans, and watched Jess in her sequins jog down the path and launch herself into Kara Merritt's waiting pickup truck. I sat there in the cold until the red embers of the taillights faded to nothing.

She'd offered to stay, but I told her to go. Sometimes misery does not love company.

Owen was sleeping, soundlessly for once. He prefers Jess over me, I think, and when she rocks him, he sleeps peacefully and obediently without any extra convincing.

So it wasn't that terrible swell of agony at his existence that echoed in my cold bones on that frostbitten night. I sat on the front step and stared out into nothing, out into all-consuming darkness, and I wished it would take me. I wished I could sit out there until my teeth stopped chattering and the cold quit creeping and everything faded away into a peaceful, empty silence. I wished I could curl up there, in that cobwebby bit of wall next to the door, and close my eyes, and sleep forever.

I thought about it: Mom, coming home in a few hours, tired from her shift, to find me there by the door, pale-faced and serene like the princess in a fairy-tale. How she'd stop at the bottom of the steps, her exhaustion turning to confusion turning to horror, to despair. I imagined her falling to her knees, crawling up the stairs, trying to rub life back into my limp hands. How my body would slump over and fall, frozen across the path of the closed door.

The worst part about it, now that I'm past that time, now that I've been through it . . . all of the things I imagined Mom doing are things that she did when she realized Owen was gone. And above all, that makes the absence of her care for me, her willingness to relinquish me to the wood, so much more painful.

But I digress. I imagined more than was healthy: the calls she'd make to Pastor Samuel, and Jess, and Dad, and Aunt Maya in Virginia; how my cold body would be taken away and unfrozen and I'd be dressed in the prom dress from junior year that I didn't get to wear.

It's a slippery slope, imagining your own death and the aftershocks that follow. A sick sort of inertia. Because you imagine, and imagine, and then before you know it, you're making plans. Wanting it.

I'd spent so much time underwater by then that I knew to the very second how long I could hold my breath. How long I could keep myself from drowning. Sitting there, in the cold, it was a gamble with the unknown: How long could I freeze before I actually froze?

That's where it came, the black maw of ideation slipping quickly toward decisions I wouldn't live to regret. That's when, for the second time, the thought occurred to me as slow and sticky as molasses.

Why do I have to be the one to go?

It wasn't like my life was perfect before Owen. But it wasn't terrible—it wasn't awful. It wasn't contorted to stretch around everything but me, everyone else but me. And I was *tired*, more tired than I was willing to admit, and so I'll let that be my excuse.

I was exhausted. Cold to the bone. Weary, and scared of the years stretched in front of me, of Owen's hate growing and growing until it was a visceral thing between us. For some girls, there was the option of going to college and leaving it all behind, starting a new life somewhere else. That was never me; that was never Winston. This town had its claws in me and there was no option of leaving. Not when I was trying so, so hard to be a good girl.

Let that be my confession.

On New Year's Eve, as the seconds trickled toward a new year, I let my head fall back and I spoke the words into the empty night:

Take him away. If you're out there, if you're real. Take this away from me.

I don't know where I'm going. I walk. I walk and walk, away from the Hollow and Tristan's pitying glances, away from Fletcher's insistence that I come in and eat with them. Away from the village and out into the forest.

I don't know how much I can trust my mind anymore. Echoes, they said of the ghosts. Echoes of memory. But I must be a ghost too, or walking through the land of them, because my memories come unbidden as I press on through the trees. They run through my brain like flashbacks in a movie, solid as the trees around me. I worry that if I look too closely at any of the shadows, they will morph into me, into the girl I used to be and the one I never became.

I don't know how long I'm walking before the ghost joins me, but suddenly, her arm brushes mine and I look over to see her and her white nightgown stepping in time with me. I can't believe I was afraid of her last night. We are the same, she and me: sacrifices, long since forgotten.

Because I know, don't I? Perhaps I knew last night, when I saw her peering at me through the glass.

"What did you offer?" I ask the ghost. Her hair is dark as an oil slick. I wonder who she is, who she was. Why she chose to haunt me. Looking at her, I feel the familiarity—but I can't place her. Perhaps it's the death cast settled over her face, the uncanniness of a girl from beyond the grave.

"Everything," the ghost says. Her voice is like metal on metal, knives screeching together.

"What did he take?" I ask.

"All I wanted to give."

I swallow hard. There's a thinning in the woods ahead, light breaking through, and the sound of rushing water. My heart is in my throat. I can't believe it—I've only been walking for twenty minutes at most, but I don't know if I can trust my understanding of time anymore—but there, ahead, through the trees . . . I think I see Winston.

The girl stops at the edge of the wood. Between me and the town, the Youghiogheny rushes, swollen with water from a rainstorm I don't remember.

It's impossible. The journey to the Lord's village took all day, maybe longer. I walked until my feet bled. But I can't pretend that the outskirts of the town in front of me isn't Winston, that this isn't the very same river I stepped out of only days ago.

"But I don't have Owen," I say to the ghost girl, to myself, to the empty air—because when I look, the girl is gone. Like she didn't guide me here.

Perhaps she was never there at all.

I chew on my lip and hug my arms to my chest. The sun is setting—inexplicably, because *surely* a whole day hasn't gone by, at least not one that I remember—and the town looks deserted. There aren't any cars driving through the narrow streets; no one walks through the cemetery or out of the white clapboard church.

I don't care. I don't have Owen, but I can't care about that either. Maybe talking to my mother will clear some of the guilt—maybe, if she looks at me like the prodigal daughter she lost, it will convince me that this is what I need to do.

The first step into the Yough sends a shock of cold water into my boots. The current is fast, fast enough that I could be swept away if I'm not careful, but I force myself to keep going. I drag myself out of the river and the Lord's domain and onto the bank.

Before I can think better of it, my feet are carrying me home. I stagger up the road, ignored by the McCaskey's on their front porch drinking iced tea, ignored by the pickup truck that screeches around a bend and nearly runs me over. I keep my eyes down, focused on the water dripping from my skirt onto the road and the wet footprints I leave behind.

I don't care about anyone else here. I'm only looking for forgiveness from one person.

It takes me the better part of an hour to get to my house, and when I do, the night is thick and dark. Crickets sound in the bushes, and frogs from the river, and fireflies cut up the darkness.

The night is clouded and the moon doesn't offer much light. When I get up to the front steps, the windows glow with light from the TV.

Mom is home.

I'm halfway across the front porch when I realize I'm still tracking dark, brackish water. I grimace down at the footprints—Mom won't be happy about cleaning up after me—and push my way inside.

She sits on the couch with her feet tucked up under her. Her brown hair is piled up on top of her head, shot through with gray. I can't say for certain, but the bags under her eyes look darker, the lines of her face deeper. She doesn't look at me as I shut the door behind me. Her hands are closed around a mug of tea, her wrists thin and frail and breakable peeking out from the sleeves of her oversized hoodie. Upon closer inspection, I register that it's actually *my* hoodie she's wearing, and that does something odd to my heart.

"Mom."

She doesn't look up. Acid floods my mouth, bile crawling up my throat. Is she ignoring me? After everything, after all I've tried to do, all I've given up for her?

"*Mom.*"

Nothing. I stride closer, kneel in front of her, shout "MOM" in her face so loud that she has to hear me.

She doesn't move. Doesn't react. And when I reach for

her wrist . . . my hand closes around nothing. Goes right through her.

I stare at her, horror and realization dawning: She doesn't see me. She *can't see me*. I am invisible, as open as air, as ether.

But . . . the door? I opened the door? Or did I just think I opened the door, my brain putting the pieces together for me when I passed through the wall like nothing?

I can't accept it. I stand, ready to smash things, to make a mess. I try to knock the tea out of her hand, try to smash the screen of the TV, to throw books off the shelf, to shatter glass in the kitchen. Nothing works. My piano doesn't turn on when I rush into Owen's room, untouched as the last time I was here. My hands go through everything. *I* go through everything.

I don't know how I've become a ghost. How I've surrendered everything for Owen, and here, it turns out, I still had more to give.

When I slink out through the house and curl up on the floor next to her feet, I realize one thing: This whole time, I wasn't tracking river water through the house. In the dim light, my footprints are dark red, drying to brown. Every step I take leaves a perfect imprint of blood.

I can't say why I go to Jess's house. She's sleeping by the time I get there, peaceful as ever. I curl myself up on the corner of the bed and watch her chest rise and fall, rise and fall. We used to have sleepovers every Friday night here at her house. The memory of all the previous versions of me stretches out next to her, legs entwined, whispering all of our secrets until one or both of us fell asleep.

"Keep my secrets," I whisper to her now. "Because I need you. I need someone. I don't know what I'm doing."

I can't keep them if you don't tell me, I hear her saying in the back of my head. I wish she'd wake up, that we could talk this out. I wish I'd trusted her more when I needed to.

I leave her bedroom behind and go to her ensuite bathroom. She must've just showered before bed because the mirror is still steamy. I swipe my hand across it, unthinking, to see my reflection—and clear the mist.

Water. I can touch it. I can *clear* it.

I don't think she's going to wake up, but I write anyways with my finger on the glass. It's a trick we used to do together: write on the mirror and wait for the steam to clear, but then when someone showered again, the message would reappear. I press the pad of my finger firmly into the mirror, trying to get as much out as I can in one line.

I might be dying. Help me. —I

In the other room, Jess stirs, but she does not wake, does not get up. I stare at my reflection in the mirror. I wish I could be anyone else.

Back over the river. Back through the woods, where my ghost waits for me. She walks by my side all night, skirting around the Lord's village, to the place where my piano waits. I sit at the bench, her arm pressing against mine, and play a hint of a melody. My ghost shifts my fingers, forces my melody into minor key.

"What's your name?" I ask.

"Maria," she says.

I nod, swallowing hard. Any thought of her running away, finding a future somewhere else, leaving it all behind—it disappears in a puff of smoke. And worse: She's here, and she's dead. She met her end in this wood. Maria came here, and she did not come back.

"Did you do what he asked of you?"

"Yes," the ghost says, her hands cold on mine. "And it wasn't enough. Nothing was enough."

I can't play. No words come, no notes, and I don't think Tristan will accept an empty, echoing scream as my song to get Owen back to me. With Maria's words, I don't know if he'll accept anything at all.

My ghost leans her head against my shoulder. Her hair is wet, and I'm not really sure why. When she kisses my shoulder and gets up, I follow. In the thick dark of the forest, I can't tell anymore what she looks like, who she is. When I look at her askance, I can see the truth of her death, the bloated face, the rot.

Her hair drips, heavy and wet and black down the back of her nightgown.

She leads me past the piano. Not very far—I don't know how far I can go with the cloying mist of exhaustion weighing my thoughts down. I nearly trip on the porch steps that rise out of nothing, the foundation that she moves so effortlessly across.

It's the ruin of a house she's led me to. It smells acrid, like burning wood and damp ash.

Maria, my ghost, looks back at me from the middle of the house. In the slanted moonlight, the rot fades. She is porcelain and perfect.

There's a skeleton at her feet.

I didn't notice it at first, not with the cloud of my exhaustion, with every brain cell focusing on not tripping in the dark forest. But the skeleton is articulated, curled into fetal position, with her hands stretched in front of her chest. The tatters of a white dress cling to her bones. When I step closer, looking down at her, a glint of silver catches my eye—she was wearing a ring when she rotted to nothing.

I look at my ghost. She looks at me. It feels like she's imparting some secret that I do not understand.

She died here, in this wood. She did not run away, and she never came back. She never left this realm at all.

None wished to stay, Ruth told me. She didn't say they'd left. She didn't say they'd lived.

It seems like a foregone conclusion when she leans over the skeleton to kiss my forehead and vanishes to nothing. It must be her body here she wanted me to see, bared and rotten. I clench my fists, nails digging into my palms—when I considered my own fate, I wished so desperately that she'd just left, gone, never returned. This fate is worse.

I don't care. I roll up on the damp undergrowth next to the skeleton. So tired. Too tired. I lace my fingers with her bones and let myself sleep.

fourteen

W hat follows in my memories is a collection of vignettes. I do not know what I remember and what I only think I do.

First: a dog barking. A wet nose against my cheek. Opening my eyes to see the empty eye sockets of a skull, bits of flesh clinging to it—but only last night, I'm sure I remember the bones had been clean.

Snuffling in my ear. I look up to see Whit's imperious eyes, his snout bearing down on my skin. Leaves crunch behind him, and a hand runs through the fur above his ear.

I lose consciousness, or it loses me. Second, not long after, the stirring of footsteps as I'm carried back. One of my arms is thrown across my stomach, but the other dangles, limp and loose. I look up and see the bottom of Tristan's chin.

Unthinking, I run my fingers over his jaw, feeling the

scratch of stubble on my palm. Dig my nails in. Not enough to draw blood, but enough to leave streaks of dirt on his skin. He is real, and solid. Tristan glances down at me, his mouth pressed into a line. In his arms, in his domain, I am no longer a ghost. There's a half-memory—me screaming, or someone else, my nails digging in as I choke on a sob. *Maria.* All those girls who died here—but I do not have the breath or focus for a full accusation.

What did you do to them?

Time, or the impression of it, stretches longer. When I come to again, I'm in the great bathtub in the Hollow. The water around me is dark with dirt and blood.

Ruth stands above me, scrubbing my arm. Her eyes flick to mine, and her expression softens. She presses a hand to my cheek, warm with soapy water.

"My sweet," she says, as if she knows me better than she does. She grips my chin, a mirror of the way I touched Tristan not long before. "Do not—"

I don't hear the rest of her plea.

There's something warm and furry pressed against my chest. The light is wrong, not the same as it has been the other mornings waking up here.

I open my eyes. Time has stopped slipping and I feel grounded, less like I'm tumbling down a hill and more like my feet are firmly, albeit uncomfortably, planted.

I'm not in my room. The warm, furry thing is Whit, stretched out next to me. My hands are twisted through his fur, but he doesn't seem to mind. He huffs wolf-breath in my face and licks my nose. I don't have the heart to push his snout away.

When I sit up, the picture grows clearer. I'm in a room just a bit bigger than mine here. The four walls are all different from one another: a forest features in each, so realistic that it looks like I can just walk through the walls and into the picture. It's a different season in each of them. Spring along the wall behind my head, behind the bed; summer in brilliant jewel-green tones to my left; crisp and colorful autumn straight ahead, framing the windows that look out to the true wood; snow-capped winter to my right. I tuck my knees to my chest and let the implication of this great four-poster bed and Whit's warm body and the season walls sink in.

I'm in Tristan's room.

One of his shirts is tossed over a chair in the corner, and a pair of boots stand in the space next to the wardrobe. On his dressing table, the copper circlet sits on an amber velvet cushion, picked through with leaves in metallic thread. A scattering of rings lies discarded in a dish next to a basin of water, rose petals floating on the top.

I take a deep breath. Let it out. Knit my fingers once again in Whit's fur, but he seems happy to oblige.

Yesterday—I think it was yesterday, but time still feels hazy, uncertain, hard to grasp—I went into Winston, the place I've always known. I walked through my house. I saw my mom. And I was nothing at all: air, a haunt, a ghost.

I think of the skeleton in the woods, the chill of her bones still a memory on my fingertips. Of the ghost girl who called herself Maria, who can only be the other girl who disappeared into this wood years ago, on the same mission I set out to complete. That skeleton—it's Maria, or one of the other girls, but the meaning is clear: She died here.

Even if she did her best and completed her task, it wasn't enough—she's still here. And I know, though I may not want to admit it, that I may not be enough either. I may face the same fate. It's not about trusting or distrusting the Lord and his machinations. I don't think it's as complicated as that—there are rules here, which must be followed. Of time, and consequence, and I am tied up in them.

Whit whines, a loud and long, drawn-out noise, and buries his head under the pillow next to me. There's the sound of footsteps thudding on the wooden stairs, and before I can get my thoughts in order, Tristan is there.

Tristan is there, and something inside of me has shifted. Or maybe it has broken.

I watch him, wary, but not afraid. It's a foregone conclusion that we have to have this discussion, even though he was kind to me. He was tender with me, forgiving when I disobeyed, when I ran—it's a minimum, but a minimum that I hadn't expected. I remember the feeling of his hands in my hair, the sure sway of his gait as he carried me back to the Hollow.

Though I had always been taught to fear the Lord . . . I can't find it in me to fear Tristan. Perhaps I wasn't lying on that first night, when I told him I didn't. Perhaps I never have feared him the way I was supposed to.

Maybe that's to be my undoing, just as it was every girl who came before. Some sort of venomous numbing, making us feel so much less of the fear we should, dulling those instincts into hazy insufficiency.

He shuts the door and comes in quietly, his mouth pressed into a line. If I could detangle my memories from the last day, I think I would find that very same expression smudged over them like fingerprints. The concern is clear, and I cannot fight the understanding that he is not worried for what I have done, but instead, for what I have gone through.

A darker part of me wonders if that's a manipulation. If this is the danger of the Lord: that every little thing is to lull me into a false sense of security; that every kind gesture makes me less and less expectant of the bite.

"May I sit with you?" he says.

Letting a boy in your bed is not the behavior of a good girl. But I'm in his bed, technically, and if there's anything I've learned . . . it's that I have no idea how to be good, and in all the time I've spent trying, I've only gotten worse.

I nod, fighting for any of the sharp anger I felt yesterday, trying to push past the numb, uncertain exhaustion.

He pushes Whit closer to me and the dog rolls, whining again, but conceding. Tristan sits on the bed on the other side of the dog, his legs stretched out over the covers. He's not wearing his boots. His trousers are cuffed, but even so, the bottoms are speckled with mud.

"If you want to be free of your duty," Tristan says slowly, "to go back to Winston, without Owen, you are welcome to leave."

I swallow hard. It's the last thing I expected him to say—it's hideously tempting, and because of that, it must just be another trap.

"Is that what you offered the other girls?" I ask. The words are tearing free before I can stop them.

Tristan raises an eyebrow. "What are you talking about?"

"Maria Sinclair and all the girls before. Maria's a ghost now—I saw her body. She's *dead*, Tristan; she's dead here and she never made it back to Winston. Is this some kind of sick joke? Is this when you tell me that you killed her, killed all of them?"

He's blinking back at me, the confusion clear and terrible, and I don't know if I can trust anything he says or his face betrays. "How do you know she's dead?"

I press my hands to my eyes. I can't handle the riddles, the misdirections. "Tristan, I—"

"No, listen. Just because someone is a ghost or an echo in my realm doesn't mean they're dead in yours. Like—Leah, when you went to Winston, did anyone see you? Hear you?"

"I . . . I wanted to speak to my mother." The memory is there, of her on the couch, ignoring me. The awfulness of being invisible. "I wanted her to tell me she misses me."

When I glance up at him, his expression is strained, brows drawn together. He does not ask. He only waits.

"But she couldn't see me," I say.

"No," he says softly. "You're . . . I mean, you're still alive, both there and here. Don't worry about that. But you're in a gap now, between the living and the dead. Between the present and memory. There are many paths, branching out, of what your life could be from the moment you rose from the river into my realm, and you're at the intersection of all of them. And sometimes—those other options get stuck, and they create ghosts in my realm. The people here remain because they've chosen *this* path, but something of everyone else who was still here remains."

"But what of those who were given to you?" I ask, tasting acid in my mouth.

"The same rules, Leah. You can go—you can leave now, and I'll give you the antidote and unstick you from time. I take no joy in keeping you here, against your will."

But that's not true nor fair, because Maria never came back to Winston, and she's not here either—she has to be *somewhere*.

"So, I ask you again, how do you know she's dead?"

Because I *do*. There's no point explaining the thumping hollow within my stomach when I see her, when I think of her. There's no warmth there. She's not a memory of the time she spent here—she *is*. She's stuck, if anything, and that skeleton was not just an echo. It was real and whole and awful. "How do you know she isn't?"

Tristan shakes his head. "I don't. I just know . . . I wasn't the Lord when she was here, Leah. My brother was. And I remember her, vaguely, but still. She finished her task. She did what she promised she would do, and my brother gave her the baby back, and she was freed from this place. Free to go back to Winston."

"Don't lie to me, Tristan."

"I'm *not*," he insists. "I did her no harm, and I can guarantee you my brother didn't either."

"And can you vouch for every other person here?" I snap, all venom. If there's some other threat here in the woods, something unknown . . .

He frowns, uneasy. "I thought I could. But I also thought she returned to your world. I wouldn't lie to you, and I'm not lying now. If something happened to her, which could be possible . . . it was not under my watch."

"How am I meant to believe that?" I ask, sounding so much

stronger than I feel.

Tristan looks at me, and something in his face shifts. "I owe you an apology," he says slowly, like the words cost him something.

It's enough of a surprise to render me silent.

"I know that me . . . taking Owen has been . . . hard on you." The words are slanted, and we both know it. It hasn't been *hard on me*—it's changed everything. But I can allow him this grace, to talk about the issue in his own terms.

"You think it was a choice. That I picked him, or followed through on some silly declaration that you, apparently, made yourself. But that's not how it is, nor how it works. I didn't make the agreement, Leah. It's been in place since the first Lord, since this village was a refuge in its infancy."

I watch him steadily as he unwinds himself. I remember his outburst in the wood, when we were discussing what he was and what he wasn't. Then, how surprised I was by his deluge of words. It's happening again, that rush, and I wonder now if he speaks to me so sparingly because if he opens up truly, the words won't stop coming. Maybe it's safer to say the minimum, because if he doesn't, the floodgate will open.

Tristan reaches over Whit and grabs my hand. Not in an affectionate way, not lacing our fingers together. He grabs, and squeezes, like he needs to reassure himself I'm here. I don't know if he's intentionally changing the subject from the other girls to me, but I don't think he's trying to hide something. Not now, not when this is closer to a confession than anything he's said before.

"Then what is it?" I ask, because I have to say something. "If not your choice?"

"I *have* to take what I'm offered," Tristan says, his mismatched eyes searching mine, beseeching me to believe him. "I can try to resist, try to stay away, but it never works. Every path starts leading to Winston, to the thing or person marked for me. The wood deceives me. Time reverses until I do what I'm bid. I am the Lord of this wood, yes, but I cannot control the compulsions. I *must* claim what is offered to me."

I chew on my lip. "You put off taking Owen for months."

"I don't want to take them, Leah. I want everyone, every-*thing* who comes to this place to seek it of their own accord. And I thought I could put it off when I took the mantle from my brother—you know I *tried*. But it wasn't my choice to open the line for compulsion, and I cannot fix it. Cannot stop it."

Something twists in my stomach. I offered Owen to the Lord—and I know I'm responsible for that. But what about Maria? What about the other babies before? Were they all offered by mothers, sisters, fathers who couldn't cope?

"And I'm sorry I forced you to run. That it was too much."

I shake my head, because no matter what Tristan is saying, this is one thing he cannot take blame for. "It's not your fault," I say. I squeeze his hand back, feeling the press of one of his rings, unyielding, into my skin.

"Do you promise you don't know what happened to Maria? That you'd tell me what happened to the other girls, if you knew?"

His eyes don't leave mine. "I swear it, Leah, on my own grave."

"And . . . can I go back? Ever?"

Tristan releases my hand and gets up. "You can," he says, but there's something different about his tone. He sits down on the edge of the bed, his back to me, and pulls his boots on. "When you've completed your task. Finished what you promised. When you leave us behind, you'll go back to the girl you are in Winston."

The words taste bitter on my tongue. "Of course."

"I have to finish my work in the village. Will you be okay here, today?" He doesn't look at me when he says it.

"Yeah. But Tristan . . . why am I in your room?"

He shoots me a sideways glance, halfway to the door. His mouth quirks up into a smile. "Your window is still broken," he says simply. When he goes, he shuts the door behind him.

Fifteen

Fletcher must've been waiting for Tristan to leave, because the second I hear the front door shut downstairs, they're bursting in the door with a tray of soup and heel of bread.

I stifle a groan. "Why are you so dedicated to feeding me?"

"Maybe my love language is cooking," they say, thrusting the tray at me. Whit takes a curious sniff of the bread. Fletcher scowls and leans back before dog tongue can infect my lunch. "What's yours?"

"Sacrifice," I say. It's meant to be a joke, but it doesn't hit— the second the word is out of my mouth, both of us wince.

"Whit, *down*," Fletcher says. The dog whines, but after another firm glare, he slinks off the human bed and into a padded dog bed in the corner. Though I wouldn't admit it to Fletcher, I miss the warmth of him immediately.

Fletcher sets the tray on my lap and glares until I obediently pick up the spoon. The soup is good, chicken and rice and hearty bits of carrot and potato. I try to eat without looking up at Fletcher, who doesn't take their eyes off me.

"Thank you," I say when I'm nearly finished. "For feeding me. You don't need to take care of me."

Their expression softens. "Somebody ought to." They wave a hand at me under the blankets, dressed in what I assume is one of Tristan's long shirts. "I daresay you don't do a good job of it yourself."

They're right. I don't.

"Can we go for a walk?" I ask.

Their eyebrow quirks up. "Haven't you done enough walking?"

I shrug. But really, I want to go into the village, where I haven't been since I got here. I want to thank Ruth for her clothes, and for whatever she did to help me last night. And I want to talk to Fletcher away from the Hollow, from all of this. According to Tristan, the people here (with a few notable exceptions) *chose* to be here. I want to know why.

I want to know, if I'd known better, if this is something I would've chosen for myself.

And most of all, I want to know that not everyone here is a ghost, a memory, an echo. I need to know if Ruth knows what happened to those girls—and though I trust Tristan enough to stay, I need to know he didn't lie to me.

After I've eaten and cleaned up, I head downstairs dressed in a pair of loose khaki shorts and a pale blue button-down with my boots laced on my feet. I feel a bit like one of the archaeologists in *Jurassic Park*, but I'm not sure Fletcher would catch the reference—and Tristan certainly wouldn't.

We follow the snaking trail to the village, and I feel shy and awkward and uncertain how exactly to break the silence. So, finally, I just go right into it.

"How long have you been here?" I ask.

"About a year," they respond. "Give or take."

"Does this outfit remind you of Laura Dern?" I blurt before I can think better of it. Perhaps this is why I have no friends.

The corner of their mouth quirks as they glance at my shorts. "In *Jurassic Park*." Their hip bumps mine, and I can't remember the last time I was just . . . friendly with someone who wasn't Jess. "I do miss TV. Movies. And, like, phones. General communication."

"Is there none of that here?"

"Nope," Fletcher says, popping the p. "And even Tristan's most entertaining stories don't compare to that reality show about people working on yachts."

I snort before I can stop myself. There's no point in telling Fletcher that I watched very little reality TV—my parents thought it would influence me to act out, drink, wear less clothing. They didn't know I could learn to be bad all on my own.

"Do you ever miss other things about the place you left

behind? People?" I ask. The edge of the clearing is in sight. The throne and dais, the remains of the great bonfire in front of it, all are there. I have the sudden memory of Tristan on that night, his eyes shining with power.

"No one that will miss me," Fletcher says. Their voice is tight. I grimace. I've poked a bruise I shouldn't have—and I know better. I'm probably covered in very similar bruises, just below the surface, ripe for prodding.

As if they can read my mind, Fletcher loops their arm through mine, and I'm forgiven. "But let's not worry about that now. Why did you want to come to town?"

"I should thank Ruth," I say. "She's had the unfortunate task of bathing me more than once."

Fletcher makes a low noise in their throat. "You know, no one here is that mad about taking care of you. I know you think you're this tough thing, but you don't have to be. We all help one another here, Leah. You can help, too. And when you get into a scrap—or when you pass out in the woods in a pile of mud and won't stay conscious—there are people here who care about that sort of thing."

I don't like being anyone else's responsibility. But I also don't have a response to Fletcher that doesn't sound like I'm dismissing their kindness. So I only shrug, and press onward.

They stop a few times: once to pet a cat, once to accept a warm loaf of bread from someone they introduce as Andrew the baker, once to pick a spool of thread wrapped in parchment paper out of a box in front of someone's house.

By the time we make it to Ruth's, the exhaustion of the last few days has caught up with me. I'm grateful when she opens the door, gives us both a shrewd look, and directs us to sit on the low stools by her table. I lean gratefully against the wall while she pours tea into three mugs.

"I came here to thank you," I say. "For everything."

Ruth and Fletcher exchange a glance. "You're welcome," she says, shoving a mug in my direction. "Now, don't go trying to get yourself killed in the woods again. We'd all appreciate it if you remained more than a body."

I don't know what to say to that. The skeleton in the woods returns to my thoughts, and I shudder at the memory.

I don't understand why these people care if I live or not.

Ruth sits with us for only a moment before she gets up and goes to the heavy wood counter. She continues fussing with dried herbs, parceling them out and wrapping them with string, as if she can't sit still for long.

I'm reminded of what Fletcher told me on the walk here. "Can I . . . help you with that?"

Ruth looks at me, eyebrows knitted together. I look to Fletcher for help, but they're staring out the window, not paying attention to me. I spot Andrew the baker coming down the street with a basket of apples.

"Why?"

I don't have a response. "Because I think I should" doesn't feel good enough. And I'm too shy, too ashamed to admit that I want to feel useful, like I belong somewhere. As far as I can tell, no one here hates me, which is a step-up from Winston.

And I don't want to ask about the other girls in front of Fletcher, or anyone else. I want it to be just Ruth and me. And if that means staying and helping . . . well. There are worse fates.

"I'm bored," I say, noncommittal. "Can't stay at Tristan's all the time. And my song isn't coming easy. If I do something else . . ."

Ruth *hmphs* at that, turning back to her herbs. She puts a few bundles in a cloth and wraps them up, then brings them to the table. Sets them before Fletcher. Looks at me, *hmphs* again. Takes a sip of her tea. "You sing, girl?"

". . . yes?"

She nods. "Good. Then I have use of you."

I don't know what to expect when Ruth leads me to the back of her small cottage, but a sprawling garden seems . . . pedestrian in comparison to the other options my brain cooked up. She basically dismissed Fletcher as soon as she'd finished her herb separating, so now it's just me and her in the little patch of garden.

A wall of brambles separates it from the garden of the next cottage over. There's a twisting iron gate in the back, half-covered in brambles, and what looks to be another garden behind Ruth's, partially obscured by trees and overgrown. I can hear the noises of the village, though: easy laughter and conversation, the far-off din of what I think might be a blacksmith's hammer.

She leads me to the back of the garden, near the gate, where the plants are sparse and brown and dying. I cross my arms over my chest, surveying.

"Ruth," I say, before she can give me instructions. "The other girl. The one who died. *Any* of them who died."

Ruth sighs, pushing her red curls away from her forehead. "It's not a good idea, to go poking into that."

I don't really care if it's a *good idea* or not. Most of my ideas aren't. "I just . . . for my own safety. Was it Tristan? Did the Lord have anything at all to do with it?"

At this, her face softens, just a fraction. She reaches out, touches her fingers against the back of my hand, just once. "It wasn't Tristan or his brother that did them wrong," she said. "None of our Lords would raise a hand against one of yours; they don't mean harm. Whatever they are, it isn't their way. I don't know the truth of what happened, but I can tell you that much. You have nothing to fear in that boy."

She watches me, and I watch her back, two feral things who've been hurt too many times. But I see something in her that I recognize, and maybe she does the same.

For now, I choose to trust her. "Okay. Then how can I help you with the garden?"

It's enough to break the solemness. "This patch doesn't seem to like me very much," she says shrewdly, kicking at a bare patch of dirt.

"I'm sorry," I say, for lack of better response.

"The plants like songs. I think they're tired of me. My songs, my voice. But if *you* could sing to them, maybe they'd respond a little better."

I laugh before I can think better of it. The look Ruth shoots me makes me bite my tongue. "Why would singing help?"

"Singing, talking, emotional things. Things they can feel. It helps, here, where there's so little change, where time moves in a trickle and a rush and it's impossible to say which is which. Singing marks the time, gives them something to grasp onto. Gives them emotions to grow big and strong."

She's talking about plants. I think that's what we're talking about, yet none of this makes sense.

"Don't question me, girl," she says, heading off back to the house without waiting for me to respond. "Maybe stop trying to be so married to rules for once. Maybe try something, see what happens."

There's no point in telling her that when I break the rules, bad things tend to happen.

I curl up on the patch of dirt next to the hedge fence. The dirt is probably staining my shorts—truthfully, I don't know how Tristan's household manages all the laundry, especially now that I'm dirtying everything I touch—and close my eyes. Perhaps I'll believe in myself more, believe all of this, if I just sing to myself.

Go to sleep you little baby
Go to sleep you little baby
Honey on the rock and the sugar don't stop
Go bring a bottle to the baby.

I open my eyes, ignoring the foolish racing of my heart and— nothing. The dirt is still dirt. The plants are still brown. I close my eyes again, resolved to do *one thing* right.

Go to sleep you little baby
Go to sleep you little baby
Come and lay your bones on the alabaster stones
And be my ever lovin' baby

And this time, this time when I open my eyes . . . there's a new green shoot in the space next to where my palm meets the dirt.

I suck in a breath. I don't understand how this is working, how it's happened. I only know that it is. I shift to my hands and knees, cradling one of the browned leaves between my palms. Switching tactics, I sing a bit of a song that Mom used to sing while rocking me to sleep: *It only takes a spark, to get a fire going . . .*

The leaf changes, green chlorophyll spreading through the leaves. It's a peculiar kind of magic, but I don't think it's magic at all. It's the same thing that calmed Owen, the same reason Tristan accepted my meager offering in exchange for a baby.

Words mean something. These songs, they tether this place to time, show some sort of change and shift besides the echoing memory of ghosts. And I am now a part of it.

Sixteen

My grammy used to say that a routine was a kindness to the soul. That we weren't meant to be spontaneous, to do things that were surprising and new. I used to disagree with her: Isn't spontaneity, excitement, change the spice of life? But now, I see what she means. There's comfort in routine, familiarity. Especially when the routine doesn't feel like it's actively stifling you as a person, swallowing you whole.

I can't explain it, nor do I know how. But I wake up and I eat the food Fletcher pushes at me, and we walk through the woods to my piano. They sit and knit or read while I struggle for a few hours, and then we walk through town to Ruth's. She feeds me lunch and lets me sing in her garden. When night starts falling, Tristan retrieves me, or I leave when the sun is heavy and low, and we walk to the Hollow where we have dinner at the great table with Fletcher. Then I sit up and read, or work on lyrics, or try to recall songs for Ruth's garden before sleep.

Wash. Rinse. Repeat.

I meet Andrew the baker properly, who leaves me still-warm cinnamon rolls on the top of the hedge in Ruth's garden. I accept steaming cups of hot chocolate from the villagers who come by Ruth's for her herbs or vegetables, who think to bring a present for me.

It is a soothing balm to my soul, this kindness. I don't know how to explain how tightly I'd wound myself in Winston until I came here, and I found myself unfurling.

There is still the question of Owen, and what I have to do to get him back. The words don't come easily—the ones that do come will not convince Tristan to return what is rightfully mine.

Besides Fletcher and Tristan and Ruth and the quiet movement of the village, the other constant is my ghost. I come out of Ruth's one evening to find her waiting for me at the edge of the village, on the path to the Hollow.

"You know better than to believe you deserve this," she says, which sends me bristling.

I frown at her. I don't ask her what happened to her—the last time I did, she screamed and screamed until my head ached. As long as Tristan or the previous Lords weren't involved, I'm not really sure what else I can do for her. "I'm just doing what is best for everyone. Helping out while I'm here."

"They'll never keep you. They don't want you."

Anxiety thumps in my stomach, a heavy stone falling. "I'm not asking to be kept," I bite out, but what else could I want if not safety? Comfort?

But my ghost is right, and she knows it. Her mournful face, bloated and dead when seen in certain lights, is honest. She doesn't lie to me. Perhaps she's the only one.

So, I follow her. I skirt around the Hollow, even though I know Fletcher is probably laying the table for dinner. I go again past my piano, up the derelict stairs, into the foundation with the skeleton. What I see makes me suck my breath through my teeth in a low, hollow whistle.

There's gristle on the bones. The remains of viscera. The once sun-bleached dress is speckled with rot. Stringy tendons hold her together, half-rotted. She still looks nothing like the ghost girl beside me, but she is more visibly human. Rotting in reverse.

I curl up on a half-burnt piece of wall nearby and look at the wreckage of her body, the chestnut hair caught in clumps and tangles, the handprint of blood on her chest. It's all achingly familiar.

"I'm sorry they did this to you," I say to Maria. And I don't mean Tristan or the village. She knows it.

We both mean Winston, or the unseen force in the wood, even more dangerous than the Lord we've always been taught to fear.

She lowers herself next to me, looking at the rotting remains of the girl. It has to be the remains of Maria, here to complete whatever plight she set out to do.

"Are you afraid?" Maria asks.

I don't answer. The tears rolling down my cheeks speak louder than I can.

When I make it back, Tristan is in the parlor room, tucked into his armchair with a book. His eyes flick to the doorway where I stand.

"You missed dinner," he says. Not accusatory. An observation.

"Sudden rush of inspiration," I lie. Though it would be much easier to go upstairs, to bed, to my memories and my thoughts, I throw myself down in the chair across from him. After the chill of the wood and the sight of that rotting body, I don't think I'm ready to be alone.

A knot in the fireplace pops, sending up a rush of sparks. I stare into the flames, oddly aware that Tristan is watching me just as intently.

"How is your song coming?" he asks finally.

I shrug. It's not coming. That's the problem. All words I have get stuck in my throat, and there's no Heimlich maneuver for creative inspiration.

"Do you need more time? I can give it to you."

I laugh, surprised, because I didn't expect Tristan to cede on anything. I don't know why. But more time is the last thing I need—if I have it, I worry I'll actually convince myself that I belong here, and very few things could be worse than that. Like Maria said, they don't want me. Not really. This is not where I belong.

"When did you become the Lord?" I ask instead of answering him. Tristan hesitates, caught off guard. He dog-ears his page and sets it on the low table beside him. He's reading a tattered paperback of *Good Omens*—I wonder how he got it.

"A year ago. Less. Probably just after you . . . offered Owen. I told you—I tried to refuse him, my first offering."

I nod. The words don't sting like they should. The memory of what I did doesn't have power over me. It's more of a weary awareness now, the things I would give, sacrifices, to be the girl I never got to be.

"And before?"

"It was my brother," he says. "And my mother before him."

He'd mentioned this before. I nod, processing the information. "Were you two close?" Something in his tone implies that his brother is not just gone from here—he's gone entirely. Dead, I imagine.

"Close enough." He's not forthright with his answers.

"A closed book, you are," I say, like Yoda. I look down at my hands, pick the dirt under my nails. "You know my deepest darkest secrets. Well, most of them."

Tristan sighs. "I don't owe you my secrets."

"I know," I say. I don't owe him mine either, but I don't say it.

He watches me for a long moment, then he gets up. There's a bottle of dark red wine on the table against the wall, and he pours two glasses. He hands one to me, then settles back in his chair, letting his head drop back.

I take a small sip. It tastes warm and sweet, heavy with cherries.

"He was a good Lord," Tristan says. "But it's a heavy burden to bear, taking what is given. Not just here in Winston—all up and down these mountains, we take what we're offered, though I can't say all have the same . . . ferocity as your town. He did it for ten years, and then he didn't want to do it anymore. He stepped out of this time, became something else somewhere else. I can't fault him for it."

I swallow another sip of the wine, fighting the guilt that surges through my veins. It sounds painful when Tristan tells it, and I feel bad for drawing the tale out of him.

"Is he . . .?" Dead, I want to ask, but it doesn't feel appropriate.

Tristan shakes his head. "No," he says. "He's very much alive. But . . . when a Lord leaves the forest, when we leave this all behind, we can't come back. It never suited him, being Lord. I don't think he ever wanted it."

"Did you?" I ask. I don't know why I'm pressing so much— it's not like me. If I push Tristan, it gives him permission to push right back.

He sighs, looking away, seeing something I can't. "I don't know," he admits. "But I don't . . . I don't hate it. Not like he did. I find it suits me, though I would never have asked him to hand the responsibility over."

"It seems people like you," I say, which is a ridiculous observation—I don't know enough to say. It just feels like the right thing.

He shrugs. "Maybe they do. I can't say it's *nice* knowing people like your friends are terrified of me, but there's a certain freedom to it. Not caring."

As if that was ever an alternative.

"We weren't born here," Tristan says unprompted, like he can read the look on my face. "No one can be born here, not in the village. That's not how time works here."

"Because it's what is and what isn't. Echoes of what is to be," I say, reciting what he told me back to him. Sensing some discomfort to come, I drain my glass of wine.

"Right," Tristan says. He doesn't look at me. The lone ring he wears glints in the firelight. Upstairs, I hear the sound of claws on the hardwood: Whit must be walking around, maybe looking for Tristan. "We were born in another town, maybe one like the one you were from. Weren't there long. My brother was, I mean; he was much older than me, but he didn't fit in. None of us did. I think they knew my mother was untamed, a forest thing, unstuck from time."

"What happened to her?" I ask, the question bubbling to my lips before I can stop it.

He frowns. "She's dead. It happens—there are risks to what we are, what we do. Don't look at me like that."

I try to wipe all pity from my face. Silence hangs heavy between us.

"Do you regret offering Owen?" Tristan asks. I *was* afraid of this, of him questioning me as I did him, but it doesn't have the edge I was expecting. He leans over to pour me another glass of wine and I take a hesitant sip, even though I'll answer better if my head is clear.

I can't be annoyed with him for asking me a question. Not after he so graciously answered all of mine.

I look at him, the curls and baby hairs framing his face. He looks back, sipping his wine. It stains his lips dark plum, and I (somewhat ridiculously) imagine what his bottom lip would feel like between my teeth.

I blush immediately. The wine. It must be the wine. I shouldn't have drunk it so quickly. Always too hasty, always rushing for a deeper glimmer of life.

"No," I say. I hold his gaze. Something shifts between us. He takes a breath, sharp, and sets his glass down. I drain mine to the dregs yet again, welcoming the wooziness that comes to my head.

"Leah—"

I shake my head. Whatever he's about to say, I probably don't want to hear it. It's probably a mistake.

I get up with the intent to go to bed, and my still-booted feet catch in the carpet. I stumble forward, tripping further over his stretched legs. He leans forward, catches me as I stabilize my hands on the arm of his chair.

His hands. One on my hip, one on my waist, braced against me. He looks up, lips parted, his eyes hazy and indistinct. Burning. Fingers tightening on my skin. For a second, we're breathing the same air, sticky with cherry wine.

Be a good girl.

Gently, I remove his hands from me. He looks away, ashamed.

"Good night, Tristan," I say. This time, I focus on every step, forcing myself to be steady.

Seventeen

Good girls don't want. They don't have thoughts late at night, ideas of things they saw in movies or read about in books, things that they could imagine themselves participating in. They don't doodle in their notebooks and imagine what it's like to kiss one of the quarterbacks or what it would be like to feel the hand of the boy they like creeping under their skirts. They certainly don't lay in bed when the house is hushed and quiet, asleep, fingers seeking and exploring and testing.

Be good, Mom always used to say.

I'll try. I'm trying. I am.

Like Jess, and Blaire, and all the other girls we hung out with, that was our objective. Be good. Be irreproachable. Do not let rumors spread. Do not do anything that would even encourage them in the first place. And the rules didn't even know how to cope with queerness, how to align with those feelings of short breath and heart-thumping desire with someone like you.

Don't go to his house alone. Don't let him drive you home. No closed doors. No kisses. No late night sneaking off. No room for doubt. No room to be anything other than a good girl.

When I was a freshman, they brought in a woman to talk to our youth group. I can't remember her name, but she was pretty in an average sort of way, with a spray of freckles across her nose and green eyes and delicate hands, with a big engagement ring and wedding ring. Blaire giggled to Olivia Pridd about how it was the biggest engagement ring she'd ever seen. Jess poked her in the ribs when the woman looked over at us, her attention caught by the giggling. But she didn't look put out by it.

That's not what matters. The woman brought a vase, a pretty blue one from a department store. She stood in front of the youth group, all thirty of us, and dropped it on the floor of the church. I remember how it smashed, the pieces skittering across the floor. All of us, it felt, drew a breath at the same time.

"Pick it up," she said. And we listened, all of us on our hands and knees, giggling and chatting. Jess accidentally cut herself on one of the shards and sucked the blood from her thumb. A bloody thumbprint marred that piece, but no one much seemed to care.

When we'd gathered up all the pieces, presented them to her on one of those foil trays people use for chicken wings at cookouts, she smiled at us.

"Great job, everyone," she said. "Now, I want y'all to put it together again."

Blaire volunteered, Olivia getting up to help her. But they didn't have glue, or anything that worked. No matter how hard they tried, the vase crumbled over and over again.

"Now," the woman said after they'd given up. "I want you to think about this. You're a vessel. A whole, complete thing. And you're perfect just the way you were made."

I was tired, thinking of my algebra homework, so I'd let my mind wander, but this brought me back. Next to me, Jess stared ahead, rapt with attention. We all were focusing now, anticipation heavy in the air. A whole group of kids, curious about sex, the big forbidden taboo, had a radar for this sort of thing. It was coming. We all knew it was.

"Imagine your soul is this vase. When you engage in intercourse outside of marriage, when you let someone inside you—it changes everything. Breaks that wholeness. Do you see? How we're meant to enter holy union whole and perfect, untouched?"

Let someone inside you. She meant us, the girls, the daughters. I snuck a look over at Trent McCoy and Brian Klink, but they were too busy snickering and elbowing each other in the ribs to notice me.

Muttering. A bit of uneasy shifting. Between us, Jess squeezed my hand. She wasn't worried—we were both virgins; we talked about sex with the sort of wide-eyed naivety that comes with the forbiddenness of it all. We didn't even have the grounds to explore with imagination.

Our parents had all paid twenty bucks for this session, for the woman to come in, and at the end, she had a whole load of silver rings. One for each of us. Jess and I put them on each other like brides, slipping on the sterling silver rings with the inscription *true love waits* on the inside. Onto the ring fingers of our left hands they went.

If anything, the session had the opposite effect on me. It ignited a new curiosity: How far could I go before I was broken?

Far enough to forget how to be good. Far enough to shatter.

I lay in bed, on my side, listening to the wind whine through the trees. Tristan fixed my window days ago, but I sleep with it partly open, no longer afraid of the ghosts outside.

Every time I close my eyes, I feel the press of his hand on my hip, my waist. I wonder what it would be like if I'd leaned into him instead of pulling away. If I'd closed that cherry-wine-laced space between us. Taken his lip between my teeth.

This is . . . bad. Blasphemy. Tristan is the Lord of the Wood, a demon, the very thing I've always been taught to fear and hate and revile. I should not be thinking of him this way. I shouldn't be *wanting* him.

Wanting like that . . . it's forbidden. I know better. It's not just the woman who came to visit us at youth group, or the purity ring that I wore until I lost it on a dark, cold night on the edge of spring. It's the gossip about other girls, the kind that I also used to participate in. Who slept with who after parties. Who hooked up after homecoming. Who was branded as dirty, broken, terrible, a *slut*.

I let the word roll through my throat, my chest, my stomach. Remember the taste of it on my mouth. Because I said it, too; threw it at other girls until they doubled back and threw it right back at me.

I think of Jess and me, at a sleepover in our sophomore year. *What does it feel like? Is it nice? Do you think we could do it alone? Is that bad? Are we still good, if we want what is forbidden?*

Time doesn't matter here, in the wood. It catches in eddies and bursts. And I catch with it, rolling onto my back, imagining again the grip of Tristan's hand on my hip. Imagining where else it could go.

I can't remember the last time my body felt like it was entirely my own. I keep my breath quiet and even. Keep my eyes closed as my hand wanders. He is a force of nature, a reminder of all the ways in which I am terrible. And right now, I can only imagine how easy it would be to slip, to fall, to get so much worse.

Eighteen

I don't *intentionally* avoid Tristan the next morning, but I certainly don't rush from my bed until I hear him leaving through the front door. I can't meet his eye, just yet—shame and want are far too entangled in my brain. I don't know how to look at him straight on.

I shouldn't let this go any further. There's already too much here that I like and that is bad—I have to get back to Winston and my days are running out. Though Tristan offered me more time, I don't want to take it. It's better for everyone if I finish my task in the two weeks I have left and leave all of this behind.

When Fletcher comes with breakfast, I'm already dressed in a blue skirt, white blouse, and heavy knit sweater that I may or may not have pilfered from Tristan's room. I take the roll they offer me and say, "I have something I need to do this morning. Can you help?"

Fletcher looks at me, not distrustfully, but not fully on board. "What do you have in mind?"

It's hard to explain past the growing lump in my throat, but I need to confront it. I cannot just keep pretending I'm here for good without doing anything—and that means I need to confront why I'm here. I need to face it.

I need to see Owen.

They suck a breath through their teeth when I voice my request. "Are you sure that's a good idea? Last time—"

"I know." Last time, I ran away, all the way back to Winston, with my tail between my legs and my trauma blooming from my chest. "I need to see him. To remind myself what I'm doing."

Fletcher nods, unconvinced. But it doesn't matter—it's not their choice. And they seem to realize that I need the support, not scolding, as they accompany me into the woods, deeper and deeper, until we come within sight of the little cottage.

We stand, together, just outside the clearing. No one is outside. Smoke pours from the little chimney. The smell of rich roasting meat, rosemary, thyme, and garlic spreads out around the little house.

Fletcher takes my hand. I squeeze hard. "You don't have to take him back," they say. "You can stay here. With us."

I nod. But I'm a good girl. I'm one of Winston's daughters, born to cling to this town no matter how much it tries to throw me out. I'm supposed to live there forever, find someone else just as doomed to stay as I am, rot in the soil my grandparents tilled, keep the disappointments of my parents tucked close. I'm not created for a life outside Carver County. I'm not a child of this wood, marked for Tristan's easy smiles and Fletcher's acceptance and Ruth's guidance.

I keep a tight grip on Fletcher's hand as I approach the cottage. Tristan said they couldn't see us, so I imagine it's something like Winston. I doubt our previous invisibility was something he arranged.

When I pass through the wall, Fletcher only makes a low sigh and follows me. I doubt they want to be entangled in my mess, and I can't blame them. I'm about to tell them to go on back, wait for me, but the look on their face when I turn back gives me pause.

Fletcher isn't put out by my quest, or my feelings. There's a hint of pity on their face, but worse, their brows are drawn together with concern. They're worried about me, maybe how I'm going to push too hard or too far, bend myself to breaking.

But I can't. I'm already broken, and now I'm on the other side, taking in the wreckage after the fracture.

I squeeze Fletcher's hand and let go.

The cabin is cozy and warm. The woman sits on a couch, hemming a sock. Her feet are on her husband's lap as he reads a book. Owen isn't in here.

I don't know if I'm still in the wood or if I've somehow

managed to go into a different time. It seems that way, unplace-
able with the lack of electronics and the simple furnishings, but
I don't know any better.

There's no need to be quiet, but I am. I leave Fletcher waiting anxiously by the stove and go into the first room. It's their
bedroom, with a great bed and a quilt that looks handmade. A
half-drunk mug of tea is abandoned on one of the bedside tables.
There's a wood crib in the corner, and from it, the slow, even
breathing of a sleeping baby.

Owen lays on his back, cheeks chubby and red, one fist balled
next to his mouth. I don't recognize the clothes he's wearing, but
of course I don't.

I lean over the crib, and the wood creaks beneath me. I draw
a quick breath—I shouldn't be able to affect anything here,
but apparently not—and Owen's breath hitches. His eyes open.
Hazel, like Grammy's were. Like mine.

I hold my breath, waiting for the screaming to start. For his
face to redden and wrinkle, just like it does every other time he
sees me.

But it doesn't. His small rosebud mouth opens, a spit bubble
escaping. He . . . *laughs*. He *smiles*. His hands reach out, grasping.

I turn to go, and Owen makes a cooing noise. I close my eyes,
forcing myself to find stillness. When I turn back, he's standing,
chubby fists wrapped around the bars of his crib. He cries out,
reaching for me.

I turn back. His hair is as soft as cornsilk when I run my fingers through it. His skin is sleep-warm, damp in that way babies get. He grips my arm with one chubby hand, fingers going through the knit of Tristan's sweater. I think of all the times we've gone through this dance, him waking and screaming, me swinging him up in my arms.

"Mama?"

I close my eyes against it all. Truth is, I do look like the woman in the other room if we were in another time, another reality. I look like my mom too. And even though Owen and I have been separated for a couple of weeks, he probably knows me better than anyone else in his life.

"No, baby boy," I say.

The door behind me opens. I freeze, certain I've been caught— but the girl just moves through me. The sensation is odd, staticky and warm, but she doesn't notice me nor feel me as she hefts Owen out of his crib and curls up with him on her lap on the bed.

"Sleepy boy?" she says, pulling him close to her, pressing kisses to his face. He coos, squeals with laughter.

"Mama mama mama mama," Owen says. He waves wildly in my direction. "Mama mama mama."

"That's right, Owen," the woman says, pulling him against her chest. "Mama."

I've seen enough. I don't run through the house, but I'm moving quickly enough, with my head down, that Fletcher gets the hint. They follow me out into the yard and across the clearing to the trees. I force the air in and out of my lungs.

"Hey," they say, laying a hand on my arm. "You can have him back. You'll write such a good song, and Tristan will give him back to you in a heartbeat."

I nod, unable to speak. They're right. The words are coming to me, clotting on my tongue. Ones that will get Owen back, and me on my way.

At Ruth's, I start by gathering tomatoes and zucchini into buckets, humming as I work. My mind wanders in and out of that little cabin in the woods, through the memories of Owen's first year of life.

Let the record show I don't hate *everything* about being an older sister, a caretaker. Owen has a way of burying his head in my neck when he's overtired, burrowing into my skin as far as he can go, his little fists balled in my shirt. He looks at me sometimes like I'm the center of his universe, and for a split second, it feels good to be needed.

But those are selfish reasons, aren't they? I can't say I make Owen's life any better, even though at this stage, he just requires feeding and changing and holding, somewhere warm and safe to sleep. We give him that.

But when I was a little girl, I spent most of my days at Grammy's. I remember the warmth, the love, the assurance that there was someone there who I could go to. Every day when Mom or Dad came to get me, swung me up on their hip and loaded me in the car, I waved to her as she stood on her porch and watched us go. Every single day, she stayed and waited to leave until we were out of sight, as if she couldn't bear to miss a single second of me.

I cannot be that to Owen. I *am* not. Even if I stay in Winston, I can't imagine us being . . . I don't know. I can't imagine being someone he goes to. Someone he loves unconditionally.

I can't imagine sticking around.

"Sweetheart?"

I look up to see Ruth standing over me. She has on one of her aprons, patterned with faded blue flowers. Her hair is piled up on top of her head, curling tendrils sticking out at odd angles. In one hand, she holds a heavy ring of keys.

"What's up?" I ask, sitting back on my heels.

For a half second, Ruth looks uncertain. But then she glances over my shoulder, at the plants I've brought back to life with care and attention, and something shifts. "I have a new job for you. Similar to this one, but . . . a bit different. Do you think you can manage it?"

"I think so," I say, because I'd weirdly rather die than disappoint Ruth. Perhaps it's a crossed wire, but she reminds me more of my grandmother than anyone else, and it makes my stomach ache with childlike longing.

She offers me a hand and helps me to my feet. Ruth doesn't go back toward the house—instead, she guides me toward the gate in the iron fence. The heavy keys in her hands click when she searches for the right one.

The gate is too high to see over, but when it creaks open, it reveals another garden. It's overgrown and thick with foliage, reminiscent of an old cemetery. I step hesitantly in after her, searching for poison ivy and poison oak and snakes.

"What is this?" I ask.

"The memory garden," she says, pulling the gate shut behind her.

She pauses for a moment, looking over the weeds, and I follow her lead. I take it all in—though I know Ruth's garden is just behind us, and Ruth's house behind that, it feels like we entered another world when we stepped through the gate. The garden is shaded with trees on all sides, heavy willows that obscure the perimeter of the iron gate. It's quiet here, otherworldly. And the plants—they're a riot of color, all different shapes and sizes of flowers and green things, curling ferns and reaching sunflowers and jewel-like violets. It has none of the order of Ruth's usual planting.

"What is all of this?" I ask—because there's something in the air, something that makes me suspect *plants* is not the correct answer.

Ruth leads farther in, stepping carefully, brushing her hand along the top of one of the peony bushes. "Everyone who comes here leaves something behind for me. And I keep it and plant it and nurture it. I hold what they must leave behind, when the burden is too heavy."

I hesitate, remembering the seeds in my pocket the other day. I hope they were errant zucchini seeds rather than the essence of someone who once lived here. "Like, a flower in their honor?"

Ruth smiles, but it doesn't touch her eyes. "Kind of," she says. She stops by a rosemary bush and pulls a few bristles, holding them to her nose. "I keep them. I take care of them. I remember, when no one else does."

"Do you know who all of these represent?"

"Mostly. And if I don't, there are ways to find out."

I nod. It's hard to figure out exactly what she's saying, what she wants me to do, but that's Ruth. "So, how can I help you?"

"I want you to sing to them. My other plants like you—these will too."

It's a compliment, but I'm not sure how, nor what to do with it. "Will it help them grow?" I ask, rubbing the petals of one of the pale pink peonies between my fingers. There's not much sunlight here, penetrating through the willows—I don't know how any of these plants are so healthy in the first place.

"Not really," Ruth says. "But they won't feel alone. It's always better that way. Just don't touch the roots. You probably won't like what happens."

Cryptic. It's all cryptic. But if Ruth wants me to do something, if she thinks there's a benefit to it, who am I to stop her?

"Okay," I say. "I'll do it."

Her responding grin is so small, barely a quirk of her lips, but she's so spare with smiles—I take it on like the sweetest praise.

Ruth leans against the iron gate for a moment, watching as I take one of the peony heads between my hands. I search for a song and settle on one that was popular last spring, about the things a heart will believe when no one is looking. When I glance over at the fence after the last chorus, Ruth is gone.

I sing until I run out of songs and the sky starts to go pink and amber. I retreat to Ruth's house, letting the gate to Ruth's mysterious memory garden close behind me.

When I came in, Ruth was making a big vat of chicken stock. She's still there, at the stove, but she's not alone. Tristan sits at the table.

In the light of the flickering candle on the table mixed with the dying sunlight from the window, he is ethereal. Otherworldly. He looks up, meets my eye. His lips twitch into a smile.

"*He doesn't want you,*" a voice whispers, right into my ear. I look around, but my ghost isn't there—it's only her voice, a constant reminder. I grit my teeth and go inside anyway.

"Hi," I say, hating that I sound so shy.

"Can I have the zucchini, pet?" Ruth asks. She knows my name, but she rarely uses it. When she's happy, it's pet, or sweetheart, or darling. When she's not, it's *girl*. Just girl. But that's fine with me, as long as she lets me feel productive.

I bring the basket in with me and set it on the table.

"I thought to catch you before you went home," Tristan says. He has the circlet on the table in front of him, and up close, I can see that he's less boy, more Lord. Gold shimmers on his cheekbones, and his eyelids rimmed in copper, his eyelashes darkened. Rings glimmer on his fingers. At his feet, Whit sleeps contentedly. "A pilgrim has joined us. Wants to integrate. We're having feasts in the village for the duration of his initiation."

I wrap my arms around myself. If he notices I'm wearing his sweater, he doesn't comment on it. "Did they come after something taken?" There's no point asking if they came for something *Tristan* took. The implication is clear enough.

"No," Tristan says.

"When they come seeking, there's only the matter of a favor," Ruth says, skimming fat off the top of the stock and putting it in a jar. "When they come of their own accord, we accept them openly."

I chew on my lip. Tristan opens his mouth, thinks better of

whatever he's about to say, and closes it. "Right," he agrees. "And Leo has come willingly, so we'll accept him as one of our own as any family might. This is a resting place. A refuge."

A refuge. For everyone else, perhaps, but not for me.

Outside Ruth's house, Tristan grabs my arm before I can flee. "Leah. You know we don't . . . you're not unwelcome here. You have a place, just like anyone else."

I wonder why he didn't say this in front of Ruth. Perhaps she would disagree—perhaps she sees me for what I am, stinking with the dirt of Carver County that I was born in. She lets me help, she shows me her secrets, but we still know what I am and where I do and do not belong. I can't imagine Ruth sees me as anything more than a temporary addition. A distraction.

"I know," I say, even though I don't.

That's where Tristan's wrong. He half-smiles, and I think he sees through me, but here's the truth: He can't be both my jailer and my savior. He can't release me from the very trap he set for me. And if I allow myself to forget that . . . well, whatever happens to me will be entirely my fault.

Nineteen

There's a great table laid down the middle street of the village. Whit sits at my feet, since I'm more willing to slip him scraps of venison than Tristan is, and he knows it from our many dinners. I'm not in any sort of seat of honor. I'm at the end of the table, as far from the dais as you can get, but Fletcher sits with me, and Andrew the baker.

The table is dotted with massive candles dripping wax, lighting up the twilight evening. Trays of venison, platters of stewed apples and carrots, heavy bowls of roasted potatoes, and baskets of sweet bread rolls fill the space between. There's so much food, more food than I understand appearing in such a short amount of time. No one is dressed up for this feast, but I like seeing all of the villagers in their work clothes. I recognize Laila and Penny, the couple who live next to Ruth, who've brought me hot chocolate on more than one occasion.

"Your voice is so sweet, in the afternoon," Laila says, her hands gripping mine. They're both in their thirties, probably. Laila's dark skin glistens with streaks of gold and silver pigment, her hair twisted into knots and tied up with glimmering gold wires. She wears a brightly patterned dress and clogs. Penny is more understated in her clothes, usually in some variety of beige cotton the same shade as her yellow-blond hair. Penny came to the village with her son, Thomas, who seems to spend most of his days looking for Whit or stealing juicy apples from the trees that border Ruth's property.

"Thank you," I say. "I hope my singing doesn't bother anyone. I'm just doing what Ruth asks."

"Oh, you could never." She smiles, going away to the place where Penny and Thomas are sitting without saying goodbye.

Andrew plops a piece of venison on my plate, then hesitates. "You're not vegetarian?" he asks, worried. "Vegan?"

"No," I say. My mom would've stopped feeding me if I'd tried something like that.

Whit whines at my feet. I tear off a tiny bit of venison and let it drop under the table.

Dinner is . . . nice. Homey. There's laughter, and flirting (between Andrew and Fletcher, not involving me), and Ruth comes over and puts her hands on my shoulders and kisses my cheek. She smells of the cherry wine I drank with Tristan.

"A good girl," she declares, running a hand through my hair.

I'm not sure how to process the surge of belonging that makes my heart feel heavy with warmth.

And above it all, there's Tristan. He sits with Leo, the new initiate, and a few others that I vaguely recognize from seeing around but never properly met. The table is long enough to seat everyone at the village, somewhere between a hundred and fifty and two hundred people.

I feel my eyes drawn to him more times than is particularly decent. His laugh, throaty and wild, catches my attention as he lifts his goblet to his lips. He stands up for a toast that I can only just hear, one that has the others whooping and Whit howling at my feet.

When the meal is over, and we're all full of wine and spiced apple cake and bread, the stronger villagers break apart the table and a few others come back with a banjo, a set of drums, a guitar, and a flute. I find a quiet space with Whit, sitting against one of the houses closer to the raging bonfire. It's warm, the wood crackling and sending sparks up into the darkness of the night sky. I wrap my arms around Whit's neck, leaning my head against his sloped shoulder. He huffs at my hair, but otherwise settles.

"I hope I'm not disturbing your evening," I say to the dog. He makes a low whine in his throat and licks the top of my head.

In the open space near the bonfire, the band is starting. I only recognize Andrew, who is playing guitar, and making serious eyes at Fletcher.

They start up a jaunty folk tune that I don't know. The remaining villagers, most of them at least, start in on a dance. I watch them wind about in complicated steps, laughing and swirling around. There's a familiar ache in my chest, watching it all happen.

They play a few more songs, and then there's laughter near the band. I watch Tristan as he talks to the banjo player, then takes the banjo himself. The rest of the village watches, rapt with mirth, as he strums a chord.

When he sings, it's like the mirth, the excitement, all of it breaks free. I sit with my fingers twined in Whit's fur, my heart-beat thudding in my ears.

Well there was a girl down south,
With honey on her mouth,
And when I kissed her, oh it was so sweet.
Her voice, it was like candy,
The heartbreak burned like brandy,
And ne'er again did we twain meet.

Whoops sound through the crowd. I don't know this song—not a surprise; I haven't known any of them, but everyone else seems to. The dancing picks up in fervor, and I watch Tristan breathlessly.

He's at ease here, the complete opposite of the evil Lord of my childhood imaginings. His fingers blur across the banjo strings as he stands on the throne. I spot Leo, the newcomer, as he swirls around with a village girl, his head thrown back, laughing.

I don't know if I could ever be that carefree. If such a thing is possible.

When Tristan finishes, he takes a grand bow before handing the banjo back to its owner. He's surrounded immediately by those who love him, adore him, defer to him.

Maybe he didn't know if he wanted to be the Lord, but he makes a good show of it. Perhaps his brother saw in him what I see now: He is dependable, steady, certain in a way that makes him easy to trust. Even for someone like me, who certainly shouldn't.

I bury my face in Whit's fur. There's such a weight of loneliness in my chest—I want to go to the Hollow by myself and mope. I want to be alone, I think.

A hand falls on my shoulder, warm and large. "Are you all right?"

I glance up. Tristan. He's left his admirers behind, all of them, and come to find me. I suppose I'm not that hard to find with Whit in my arms.

"Yeah."

"Why are you hiding?"

"I'm not hiding," I lie.

He doesn't leave me. Instead, his lips curve with a warm smile and he drops to his knees next to me, so he's at eye level with me—and Whit, who makes a solid attempt to lick his eye.

"I'll shave you," Tristan threatens, pushing Whit's great head away. The dog only huffs out a breath and curls into a ball next to me, head on his paws. Dog settled, Tristan turns his gaze back to me. "You're hiding. I know you are."

"I'm not," I insist, tucking my knees to my chest. "I just . . . don't know . . . I've never been to a dance. I don't know how. I'll look like a fool."

"Excuses, excuses." He stands back up, one hand held down to me. "Come on."

"Tristan, I—"

He raises an eyebrow, but his mouth is still full of mirth. "Would you deny me?" he asks, and there's something low and desperately thrilling in his voice. He's not speaking to me as a boy, but as the Lord, the ruler, the power behind this land. I remember how he deflated in my room the other night, shifting out of his authority and back to a boy. This is quite the opposite.

And the truth? No. No, I wouldn't deny him, and that's terrifying. Not as the Lord, and not as the boy. Even though I don't know what he would ask of me.

I put my hand in his. He pulls me to my feet hard enough that I overcompensate and fall forward into his chest. But Tristan doesn't care. He just smiles and drags me out to where the others are dancing.

"Just let me lead," Tristan murmurs. I look up at him, oddly shy, unable to speak. The circlet dips low over his brow, some of his curls spilling messily over the top. His cheeks are flushed with drink and dance and laughter.

The breath catches in my throat—I know what he is, unequivocally, and I cannot find it within me to care.

One of his hands goes to the curve of my waist. I rest a hand on his shoulder, trying to ignore the strength of his muscles under my grip. I can't forget noticing him chopping wood outside in the yard in one of my lesser moments, watching the ripples of his shoulders, his back, his arms as he lifted the ax and brought it down. That day, I wondered what his shoulders would feel like under my hands, and now that I know, I won't be able to forget it. Our other hands lace together, chests pressed without any space between.

When he takes a breath, it's like I can feel the oxygen going all the way to my lungs.

I've never danced with someone, not really. At youth group, we had one dance, and it was all about "leave space for Jesus," with a bunch of us dancing in a circle as a group and no pairing off. I skipped freshman homecoming, was grounded for basically all of sophomore year, homeschooled for junior, and . . . well, I'm missing senior year homecoming because I'm in a commune in the woods, for better or worse. Any dancing I've done with boys has been awkward swaying, held an arm's length apart.

But that's not what dancing with Tristan is like. I never understood how leading worked, but it's impossible not to follow him with his body drawing me in, his heartbeat thudding against my chest. His legs don't leave me an option to disobey. In the space between our arms, we are one, moving together.

I'm conscious of the sweat pasting my hair to my forehead, the back of my neck. Of how tightly his hands hold me, his fingers digging into my waist. I am hyper-aware of everything about him: the light in his eyes, the pacing of his breath, the thudding of his heart, the heat of his skin against mine. Unthinking, I shift the hand on his shoulder and cup the back of his neck, relishing in the brush of his soft curls against my fingers.

I'm conscious of how *happy* I am. Light, effervescent, in a way I don't remember ever feeling.

He knows this song, dances to it like he has a million times before. But I haven't, and I can pretend that he makes it all up for me, that it's some deep understanding between the two of us that makes the steps work rather than his talent alone.

It's nice to pretend that I'm special.

Tristan lifts me, his hands around my ribcage as he spins us in a circle. I throw my hands up, let my head fall back. When Tristan lowers me, his nose skims my cheekbone. Warmth pools in my belly. I let my hands return to our positions, even more aware of the intensity of his gaze on my face. I can't imagine how I look: breathing hard, lips parted, flushed with happiness.

I barely even notice the music has stopped, that *we* have stopped, I'm so carried away looking up at him.

He raises my hand to his lips, kisses the back of my fingers.

"Thank you for this dance," he says. "Thank you for trusting me."

I need to get away soon, or I'm going to end up trusting him with a lot more than just a dance. It's the worst part of me speaking, the part that wants, that doesn't know when to quit. I know he's watching me when I turn around, skitter back past the campfire and through the rest of the clearing, out where the coolness of the wood embraces me. When I'm far enough away that I'm certain he can't see me anymore, I lean against a tree, digging my fingers in the bark. I take a deep breath, then another, and one more after that.

I don't even *know* Tristan, but he makes my veins feel warm, alight with electricity. I don't understand how he does it, or if he knows, but he does. He's my absolute worst nightmare.

"Did you forget why you're here?" Maria asks from behind me.

When I turn, she is not beautiful, nor ghost-like. She is a dead thing. Rotted, bloated, her skin mottled and purple, a cord tight around her neck, the skin puckered. She reaches for me. Two of her fingers are broken, and one is missing the flesh at the tip. A bare bone pokes through.

I let her grab me. Touch me. Bury her terrible, fleshy face in my neck. She sobs tears of blood and putrid matter against my shoulder. I force myself to embrace her, this girl, this *corpse*.

"Help me," she begs. "Help me."

MY THROAT AN OPEN GRAVE

I swallow hard. This close, even as a ghost, the stench of rot on her is hideous and cloying, turning my stomach. I lean back against the tree, sliding down until the corpse is collapsed in my lap.

"How can I help you?" I whisper. The words taste bitter on my tongue. I knot my fingers in her nightgown, gagging at the give of the flesh beneath the fabric. She is barely human any-more, barely real.

"Find them," she begs. "Make them pay."

I close my eyes. Tristan wasn't the Lord when she came here, but his brother was, and something attacked her under his watch. Something kept her from leaving.

Whatever happened to her, whatever she did, she came here and died and no one even cared. No one protected her. I've spent the last few weeks pushing those thoughts away, but they're back with a vengeance: *Something* happened to her here, and I am the only one who seems to care.

"My sister," Maria begs. "You're all I have left. The only one who can help me. Help me. *Help me.*"

"I will," I promise. I want to puke. I *might* puke. "I'll make them pay."

The ghost vanishes, body slick under my hands one second and gone the next. I am covered in gore and viscera, stinking of her watery grave. I roll onto my side and throw up all that ven-ison, bread, and apple cake into the detritus of the forest floor.

185

Twenty

When I wake up the next morning, I go straight to my piano. Maria doesn't bother me there most of the time, and I don't have to worry about Tristan, or Fletcher, or anyone else. It's just me and the keys, my fingers slipping across them, the memories coming and going in an endless tide. I shift through the only songs I have memorized: a lullaby Owen used to like, the chords of a Billy Joel song, snatches of *Moonlight Sonata*.

It's coming together, even though I don't want to admit it. It marks the end of my time here, the culmination of my song, but maybe that's for the best.

There are to be six more days of feasting to welcome Leo into the colony, Fletcher told me, with his official initiation rites taking place on the last one. The moon has passed full and is waning day by day—I'd give myself a week left, maybe a little longer. It makes more sense for me to use this distraction of feasting to spend as much time here in the woods, by myself. To figure out Maria's death as much as I'm able, to help her. To lay her to rest. And once that is all done, I can leave the hurt behind and take Owen home.

Home.

The word feels empty and dull. But there are obligations to get back to—my job, for one; school, and Jess, and all the other little pieces. And maybe I'll apply for college after all. Maybe I'm not meant to be a girl forever bound to this town that never loved me back.

I trail my fingers along the keys, a great jumble of notes. It's time to stop thinking of wolves and folksongs, time to leave behind this place with its echoes of memory that cut the softest, most bruised parts of me to nothing.

I owe her.

I don't know how to explain it, or why the feeling is so strong in my chest, but I do. So, when I finish my session, tuck the scribbled lyrics into a pocket of my dress, I set out for that burnt-out foundation where my skeleton waits.

Maria is nowhere to be found. I don't let myself fear as I go up those stairs, across the foundations. Memory stirs in me, like I'm crossing the foundation of the home I left behind.

She's more flesh, more gristle. I try to breathe slowly and evenly, to keep the bile contained.

She is still unrecognizable besides the vague shape of her body and stature. Her skin is mottled blue and green and black with rot, maggots crawling through the tattered dress over her ribs, making homes in her collarbones. Her eyes are almost back, milky and soft, one spilling across a half-fleshed cheekbone.

I pace the room, waiting for my ghost, but she does not come.

In last night's imagining, she was waterlogged and bloated, and that's not the case here. But how many deaths has she died in this place, where time is little more than an illusion?

"Maria?" I call. No one answers. No one comes.

I take a deep breath, and inch closer to the girl's body. There's that ring I noticed, and I suddenly realize why it's so familiar: almost every girl in Winston had one. I had one, too. Silver, thin like a wedding band, on her ring finger. If I pried it off her rotted finger, wiped away the gore, I'd be able to make out the words *true love waits* etched on the inside. A purity ring, like all of us in Winston got when we turned fifteen.

I suck a breath through my teeth and try to remember all I can about Maria Sinclair.

Her baby was taken by the Lord six or seven years ago, when I was almost thirteen. The story is that she was drunk and the baby was taken when she'd passed out. She'd just graduated from high school, or dropped out. She was old to me, at the time. A fully formed adult. But now, reflecting . . . she couldn't have been older than eighteen or nineteen. Just about my age now.

I can't remember who the dad was, or what the story was, or the drama. All I know is she had her baby, the baby was taken, and Maria was sent in after them. It doesn't paint a very clear picture.

But that's the thing about the Lord. He targets the young mothers, the unmarried, the ones that can't actually keep up, might not have wanted to be mothers in the first place. Maria's the only girl I knew, but their stories stretch back as far as anyone can remember, these girls that were sent back to claim what was taken.

I don't know if any of them came back. If they did, their stories weren't told—which makes sense, because in a story about the Lord, who cares about the survivors?

Tristan told me that the Lord can only take what is offered. I know who offered Owen, on that crystal clear winter night; and I know I'd offered him before, too. It was *my* fault Owen was taken. But I don't know for sure that every baby was offered in the same way, that Maria carved this fate for herself.

I'm not going to get any more clues from this body. I stare at her, and she stares back, and maybe her grave will claim me too, in the end. I go back to the warmth of the Hollow and wash the stink of death away until all that remains is clean skin, washed anew.

Under water, no one can remind me of all the things I've done wrong. All the ways I've brought this misfortune upon myself.

When Tristan comes in, I'm in his chair in front of the fire, eating a hunk of bread with sharp cheese and an overfull glass of his good wine. I nearly drop my book when he clears his throat from the doorway.

"Sorry!" I say, dropping my feet, wiping crumbs away from my skirt. "I didn't think you'd be home anytime soon."

"Why didn't you come to the feast?" he asks, shrugging off a jacket and hanging it on the back of a chair.

Because I wouldn't deny you if you'd asked me again to dance. Because I wouldn't deny you anything, if you'd asked, and that's a dangerous game to play.

"Too tired from last night," I say. "And I . . ."

His expression softens. Tristan takes the chair across from me. We could be anyone anywhere, me waiting up for him, him coming home from a party. It's too easy to sink into the idea of an alternate universe where this is okay and normal. Maybe we met at a coffee shop in upstate Vermont, Tristan and his rings ordering black coffee and me making sweet drinks that got more and more ridiculous by the day until he finally asked me out. Maybe we've been together for years, and he's just now coming back from some friend's birthday party, warm and sleepy, and we'll go to bed, and it will be normal.

A comfortable normal. Safe. I don't think I'm ever going to have a future like that.

So I pretend. I take in the column of his throat as he lets his head rest back. I see how the firelight glimmers in the hammered copper of his circlet, sets the rubies and onyxes and opals in his rings alight. I watch his slender fingers on the arms of the chair and remember what they felt like on my body, what they *could* feel like on my body. It's all there, a road map of hard work in the forest and dedication: the strength of his thighs, the marks of mud on his trousers, the corded muscle in his forearms, the breadth of his shoulders. If I could cross the space between us, tuck myself against him and bury my face in his neck, he would smell like rich pine and smoke.

"You're allowed to belong here," Tristan says, his voice husky after his evening of singing and dancing. Sometimes, when he says stuff like that, I fear he can read my mind. Perhaps it's all too clear on my face, and that's the worst thought of all—I can't even hide my most forbidden thoughts.

"But I don't," I say, tucking my knees to my chest. One day, a week or so ago, when we were walking home from Ruth's, he dug his fingers into the soil and presented me with a handful of dirt.

"Thanks," I'd said.

But he'd only smiled, and said, "Trust me." I waited, even though my stomach was growling and Fletcher was probably getting antsy, because dark was falling. But then, between Tristan's hands, a bud appeared. It grew into a perfect bloom, marbled white and blood red. He'd discarded all but the flower, and stuck it in my braid.

"The soil sings your praises," he'd murmured, making me blush. It was a full moon that night, and I'd sat up late, watching the caress of light over the petals. Something about it felt too close, too much.

But now, I remember that evening in the dying sunlight, the soil in his hands, the single flower. Maria's bloated corpse last night, her changing one today. The ring on her finger.

True love waits. Bullshit.

"I have a question for you," I say. "About my ghost."

His eyes slip from the fire to my face. "Hmm?"

"The... echoes. Memories. Whatever."

"Ah." His cheeks grow pinker, and it takes me a second to recognize the look on his face. Tristan isn't embarrassed: He is *ashamed.* My stomach twists because something terrible happened to Maria, probably here in this wood, in the Lord's care, and she tried to warn me.

"You wouldn't lie to me, would you?"

His fingers dig into the chair, but his eyes don't leave my face. "No."

I nod. I don't know how much I believe him, but he's right— he hasn't lied to me before. Not telling me he was the Lord wasn't really a lie, but rather an omission, a procrastination. A protection from the assumptions I would make before he had his armor on.

"When I go," I say slowly, choosing each word. "Will something of me stay behind?"

He's quiet for a moment, frozen. I take a sip of my wine, watching his face carefully, searching for any sign of weakness, any crack. "Yes," he says.

"How much?"

"Nothing you would notice."

"But would you. Notice, I mean."

He leans back, eyes closing. "Of course I would notice your ghost, Leah," he says, like it's a foregone conclusion, and suddenly I'm not sure what we're talking about anymore.

"Will you even notice I'm gone, if you have some of me here?" I ask.

"It will be a memory of you. Not the real thing." He doesn't look at me when he says it. I can't process what that would mean but I remember us dancing last night—and I'm suddenly so jealous of the part of me that gets to stay behind. I wish, with an aching sincerity, that I could dwell in that scrap of me, in the memory.

It's a dangerous line of thought. I leave it where it is.

"And my ghost visitor," I say, clearing my throat. There's a line of questioning here that's more important, more necessary than any thoughts Tristan may have of me. "Would she have left so much of herself, if she'd survived?"

"I don't know," Tristan confesses. "Probably not."

I press my hands to my eyes, thinking of all the things Tristan has told me and my own experiences: He only takes what he is offered, how I was a ghost myself when I crossed to Winston on my own.

"Did you watch her go back?" I ask.

He shakes his head. "No. We never do."

Something happened to Maria between leaving the village and making it home to Winston. Either some assault in the woods, or some attack in the town itself that led to her death. Unless she never made it to the other side—with her waterlogged corpse, it's possible that she drowned halfway across.

I can't blame Tristan for her death. He seems to be about my age, so he couldn't have been older than thirteen or fourteen himself.

"I have to find out what happened to her," I say. "I . . . owe it to her."

Tristan looks concerned, but he doesn't question it. "I'll help you," he says instead. "We can find out what happened, how she died, and give her peace. And if something happened to her in my realm, under my watch, then I need to know what it was."

His desire to help warms me, but I have to be realistic. "How do we know who . . . offered Maria's baby to you?"

Tristan shrugs. "I don't," he says. "I don't know who offers what, or why, but only that it is. So, when Thaddeus—my brother—went to get the baby, it was because he was rightfully left to us. But there's no way to tell, not really. I'm surprised you're the one who offered Owen, though I suspect—"

"I didn't know what I was doing," I say quickly, and Tristan nods.

"I figured."

The weariness of it all is too much. I take my leave of him after we agree to meet tomorrow morning to find Maria's ghost and see if we can get to the bottom of what happened to her. I go to my bedroom and change into my nightgown. When I look out the window, she's there in the space below, beautiful as ever in the moonlight. I lean my forehead against the glass and watch her.

Somewhere between here and Winston, after Maria left the Lord's protection in the wood, she died. I'm going to find out what happened to her. I *have* to.

There's a worry forming in the back of my mind, one that I can't quite give voice to. I don't think Tristan is the one that I should be afraid of . . . and that terrifies me more than anything else.

Twenty-One

My dreams are full of blood and gristle. When I open my eyes to the weak light of a new day and Tristan knocking on my door, I am still exhausted. I whip the door open to see him there, fully dressed, with a spade strapped to his hip. His expression shifts when he takes me in and I realize how thin my nightgown is, how tangled my hair is with sleep. He looks away.

"Sorry, thought you were up. I'll wait for you downstairs."

"Thanks," I grumble. It's cold in my room with the fire out, and there's a drizzle outside that threatens to break into a full-out storm. I put on tights under my dress, and sneak into Tristan's room to steal another sweater and a knit hat.

"Is that mine?" he asks when I come downstairs and accept the sweet bun from his hand. Fletcher must already be in town, helping Andrew with preparations for the feasting for the rest of the week. It seems to be an all-hands-on-deck situation.

"Yes."

He doesn't protest.

We make our way out into the wet. "How's your song coming?" Tristan asks, leading in a different direction than we normally go.

It's as good a reminder as any that that my time is running out. "Fine," I say. "Basically done." It's not a lie. I just . . . don't know how I'm going to rustle up the courage to sing it to him.

He nods. "You can present it whenever you want, you know. Whenever you feel ready."

"I have to find out what happened to Maria, and I don't know how much of it I can do in Winston."

He nods. What I'm not saying is I'm not ready to go, not yet. Not ready for my real life, for some feigned normalcy that I no longer understand.

"We'll do what we can," he says.

And to my surprise—he takes me to *Ruth's* house. She only sighs when she opens the door, looking the two of us over, taking in the spade at Tristan's hip.

"Is it necessary?" she asks.

He shrugs apologetically. "Looks that way."

"They don't like you rustling around in there," she says, arms crossed as she leans against the doorway. The air in the house is heavy with the smell of cooking onions. There's some sort of bird carcass on her table, huge, halfway prepped. It has to be a turkey.

"I know. I'm sorry. I don't think Leah will do much to distract them—"

"*Leah* isn't the problem," Ruth says, turning back to her hut. She is halfway through making bread—she slams the dough down on the workbench with a heavy *splat*. "They like Leah. Can't say the same about you."

Tristan grimaces, and I feel utterly lost. But he and I move into her cottage, Tristan seeming to take up less space than usual.

"Don't take it personally, love," Ruth says, slamming the dough down. "It's only the idea of you. Not the reality."

"That's not particularly helpful," Tristan says.

"Can I ask what's going on?"

Tristan glances at me, his mouth etched into a frown; Ruth does not. "Ruth keeps the memories of those who left. She's the protector of whatever they left behind. So, whatever memories we have of Maria's . . ."

The memory garden. I glance at Ruth. "The one you had me singing to?"

This is a surprise for Tristan. "You went in the garden?"

"You were literally here," I say, defensive despite myself.

Ruth only shrugs. "They like her."

"Ruth, she's not—"

"Not your business, nor your responsibility," the woman says in a singsong voice. "You don't get to determine who goes where within my keep."

MY THROAT AN OPEN GRAVE

Tristan mutters something under his breath, but he looks more wearily resigned than angry. "Did you tell her the mechanics?" he asks. "Since you seem to want her there, for some reason?"

"Of course not," Ruth says, replacing her dough in a big bowl and covering it with a tea towel. She wipes her floury hands on her apron. "She was keeping them company. That's all."

Tristan sighs, long suffering. "Well, if that's all . . ." He gazes toward the back of the house, toward the garden.

"What do you need from there?" Ruth asks.

It's my chance to intercede before the conversation gets away again. "The ghost girl who keeps haunting me," I say. "I can't shake the feeling that she was murdered. I want to know who did it. Do you think the garden can tell me that, somehow?" I know it sounds ridiculous as I'm saying it, but if Tristan and Ruth think the memory garden could be helpful, I trust them more than my own doubt.

Ruth shrugs, pulling a piece of paper toward her and checking something off. "Maybe," she says. "Hard to say what makes it here, what doesn't. Tristan, I'm up to my neck in work for tonight—I'll give you the keys if you promise to be careful."

"I'm always careful," Tristan mutters.

"Don't upset them," she says. "The last thing I need is a horde of angry ghosts in my kitchen." But despite her warnings, she goes to the hook by the back door and withdraws the heavy iron ring from the mess. She tosses it and Tristan catches it easily.

He doesn't say anything else as we pass through the normal garden and through the heavy iron gate. I breathe in the scent of pollen and flowers, of fresh dirt and green things. It's calm in here, just like before. Calm and quiet, like it's miles from the village.

But Tristan doesn't loiter. "We only have to find Maria's patch, and we'll get some of her memories. I don't know when or if she'll appear today. I'm not in the habit of calling ghosts, but I can teach you what to do, and we can start with our own. That way, you know what to do when you see her next."

"Oh," I say breathlessly. There are just . . . so many plants, all tangled and growing over one another. So many memories. "Ruth told me not to touch the roots."

He stops by the peony bush, glancing back. "Yeah, she would've. Ruth is the Keeper—she's the one who watches over them, keeps them safe. She'll take care of them when we're gone. But we need the roots to get to the memories."

"Does it . . . hurt anything? Erase them, if we dig them up?"

"No, we just need to find the right ones. We won't be causing any damage. Do you want to see your memories?" he asks.

"Would that . . . ?"

Cheer me up? Probably not. In fact, there are terrible things in my memories that I would prefer to forget, bury forever and ever and ever.

But I can't pretend I'm not curious, so I nod, and follow Tristan as we crawl across the memory garden. I catch flashes of other lives, other memories as our hands search for any piece of me: a cup of tea handed over, the smile of someone else's grandma, burying a wife, picking flowers with a granddaughter.

Finally, Tristan stops, the spade resting over a piece of land. "I think you're here," he says.

I hesitate. It would be wonderful to see Grammy again, or a tender moment with Dad, but . . . there are other things in there. Things that I'm certain I don't want Tristan to see. "Can I pick what it shows me?"

"Sometimes," he says. "Would it make you feel better to see a few of mine first?"

There's a strange vulnerability in that, and judging by the way he won't quite meet my eye, he knows it. I nod.

We shift back a few feet. Tristan pulls a plant, the roots shining with pearls. He holds them in his cupped palms. "I'll be with you," he murmurs. "But I warn you . . . sometimes there's a physical reaction. The things in the memories, the things we experience, they don't stay contained."

I shudder, but it's too late to back away. I meet his gaze and nod. "It's okay," I say. He swallows, looking away for just a moment, before he brings his hands closer to mine.

I lay my hands over his, feeling the moist soil and the grit of dirt. I close my eyes, feeling the tug of something on my consciousness. With my eyes closed, it feels like I'm falling, tripping through lights and sounds until an image forms around me like my eyes are open, like I'm right there and living it. And I'm transported to—

The Hollow. In my room, though it's not mine then. Tristan is a very little boy, and there's a rocking chair in one corner. A woman sits there, hair loose and curling over her shoulders, rocking back and forth. She looks like Tristan: They have the same nose, the same chin, the same curls. She holds a book in her hands, reading to him. Sleepiness overtakes me as I look at her, her graceful fingers turning the pages. I am him. I feel what he feels, smell what he smells, see what he sees.

The memory shifts. I'm in the memory garden with Thaddeus and Ruth, tending to it. Thaddeus shows me how to water it, how to nurture the memories, the right songs to sing. I watch as he takes a string of bulbs and offers them, as we travel together through his mother's last moments. Thaddeus plants the bulbs.

Next, we're at Ruth's house, a heavy fur wrapped around Tristan's shoulders. There's a teapot on the table. My hands are bloody, and distantly I know it's Thaddeus's blood, that he's not dead but he's not coming back. Ruth cries softly over the stove, but she doesn't hide it very well. I want to comfort her, but I can't.

Time passes. I learn. I grow harder, into my role. I feel the tug of something, a thread pulled taut, and I'm in the forest, staring into the lights of the night. I catch the sight of my own face in my kitchen window. Tristan watches me, real me, as I make a bottle, humming under my breath. It's cold, so it might be relatively soon after my New Year's offering. I look . . . exhausted. But when I pick up Owen, there's a look on my face that even I don't understand, that I didn't know I could make.

We skip to the other night. He's watching my face, hoping I don't notice how intently. *Gorgeous.* It's his thought—not mine. He's breathless, trying to figure out words, and he knows that every time he opens his mouth in front of me, he says the wrong thing. He cannot find words. He wants to say everything, to tell me every thought that comes into his head.

I get up. Trip. Tristan doesn't think, and his hands go to my waist, my hip, and it's like the world stops moving. My skin is hot through my clothes and he shouldn't want, he can't want, he doesn't *want*—

Tristan pulls his hands away, shattering the memory. When I open my eyes, his face is bright red. "I'm sorry," he says. "I'm, um. I."

I shake my head, brushing off the arousal that followed me from the memory, trying to shut it down. I can't understand how he sees me in his memories: He . . . he thinks I'm beautiful.

"Let's see some of mine," I say, deflecting, so I don't have to talk about what I just saw. If I talk, then I'll confirm that I feel the same tugging, that I want the same things he does, and then where will we be?

Tristan is quiet as we repeat the process. My memories grow into long pinkish green stalks, like Grammy's prized rhubarb. It's not long before I come across bulbs under the dirt. *Memory pota-toes*, a dimly frantic part of my brain provides, but that's not quite fair. I pull one nearly above ground and see that it's milky white, pearlescent, crusted in dirt. I put the memories in his hands. I'm not sure how it works, now that I'm the one in charge, and I'm not sure how to get the right memories but . . .

But we're in my Grammy's living room. The TV is on. She's made macaroni and cheese for lunch, and the bowl is on my lap. She looks at me and says, "You're a good girl, Leah. You know that, right? A good girl."

"I try," I say, but I just want to go back to my show. She reaches over and swipes some of the hair across my face and—

Don't think of it.

Blood. It's on my thighs, too much of it, soaking through my shorts as I stumble to the bathroom. Blood, and pain, and I feel it in my stomach, my back—

No. I push the memory away, trying to find anything else, *anything else*—

And I smell peppermint, my hands buried in Trent McCoy's hair, his lips on my shoulder. He moves, biting my neck, and I wince as the pain rushes through. There's friction between us, his hands gripping my thighs, pushing up my skirt, and I want it so much and he knows; it's not a matter of giving in. I'm in the corduroy skirt I wore to the basketball game and he makes a low noise against my skin. His voice is ragged and all I feel is curling desire exploding into action and—

I push it away, all of it, push him out. I come out gasping . . . and I am on Tristan, on top of him, pressing his face to my neck, my fingers knotted in his hair. His hands are on me, holding me close, and we were both in the memory—we both feel it.

I skitter back, a hand pressed to my mouth. Tristan looks at me, wide-eyed.

"That was . . . not supposed to go that way," I say, oddly ashamed. I can't believe he saw me like this. At my worst. At my weakest. I bite down on my fist.

He is backtracking, red-faced, trying to make it better but making everything worse. "Leah, that's not bad. Um. I understand you not wanting me to see it, and, um, I'm sorry if it was invasive. It's probably made worse by—when you have a feeling, going into it, like coming out of my memories and going into yours . . . I didn't mean to—I absolutely am so sorry for intruding."

"No," I say, shaking my head. "No, no, it's okay, and I don't hate you, and I'm sorry, I didn't mean, um. It's okay. I hope it's not. I don't know. Weird."

I stand up sharply, my body a riot of feelings. I haven't yet recovered, and I can't control the waves of desire that continue to roll through my stomach. I can't look at Tristan. There are too many things here—God, what if he thinks I pushed that memory on him? What if he thinks it's some awful sort of forced voyeurism? I can't imagine what he's thinking, what he believes

I did.

But when I force myself to look at Tristan, he does not look horrified. His lips are red, bruised, as if I kissed him—and I have no idea if I did. If he wanted me to.

I can't do this. "We should look for Maria's."

He looks up at me, and I have the oddest sensation that the roles are reversed, and he is a supplicant and I am the powerful one.

"Of course," he says.

We spend the better half of the morning searching, crawling in the dirt, backs aching. I hum and sing, trying for songs she would've known—but nothing helps. My ghost does not come. And when I sit back on my heels, take in the garden and Tristan a bit away, dirt streaked across his face, I feel the sinking pit in my stomach.

"We're not going to find them," I say. "Are we?"

He sighs, pushing his hair back with one dirt-streaked hand. "Not if she doesn't want to be found," he says. He chews his lip for a moment, thinking. "It's me, probably. I doubt she wants me to . . . see her."

"Because . . .?"

He digs his fingers into the dirt, taking a big pull, letting the soil patter through his fingers. "Because I'm the Lord. I might not have been when Maria was here, but that's who I am now. And you hate me. All of you have been taught to."

He says it like it's fact. A foregone conclusion. And maybe

once, for me, for all of us in Winston, it was.

"I don't hate you," I say, the words slipping out before I can stop them.

He manages a small smile. "A small mercy," he says, "that I don't deserve."

I shrug. He might be right—maybe I should hate him. But I don't. I don't think I can. I get up, offering him a hand, trying to ignore the slide of his fingers on mine, trying to push out any memory of what it felt like to be in his arms.

Twenty-Two

I manage to hide for most of the week, bury my anxiety in productivity, in work, and avoid most of the celebrations. Maria doesn't find me, even though we need to see her memories before I go and I don't think Tristan's hospitality can extend much past the date of my offered song. She doesn't even come to find me when I'm in the memory garden alone—perhaps she fears the truth as much as I do.

My days are spent avoiding Tristan as much as possible—I can't believe my memories betrayed me even more than his had. He literally, physically *remembered me basically having sex with someone else*. And I'm not sure how the memories work, how easy it was to . . . to just . . .

He's reassured me that it's fine, that there was no lapse in consent. But I can't face him. I just can't.

The morning of Leo's initiation comes, and when I wake,

there's a bundle outside my door. I want to ignore it, but that's bad behavior for an honored guest. So, I unpack it on my vanity, and I'm only marginally surprised to find a flower crown of pale pink peonies (which are massively out of season, but I cannot question Tristan's methods) and ivy. Inside is a dress of soft, frothy white tulle and gossamer, embroidered with pink flowers and green vines and gold leaves and pearls that remind me all over again of our memories.

There's a note underneath. I unfold it, scattering petals across my vanity table.

> Leah,
>
> There is not a single memory you could show me, accidentally or otherwise, that would make me think less of you. Come tonight. Feast on wine and be drunk on mirth. Sit in the corner with Whit, if you must. But be there, and for one more evening of freedom, let us pretend.
>
> —Tristan

I suck a breath through my teeth. But who am I to deny him, when I want to go? To pretend that my bargain does not hang over our heads, that I could dance with him under the stars without consequences?

And what does he want us to pretend?

I'm not strong enough.

I spend the morning drinking strong cups of tea and refining my lyrics, but I take the afternoon to bathe, using the scented oils in the bottom cabinet of the bathroom. I braid my hair and pin it around my head, then stare at my reflection and fret, and take my hair out again, letting it fall around my shoulders in loose waves. The flower crown is enough.

Tristan is gone for the day, but Whit is in his room, and he shuffles over to sit at my feet while I "borrow" pigments from Tristan's supply. Gold across my eyelids, rouge on my cheeks, and I leave my lips as is. By the time dusk is falling, I'm satisfied.

It reminds me of getting ready for a dance with Jess, both of us preening for hours. But there are no moms with their cameras, no boys coming to pick us up. There isn't even a Jess, a fact which makes my heart physically hurt.

I'll see her soon, though. Her and all of Winston. Unfortunately, that thought might hurt even worse.

I lace my boots and trek through the forest with Whit at my side. Already, I can hear the noises of the party, the laughter and music. Ruth sees me first from where she stands, putting bright orange and gold leaves around Tristan's throne. She nods to me once and goes back to her work. I feel a bit ashamed—I haven't helped her all of this week, not with her garden, not with the preparations for the feast.

But it doesn't matter. "Leah! You look gorgeous!" Fletcher shouts when they see me, wrapping me up in a hug. They're already tipsy on mead, their fingers laced with Andrew's. I think

I missed some developments in my moping, but it's okay—I'll get all the details from them later.

And there, with Leo, looking otherworldly as ever, is Tristan. He watches me while I take my seat at the table, his gaze lingering and unreadable.

I wonder what he's thinking. If he hates me. He's reassured me every time he's caught me over the last few days that it's okay, but that doesn't matter. What if he thinks worse of me by the day?

It's become easier and easier to bear much of what his realm has thrown at me. I can handle the gore, the ghosts, the bodies, the terror. But I don't know if I can handle Tristan's former regard for me twisting into something terrible. Every time I think of him dancing with me the other night, it tastes bitter as bile in my mouth—I can't imagine him doing that now that he knows the truth of me.

If he was a boy from Winston, a boy like the ones I grew up with, he knows I'm not worth anything.

I sense his gaze on me all through dinner, but I do my best to focus on my own conversations, my own plate. There will come a reckoning, but he said tonight was for pretending. So, I'm going to pretend.

"Tristan is very . . . focused," Fletcher observes quietly to me as they spoon more honey-roasted parsnips on my plate.

"Mmm." What else can I say? Anything, everything—it would

only serve to reveal me. They take the hint and leave it alone.

When the plates are cleared and the tables are shifted away, there is no raucous music, no move to clear the tables to make space for dancing. Tristan stands and retrieves the heavy cloak that Ruth holds out to him. He fastens it around his throat with a pin that sparkles dimly in the firelight. He looks every bit the terrifying Lord that the stories say he is.

When he moves to his throne on the dais, it's like every breath catches—and I'm no exception. I wonder if the other villagers think he is inhumanly beautiful, or if he's just normal to them now. I don't know how he could ever be anything other than extraordinary.

A hush falls over the rest of us as Leo stands before him. Magnus, one of the villagers, stands by with a great bowl in his hands. It's intricately beautiful—and unspeakably familiar. I stare at it, trying to figure out where I might've seen it before.

I wonder if Leo is nervous. I haven't had much time to talk to him—barely any, besides a couple of nods and a spare word or two—but it's no small thing to stand before Tristan when he is in this form. And yet, everyone here has done it. I remember the hushed, unexpected awe I felt when I stood before him to ask his favor.

Tristan's voice is smooth and dark. "Leo Klein," he says. "You have come here with the intent of leaving behind time and civilization. You come with your own purposes, your own desires, and

MY THROAT AN OPEN GRAVE

values you believe align with ours. Are you willing to separate yourself from the world of men?"

To his credit, Leo doesn't hesitate. "Yes," he says without a hint of doubt. I wonder what that kind of certainty feels like.

"Do you swear your protection to this place, this wood, and all within it?"

"Yes."

"Do you swear to nurture this wood with all that you are, all that you have, until the end of your days?"

"I do."

It feels oddly like a wedding ceremony, and maybe it is. It's an oath of loyalty, after all. I let my mind wander to dangerous places: I imagine myself in Leo's place. How Tristan would look down at me, his eyes shining, as he asked me to swear fealty to him, to this place. How my heart would trip with every word of the vow.

If I did it—if he would have me, if they would have me, if I'd never again go back to Winston—I think the oath would taste sweet and forbidden as liquor on my tongue.

But it is not me swearing myself to him and his commune. At Tristan's behest, Leo kneels, and Magnus approaches with the great bowl. There's water in it, and I'm reminded of the baptisms I watch in church.

Tristan dips his hand into the water. He nods at Leo, something they've pre-arranged I think, and Leo strips his shirt off. Tristan moves forward, off the dais, and presses his hand against Leo's heart.

"Belong, always. Let your feet guide you home no matter what trails you find yourself on."

Tristan takes the bowl from Magnus and lifts it high. I'm mildly impressed he doesn't spill it—it looks fairly heavy. He holds it to Leo's lips, tips it slightly to allow a dribble of the water for Leo to drink.

Magnus takes the bowl back. Tristan grips Leo's shoulders, kisses both of his cheeks. "Welcome home," he says.

Something in me twists. I wonder what it would be like to hear those words myself, to feel the weight of belonging—to know that there was a true home that I could never leave.

I'm eating another sticky bun, watching Andrew and Fletcher dance, when there's a hand on my waist. "Can I borrow you?" a voice says, warm near my ear. Tristan. There's that embarrassment, now. The anxiety. But I nod, suck the sugar off my fingers, and follow him into the wood.

He walks without turning until we come to a creek that must flow to the Yough, and then even farther than that. Water babbles in the distance, and I'm about to ask how far he's going to take me when the trail opens to a waterfall, the pool at its bottom deep and clear. Tristan takes a seat on one of the big, smooth rocks by the pool, and pats the space next to him.

It might stain my dress, but I don't care. I'm here, and full of wine and mirth, like he said he wanted me to be. I'm pretending.

"I just want to apologize for the other day, for anything I might've done to . . . lead you astray."

My thoughts turn sluggish, my stomach full of lead. This is where it ends, where reality catches up to me, where it all goes sour. "What do you mean?"

He runs a hand across the back of his neck, clearly nervous. "I just mean, if there's a boy or someone there waiting for you in Winston, I'm sorry if I've . . . crossed boundaries. I didn't intend to . . ."

The laugh bubbles out of me before I can think. Of course he—Oh, I should've just put my pride and embarrassment aside, should've just explained. I have the sudden realization that per-haps, this won't be bad after all. Not as bad as I was expecting. I've spent so long guarding every single thing about myself against judgment in Winston that I've forgotten that there are people out there who don't automatically assume every bad thing I've ever done.

"You think I'm still involved with Trent?" I ask.

"Um."

"I'm not," I assure him. "I'm sorry about the memory. It was . . . a lot. But I am not dating him—and I'm sorry if it made you uncomfortable in any way. Really."

He looks at me, chewing on his lip. "It's okay. Memories can be . . . invasive. I didn't want you to feel like I was stirring up things I shouldn't be."

I nudge him with my shoulder. I feel lighter, now that we've cleared this up. "Stop apologizing. It's fine."

He nudges me back. "And I didn't stress enough that some memories have . . . physicality."

I laugh again, despite myself, remembering the surprise on his face when we came out of the memory entwined. "I'm okay with it if you're okay with it."

The look he gives me . . . oh, it sends a shot of heat straight down my spine. "I'm okay with it," his voice strange. He swallows hard, then, "Leah?"

"Yes?"

I can't imagine him doing something so pedestrian as *fidgeting*, so the way he's twisting the ring around on his right hand must be some other sign, some other tell. "In Winston, you're taught to fear me. To *hate* me."

There's no point denying it. "Yes."

"But you never have."

It's not a question, and I'm not sure what to do with it— because it's a half truth. "I think I did fear you, at one point," I confess. "The first night, maybe, even though I tried not to. The first few days, always waiting for you to do something to hurt me."

The shock is clear on his face. "I would never—"

"I know that *now*," I say. There's a patch of tiny white flow-ers, growing in the moss. I pull up a couple and rip them apart, petal by petal. "But you have to understand . . . You're not human, Tristan, and you take things you shouldn't, and you've been made into a punishment. You have to see how that could be terrifying."

He shrugs. "But you came seeking me anyway."

I bite my lip, considering. "Perhaps I always wanted to be punished. Perhaps I was begging you to come do your worst, to unmake me and everything I've ever done wrong."

He snorts, perhaps seeing this as a joke, but I'm not sure it is. I've seen the teeth. I've felt the venom. And I can't say for certain that the poison is a threat anymore.

I can't think of what to say, what to do. How to make a step that makes sense. I'm caught between wanting and knowing what is good for me, what is better. So, like every other time, I deflect.

"Can we swim in this pool?" I ask, nodding to the water. It's cold enough, the bite of autumn in the wind, but I don't care. It's something, and I want to be immersed, in the water, where everything is clearer.

His smile is slow and sweet as honey. "Of course."

It's a race to get our boots off, and I loop my flower crown around the top of mine. He takes off his copper circlet and leaves it on the rock next to our shoes. He's in first, not bothering to take off any of his clothes, and something about the Lord of the Wood returning to his party sopping wet is far too entertaining to me.

He pushes away from the rock and treads water, his wet hair pasted to his forehead. "Come on in," he says, opening his arms for me to jump into like a child.

And I do. I jump, and he catches me, and if this was meant to diffuse the tension between us—*well*. It is shockingly cold, but that does nothing to ease the ache.

But I push away, and tread water. "I've always felt best in water," I say. "Like I'm come undone. Clean."

He smiles. "You like your baths, too. God, you take *so long* in there."

I splash him, feigning shock, and he catches my hand. From there, it's a small thing, a simple thing, to push him underwater, to go under with him.

The water is on all sides. I am whole and known, and under the surface, Tristan laces his fingers in my hair and I fist my hands in his shirt. I open my eyes, the world around blurry and stinging and dark, but I can make out the shape of him in the moonlit pool.

I cannot say who moves first, who causes the shift, before his lips are on mine, warm despite the icy water.

It's shallow enough for him to stand, but not me. Keeping me tight in his arms, he pushes up. Pulls both of us above water. We break through the surface and I've never been rescued, saved. Never had to surface before my lungs were screaming for oxygen.

His mouth is sweet and warm against mine. Our clothes are soaking wet and sticking to skin, both of us, but it doesn't matter. I wrap my legs around his waist, his hand catching in my dress. I am lost in him, overwhelmed with the feeling of it all. The other day, seeing his emotions of when he caught me, the desire in the spark under his skin—I understood it then, but now it's magnified, all of the pieces of him and the shards of me lining up to create something new and whole.

He pulls away, breathless, to look at me. It's so, so dark, but his mismatched eyes seem to glimmer in the moonlight, and I have already memorized every detail of his face. His lips brush mine, and I'm so close to breaking, undoing all the posturing and work I've sealed myself up with.

"Tristan!"

The voice comes from the woods, from the expanse of densely packed dark. His eyes go wide, and I'm sure mine are too. Tristan hoists me up, back onto the rock, and I am dripping and immediately cold without the press of his body. But I drag my socks over my wet feet and lace my boots, only vaguely fixating on the definition in his arm muscles as he lifts himself out of the pool.

"Here!" Tristan calls back. "I'm here." Hastily, he lifts the circlet, pulls it on over his wet hair.

Ruth comes out of the wood, a lantern held high. She raises an eyebrow at the two of us, sopping wet, on the rock—and I'm sure she can see the flush in both of our faces, but she doesn't comment. She only says, "There's a visitor."

Tristan stops, halfway up lacing one boot. The gold he's used on his cheekbones has smeared up his temple, into his hairline. I think my hand is responsible for that. "Another one?"

Ruth is quiet, and that's when I realize she's not alone. She calls over her shoulder, "It's fine now," and turns back to us. To *me*.

Only then do I understand why. It's not just anyone who comes out of the shadows of the wood, into the dim golden glow of Ruth's lantern.

"Oh, Leah," she gasps when she sees me, alive and well, if not completely soaked. "I got your message. I thought . . . I thought you were dying."

I can only stare at her, because I missed her so, and yet it's all wrong because she is here. Jess, came all the way from Winston to save me from a fate I no longer fear.

Twenty-Three

We're wrapped up in heavy towels and blankets, both of us dripping onto the floor of my room in the Hollow: Jess, because she crossed the Yough to save me; and me . . . well, because sometimes I let the things I want get in the way of good sense.

She looks the same but different, more tired; and I know that it's been less than a month since I left Winston but it feels impossibly longer. Her dark curly hair is tied up into a knot on top of her head. She hugs her knees to her chest, staring at me.

Though Tristan asked how she got here, and Ruth offered to help, Jess didn't want to talk to anyone but me, and not unless we were alone. They exchanged uneasy glances, but they let her. I could practically see the carefully constructed fear within her burst apart when he let us go on alone.

You can trust them, I tried to make every gentle look say.

But her looks were as fierce as mine were gentle, and they seemed to say, *He's going to kill you, and you would let him.*

Now that we are alone, silence stretches between us. I don't know what to say to help things, to make her feel better, so finally I settle on the only question that really matters: "How did you find me?"

She snorts. "I crossed the Yough, then followed the sound of voices."

I frown at that. You're not really supposed to just be able to stumble on the village . . . but then I think of Fletcher, and Leo, the new initiate. It's easy to get to, if you want something enough, and Jess wants me. Not everyone who ends up here was brought on by sacrifice. Fletcher, for instance, wanted something else out of life and found the wood on their own; I can only imagine Leo and every other person did the same. Jess is following the natural path to Tristan's village, the path that never occurred to us in Winston. And perhaps she found me so easily because she wanted me with a desperation I can't fathom.

Maybe my problem was that I just didn't want Owen enough—and I push that thought away before I can inspect it further.

"You said you thought you were dying," Jess says, voice catching. I remember that night, New Year's, almost a year ago. Her, laughing in her sequins, running off to a party. *No,* I want to say. *I'm not dying now, but I certainly was then.*

It's not her fault who I was then, what I did, what I became. I did ask for her help, crave her presence, want her support. And now she's here—and it was like I didn't believe anyone could ever possibly rescue me in the first place.

"I'm okay. I promise."

Her fingers trace my cheekbone. "Has he hurt you? Leah, I swear—"

"He hasn't," I promise. "He's not . . . it's not . . . It's nothing like the place we've always been afraid of."

There's that distrust in her eyes. "But what if that's only because he's ensnared you? What if you only see what he wants you to see?"

I shake my head, but it's impossible to explain it to her.

"Tomorrow," I say. "You need sleep—you look exhausted. And tomorrow, I'll explain everything. And I need your help, but not in the way you think."

Her dark eyes are weary, probably tired of my bullshit, but she doesn't protest. She takes off the blankets, strips off her wet clothes, and puts on the nightgown I offer her. I blow out the candles and slide into bed next to her, listening to the fire crackle in the grate. She immediately links her hands with mine, our legs tangling in a practiced way.

It's so devastatingly comforting, familiarity making my heart ache. She lifts our hands and kisses my knuckles.

"I thought you'd died," she murmurs. "Just like all the other girls."

My stomach turns, and all I can think of is Maria. "I need to find out what happens to them," I tell her, because that's the truth, isn't it? I can't say if it was just Maria, or every other girl, who did what was asked of them and walked out of this wood and died somewhere between here and Winston. Lost along the way.

"Does anyone know you came?"

"No," Jess says, nestling closer, warm. Her voice is heavy with sleepiness. "I told Mom I was on a college visit. No one knows."

I swallow hard and nod. I'm not sure what my gut is telling me, why that's a relief, but it is. I leave off my questioning then, let Jess drift off to sleep. I'm awake far too long, listening to the crackle of the fire, wondering how this can all go phenomenally wrong.

"I would come for you," Jess says, after I already think she's sleeping. I glance over to find her staring straight up at the ceiling. "No matter what you got into, no matter what you did, or if you did nothing at all. I would come for you."

She can't know what I've done, how I've forced this upon myself. But I nod all the same, knot myself against her, and wait for sleep.

Tristan comes along with us when we set out for Ruth's house and the memory garden in the late morning. Jess doesn't trust him yet, and I can't entirely blame her—we've grown up fearing him. I can't look at him straight on, either; not with the memories of last night seared against my brain.

After Fletcher fed us both breakfast ("Do we have bread like this at home? It's basically indecent," Jess declared, eyes closed, around a mouthful of their sourdough) and Ruth brought over an extra pair of boots, Jess decided it was okay for us to venture out. She didn't quite believe me when I told her about the bargain, what Tristan told me about the offerings, and my encounters with Maria's ghost, but she agreed to help. So it was only a matter of gathering Tristan and properly introducing the two of them.

She seems to like Ruth better; Ruth who lingers in the kitchen of the Hollow with us, even though she rarely does that. It seems to surprise Tristan as much as me when she says, "I'm going to help you with the ghost."

He raises an eyebrow. He has a mug of tea in his hands as he's perched on the wooden counter, steam curling up in thick rivulets. "I thought you didn't do that," he says.

Ruth only shrugs. Jess is doubled over, lacing her boots, so she doesn't watch the peculiar exchange of expressions between Ruth and Tristan—not that she would interpret them the way I do if she did watch.

"We should head off," Ruth says. "Much to do before the

wind turns." Tristan nods like he has any idea what she's talking about, ducking into the other room to get his tools.

"How can you help?" I ask.

"It's my garden," Ruth says, as if it's obvious—which, it is, but that doesn't clarify the ghosts.

"But Maria has been . . . difficult," I say.

Jess straightens to move next to me, leaning her hip against the table. "When you say it's the ghost of Maria Sinclair . . . what kind of ghost are we talking?"

"She looks like herself," I say. "Corporeal." Unless she's rotting, but it's not worth telling Jess that. It'll only freak her out. "Can you get her memories for us?" I ask Ruth.

"I can," Ruth says archly, "but I won't. I'll ask her permission, like I always do. But I can get *her*."

"Ruth is the Keeper," Tristan says, reappearing in a coat with the spades at his side. We follow him out of the house, falling into step in a line as we wind through the forest. There's a light misty drizzle, not enough to wish for a hood, but enough that the leaves and path underfoot are damp and a little muddy.

"The ghosts are mine," Ruth says, pushing her hands deep in her pockets. She glances at me sideways and seems to come to some decision. "I don't force them around. But if I ask them for something, they tend to listen. And in return, I make sure they live on, in whatever way they choose, until they're ready to go. They're mine, all of them, and I'm theirs, and I hope that means something to Maria."

I chew on my lip, trying to work out what exactly that means. Jess shoots me a little look like she can't believe any of this, and I can't say I blame her.

"You think you can get Maria to help?"

"I'll bring her back," Ruth says. "I'll ask. But it's up to her."

It's inconclusive, but it's the best thing we've got. "Why didn't you bring her to us any of the other times before?"

Ruth shrugs then. "I'm not going to force her around if she's scared."

I can't imagine that, being dead and *still* being scared. I always hoped that death would be some kind of release, some easing of the fear weighing me down always. The idea that it's just more fear—well, I don't know what to do with that.

But I can understand the fear. Knowing what Maria has shown me on her own . . . there's nothing good in those memories. Perhaps she can't bear to see them or share them, even though she knows we need them. *I* need them.

We reach Ruth's house, and she pauses to grab the keys, then leads us to the memory garden. Jess's hand grabs mine, fingers tangling, and I wonder if she can feel the odd stillness the place has. It's like going into another world, stepping into the garden—I can't say the rest of the village feels odd and magical, like I expected from the Lord's domain, but there's something different about the garden. A reverence. A stillness. Of course this place is magic; of course there is something otherworldly in the soil.

"Should I wait outside?" Tristan asks Ruth quietly.

"No," she says. "Just stay near the edge, if you will."

He nods, fading back toward the willows, the damp fronds brushing the shoulders of his coat. Ruth glances back at Jess and me, then heads farther into the garden, stepping carefully over the fronds. She makes a sound as she goes, starting as a hum, rising in intensity. It's not words—I'm not really sure what it is. But it's odd and heartbreaking and beautiful all at the same time, and it's so very quiet in the garden, and the lump in my throat makes it hard to breathe.

Ruth turns as if she senses some change, the tune of her humming-keening-cry turning and shifting as she makes her way to a small patch of garden where the air now shimmers, and in the space between one blink and the next, the girl appears.

She's just that—a girl. Barely a ghost. She sits in the weeds, knees tucked to her chest, hair falling in a tangle over her back. Her fingers are interlaced over her shins and she looks like she's spent the time away from haunting me in silent contemplation and weeping.

"*Oh,*" Jess breathes next to me, and I wonder if she feels it too.

I make my way over to Ruth and the ghost, lowering myself to the ground next to her. Her arm is cold against mine, even through my sweater—she feels more corporeal than she ever has before.

She looks at me, then at Jess—and I'm not imagining it. She *does* look more real. More human. More *alive*. "I know you," she says.

"Maria?" Jess's voice is small against the silence Ruth's singing left behind. Jess knew her better. She's always been more social, always more caring; she's always had a much better memory than me.

Maria's eyes skim over us, and something shifts in her gaze. She even nods to Tristan, standing over by the willows, so he comes closer. "You want to know what happened," she says. It's not a question.

"If you'll show us," Tristan says.

"Not you," she says quickly, blushing as if she's alive. But her eyes find mine, and I remember what they look like milky and dribbling out of her skull, and I have to swallow hard to keep the bile down. That's the truth of her—not this. "But I'll show you if it helps."

I nod. "It would help."

Ruth holds out a hand for the girl. She stands up, letting Ruth brush the hair away from her face—it's damp from the rain, or from the river. "Be safe," she says. Then, to us, Ruth nods and says, "I have some work to do. Get me if you need me." She departs without another word, like she can't bear to watch what happens next—and maybe she can't.

Maria takes my hand and guides me to a small section of the garden. Tristan follows quietly. He doesn't intercede, doesn't come closer than a few feet away, as if Maria is a wounded animal that only trusts me. Perhaps that's not too far off.

Jess hangs back with him, uncertainty plain on her face. She doesn't understand all of this, and I didn't prepare her well.

When she kneels on the ground, I follow, making sure not to break the link between our hands.

"Should we all . . .?" I ask.

Tristan shakes his head. "It won't be as strong if we're crowding into the memory. If you're okay doing it, it should be you. She trusts you."

I chew on my lip, nodding. It makes sense, possibly, why my memories the other day were so terrible—I trust Tristan. Of course I would show him the worst of me.

Tristan offers me the spade, but I ignore it, digging into the rich dirt with my hands until I feel the pearls of Maria's memories. Jess makes a weird noise when I pull them free, expose them to the air.

"I'll be with you the whole time," I tell the ghost, as if I could reassure her. Nothing I say matters. She's already dead.

But she nods all the same. I think we would've liked each other, Maria and me, if I knew her better when she was alive. If she hadn't just been a girl down the street. If, later, she hadn't been such a topic of gossip at the ladies' pancake luncheons most of the moms went to bimonthly after church. I wonder if I knew her at all before I knew the gossip around her, before I knew of her and her baby, her and the LoW, her and her death.

"Focus," Maria says. She grips my hand tighter, tighter, and I almost feel like it is solid flesh, and—

I'm not in the forest, not in the memory garden. I'm in the woods, just within reach of the banks of the Youghiogheny, holding a baby, a man on one side of me and a boy on the other. The man looks like Tristan, and the boy *is*.

I can hear the shape of her thoughts over mine, feel the physicality of her body. She's tired. Her feet hurt from walking. Her fingers are sore—her show of devotion was enough to win her son back, and now she's ready to go home. It was something creative, threads melding into an image, rich greens and browns and sultry golds. But that is over and done, and she is ready to move on back home. I feel the urgency in her, the weight of her steps.

She drinks in the sight of the cemetery on the other side, the sloping hills, the clapboard church. Shadows wait on the other side of the bank—her family, Maria thinks, even though she can't make out the faces in the pre-dawn light. Waiting for her to come home.

She's certain they miss her on the other side. Her mother, who loves her baby boy despite everything. Who loves *her*. Aunt Clara, who will probably be waiting at home with breakfast and a big hug.

"They can't see you," Tristan's brother, Thaddeus, murmurs to her. "Not until you're back on the other side."

We look at him. There's a dull, animal fear. She hated him once; she was taught to hate him, and she drank all that dislike and fear down like water. Since she's been here, she's kept her distance from him and the other boy: only speaking when spoken to, only eating the minimum. It's better to keep herself to herself, interact as little as possible, as if she can keep the mark of the devil off her back when she goes home.

"Thank you for your hospitality," she says, kind to the last. It'll be a relief, to be back where she doesn't have to be so *afraid* all the time.

Thaddeus hesitates. "If you decide against it . . . just look back. Look back, and we'll be here."

"Of course," she says, but that's an impossibility. All of the Lord's kindness is a gilding of the demon she knows lies beneath.

She's already distracted, thinking of the celebratory pizza she'll order for dinner. The money's tight, but she can do with this extravagance. Maybe she can get takeout for the whole family, if they let her.

"Go on, Tristan," Thaddeus says. The boy gives her a nod, and races back into the wood. Thaddeus offers Maria a drink of something, a tea or brew that's bitter on her tongue.

Thaddeus stays behind her, though, as Maria turns and faces

the river. She's not looking back, not for all the money in the world. On the other side of the bank is a new life. A new world. She's never going to be this stranded girl again, never going to drink. She's going to make a good life for the baby in her arms.

She goes forward, farther down the bank. The water rushes around her, threatens to pull her along. Maria knows what she has to do: She has to go under, and when she comes up, she'll be visible. Back, home, a Winston girl, back in the town she loves desperately.

That's how I know for sure it's Maria's feelings—I never loved Winston with the ferocity she did. But through her mind, everything is rosy and bright, from the wildflowers that grow in the cemetery to the sparkling broken glass that shines like fireworks on the side of the road.

She is waist-deep. Water rushes up to her chest. She keeps the baby close to her, head pressed to her shoulder. It won't hurt him, to go under for a moment, but she doesn't look forward to it. He's already fussing, already working up to a cry.

She presses a protective hand to the back of his head. She does not look behind her.

She takes a deep breath, murmurs a prayer, and goes under.

Thaddeus said she'd come up in the other world, on the other side, like nothing had happened. And she does—she tries to. Maria breaks the surface, sputters a breath, but there are hands on her shoulders, pushing her down. Someone is behind her, pulls a cord around her neck. She can't breathe. She *can't breathe.*

She can't tell if the person holding her down is behind her or in front of her. All she can think is—*of course he wouldn't let me go. Of course I'm not free.*

In the Lord's domain, there's no such thing as freedom.

The baby is screaming. She's screaming. She cannot think, and the river water rushes into her mouth, and she cannot let go and she will not let go and—

I force myself out of the memory of choking and being strangled, still tasting blood and river water on my tongue. Maria is a corpse for just a second, waterlogged, strangled, rotted, and then a girl. A girl gripping my hand as if I'm her only remaining lifeline.

I choke on air, trying to get as much oxygen in as possible. She died there on the edge, between the truth and the memory, and as I come into myself I can't fight back the fear that clouds my brain at the memory of Thaddeus's face, so close to Tristan's.

"Leah?"

It takes me a second to realize that Tristan's hands are on my back, smacking as if he's trying to get the river water out of me too. I must've been choking on nothing, drowning on air. I sit back, keeping my grip on the girl's hand, and let my back rest against Tristan's legs. Jess is over me too, fussing, pulling the hair out of my face.

"She was murdered," I say. "Someone held her under."

He doesn't say anything. Just keeps rubbing my back. Then, finally, "Who?"

"I don't know. I couldn't see them."

"Oh, Leah."

I close my eyes to stop them from burning by phantom river water, but her hand vanishes. I open my eyes, and Maria is gone. Perhaps she couldn't relive the grief of losing her baby, of losing her life.

"I think . . . she thinks it was your brother. The last Lord."

Tristan's gaze is hard as flint. "Did you see him do it?" he asks.

I shake my head. "I don't know. Are his memories here?"

Tristan chews his lip. "I've already been through them— what's left of them. There's no mention of that, for any of them, in his or my mother's."

I cannot stop shivering. Tristan wraps an arm around my shoulders, drawing me against his chest. I grab his arm like it's a lifeline.

"I don't understand," I murmur. "There were too many hands," I say, realization dawning. "It couldn't have just been one person. I don't think it *could've* been your brother, even if Maria thinks it was."

"I don't know," Tristan says. "I didn't know, I promise you. I . . . Thaddeus came back, and he didn't tell me. He just said she went back to them."

I bury my face in his arm. There are no words to encompass

all of the things that I'm feeling, all the misunderstandings come together.

It's Jess who draws me out of it. "If it wasn't the LoW, and it happened when she was in the river, it had to be somebody from town. *Nobody* leaves Winston. Are you positive she was murdered and didn't, like, slip?"

I feel the cord around my throat as if I'm the one who was strangled. "She didn't slip," I say. I cough, and it's terrible when river water comes up from my lungs.

I was there. Even though it was a memory, even though Maria died years ago. I was there with her, inside her conscious when she went through it. Enough for it to hurt. Enough to matter.

Jess and Tristan spend the walk back bickering over what could've happened, who could've done it, but I can't contribute. I'm too cold. Too numb. When the Hollow comes into sight, I hesitate.

"I think I need some time alone," I say. "I'll . . . just go to my piano, and come back."

Jess looks at me, concerned. "I'll come with you, if you want? You don't have to be alone. I can watch the memory too, see if there's anyone I recognize."

I shake my head. The memory is through Maria's

perspective—she couldn't see them. There's no way to identify the shadows who waited for her on the other bank. Who killed her.

Besides, I'm not going to call the ghost back to make her go through her death all over again. And I'm not going to put Jess through that.

But I think . . . There's something else going on here, pieces coming together only to shatter in my hands. I need time. A minute alone, to figure out my thoughts. Untangle the jumble.

My feet carry me into the woods, and it does not surprise me in the least when the familiar stairs come into view. I stop and look at it, the crumbling staircase and burnt-out foundation, confronting the aching familiarity of the place.

I thought, at first, that maybe it was Maria's house. But that doesn't seem true anymore.

I go up the stairs. It's three steps, then four paces across the deck to the place where the door clearly was. Something is unfurling within me, some realization that is terrible and true.

The familiarity. It's all too . . .

I cross the threshold. I can see the shape of the girl at the end of the house, but I don't look at her. Not yet. I close my eyes, and pretend. Imagine. There, to my left, I can see the shape of the living room, the place where the old brown couch lives, and Dad's easy chair. The old TV. I turn and survey the remains of the house. There, to the right, a dining room that no one uses, a table covered in dust and overdue bills. A hall splits them.

My heart is pounding, thundering in my chest. If I passed through the dining room, I'd find the kitchen, with the burnt-out remains of linoleum clinging. The walls are all gone, but the imprint is there. Past the living room, the master bedroom. Past that, a room the size of a broom closet, then another bedroom in the back. That's where the girl's body is.

In Owen's room. In the room that used to be mine.

I stumble through the house, through the ashes and debris.

Nearly all traces of rot are gone from her body. Her flesh is whole, pale, only barely mottled with death. Her chestnut hair is no longer matted with gore. The dress she wears is short—I thought it was moth-eaten before, but it ends at mid-thigh. She's barefoot. There's the handprint of blood pressed to her chest.

Eyes open, no longer milky. Lips slightly parted. One hand is above her head, one is over her stomach, flat on the floor. This is the hand with the silver ring.

She is beautiful. Even in death. Even after all the things we let pass us by. She is not Maria, nor any of the other lost girls, abandoned in the woods.

The body is mine.

Twenty-four

Echoes. Memories. Things that might come to pass, things that would never happen. That's what Tristan said this place was.

But I sit on the lip of what was once a doorway, and I stare at my body. With every passing moment, the death-cast leaves her; the lividity runs in reverse. There's a cord tight around her neck. *My* neck. It's all uncanny, terrible, and . . . and for the first time, it's a reminder that I *don't* want to die. No matter how much I push, how long I keep my head below the water.

I want to live. Dammit, I so dearly want to live. I am no longer the girl on the porch on New Year's Eve, the girl who could slip so easily one way or the other. I do not want to be that body on the floor, and I will do anything I can to prevent it.

I lower myself onto the floor next to her, my hand over her

cold one. I feel the metal of the purity ring against my fingertips. The last time I saw it was the March before last, before it was lost to the woods.

I cannot become this girl, cold and dead. No matter what I do, what I choose. I won't allow it. And that is the fire in my veins that drags me back to the Hollow, where I find Fletcher, Jess, and Tristan in the kitchen, writing on a loose sheet of paper.

"Leah!" Jess shouts, jumping up when I'm back. She hesitates, taking in my expression. "What's wrong?"

"The body in the wood," I say to Tristan, to Fletcher, to Whit, curled up under the table. "It's mine."

None of them say anything. Tristan's brow furrows. "It's . . . yours?"

"My body. My house." I can't stop pacing. Echoes. Memories. It's a warning of something that's about to happen. "I think . . . I think there's the potential that when I leave this place, I'm meant to die. That's why Maria showed it to me. Not because she wanted me to solve her murder, not necessarily, but because she wanted to warn me. Maybe that's why she was so afraid to show me—she knew. She *knows*."

Tristan and Jess exchange an uneasy glance. "What are you doing?" I ask.

"All the girls that came from Winston," Fletcher says, holding up the paper. "Tristan has a list of the babies his mom took, and Thaddeus, and the outcomes. And Jess is trying to remember if they came back or not."

I chew on a hangnail by my thumb. "And what are you finding?"

"Well, I don't know all of them," Jess says, trailing off. "But the ones I do? They didn't come back."

"But they did," Tristan says. "They were *sent* back. But they didn't make it home. And this spans more Lords than my brother and mother—if it was some kind of knowledge, it was not handed down to me."

I continue my pacing, back and forth, back and forth. "Did they leave their memories behind?" I ask.

Tristan nods. "All are in the memory garden."

"So their deaths . . ."

"Leah," Jess says, watching my face. "You can't. Maria's was bad enough. You can't keep putting yourself through this."

But I can. I *have* to. Because if I don't, I'm going to end up like the girl dead in the middle of the woods, a cord around her neck. Maria didn't take me there for nothing. She wanted me to know, to put the pieces together. If I don't figure out what is happening to the girls . . . I'm next. I'm already here, already preparing to go back. Right now, I'm as good as dead, and no one from Winston will even question it if I don't make it back to the other side.

So we go.

I'm the one who has to do it—Jess isn't fully tethered to this place, and Tristan warns us that any memories she finds can suck her in for good. The spirits don't trust Tristan enough to let him see. Fletcher could help, but they wouldn't recognize any of the faces, if we were to see them. Ruth refuses to—"It's the one thing I'll never ask of them," she says as she marks out the different spots in the garden, weariness deepening the lines around her mouth, "the one thing I won't ask them to show me"—but I need to see. I need to know.

We don't bother calling their ghosts. With Ruth's guidance, I can do it alone. By the time I come up from one girl's death, she has the next staked out and ready to go.

I suppose this is my punishment. The repayment I get for being terrible, for sinning. That's what I think as we go through the garden, Tristan seeking out the memories of the girls long-dead based on Ruth's careful instructions. I drown over and over again, invisible hands pulling me under, choking on river water.

Always, the same shadows on the shore. By the third death, I understand that they wear heavy cloaks of black netting. I'm never going to see their faces. Never going to find out who exactly they are.

In between, Tristan is grim-faced, unable to meet my eye. He hates this. Hates watching me drown and choke over and over again. Fletcher moves away, facing the other direction. I throw up river water until my stomach only has bile in it as I die over and over again.

After I come up, sobbing, losing count of the deaths, Jess is crying, "We have to stop. You can't keep doing it to her."

"I don't want to do it either," Tristan retorts.

I nod, falling back before I can catch myself. Fletcher is there, wrapping an arm around me, pulling me against their chest. My head lolls against them. I allow myself to be comforted.

"She's right," I agree, my voice choked and raw. "I can't do it anymore." My throat is raw. Everything hurts—I don't know how to get the constant memories out of my head. Every time I close my eyes, I'm drowning all over again.

We need another way to find out who is drowning the girls. But I look at Jess, and she looks back at me, uneasiness on both of our faces.

"Who was the father?" I ask. My voice is rough, raspy with choking. "Of Maria's baby?"

Jess shakes her head. "I don't know."

I think that's the key, but I cannot . . . I cannot make myself go back into Maria's memories for that. It's too much of a betrayal.

I don't know what it says about me, that I can die over and over and over again. But I cannot find the truth of it, of the baby, of her shame. Maybe that makes it dignified, to let her rest with her secrets. And maybe it just means I'm a coward.

Ruth is reading a book at the table when I slip quietly through her door. She looks up, searching my face.

"You're the Keeper," I say, declaring the title Tristan used for her. "You keep the memories."

"You know that already," Ruth says, slipping a finger in her book to keep her page.

I chew on my lip. "If I gave you something, would it hurt?"

"A little."

"Would I forget?"

She doesn't say anything. Ruth nods to the seat across from her, and I lower myself into it. She makes me a cup of tea, silence swelling between us. There's time being lost here, and I'm aware of it, slipping under my feet. I should be solving Maria's death. I should be trying to figure everything else out with the others. I should stop being so selfish.

She sets the tea in front of me, cloudy with milk, over-sweet, just how I like it. She remembers enough of me to do that, and even that makes something in me ache.

"I can't take it completely," she says. "But I can hold some of the hurt. If you think that will help."

I chew my lip, poking at bruises. "And will you show it, if I need you to? If I can't do it myself?"

Her hand cups the side of my head, gentle as anything. "I'll hold it for you, and keep it for you, and take as much as I can. And I'll be there with the memories when you need them. That's what it is, to be the Keeper. I take all the memories and keep them when they're too much to hold. You can let them go."

I sip my tea. It's not too hot—in Ruth's kitchen, it's always the perfect drinking temperature, never hot enough to scald.

Back at the house, I bathe, hold my breath until I'm sure I'm in control of my own lungs. Afterward, I dress in one of Ruth's soft dresses with Tristan's sweater over top. I braid my hair. Try to grasp some semblance of normalcy.

Downstairs, the others sit in front of the fire. I join them, sitting at Jess's feet with my head against her knees. Only two days remain in my time here and I need to sing my song to Tristan or ask for more time.

"I was thinking," Jess says quietly when we're all together. "And . . . you're going to think badly of me."

"Doubtful," I say. There's no way I could think badly of Jess. If she doesn't think badly of me, with all she knows . . . Yeah. She's fine.

"Susan Morrison. The girl before Maria."

I wince, nodding. Her death is still fresh in my mind. I accept the cup of tea Tristan offers, and distract myself by stirring in milk and sugar.

"It came out later, when she didn't come back. The baby's father was married. He worked at the factory on weekdays and had a place with his wife a few hours away, went home every weekend. Susan was his weekday girl."

I chew on my lip. "So, he's not from Winston?"

"He was," Jess says. "Mom said he's a Kubler. Like, cousin to Mr. Kubler."

I nod. Mr. Kubler is a teacher at our school. His family's been in this town for decades.

"But my point is, Tristan—you said you don't know who offers the babies. And we always heard that you, the Lord of the Wood, claimed them as punishment, because of wickedness."

I stare at Jess, the pieces coming together. *This* is it. Maybe it was missing to me because I was the one who offered Owen, and I hadn't thought too hard about other scenarios. "Oh, you're brilliant . . ." I mutter, jumping to my feet. Tristan watches with some alarm.

"Maria wasn't married. I mean, whatever. But we don't know who the father was. And just judging by her memories, I don't think she's the one who offered her baby to the woods. Not like I did."

"And Susan's . . . boyfriend was Winston stock," Jess agrees. "So, he would've known about the woods, about the girls who went there. Maybe he would've known . . ."

"He would've known to offer the baby, if he was trying to cover something up," Tristan says, realization dawning.

I nod, watching the pieces slide into place. "You *have* to

take what is offered. Even if time goes by, you have to. So, isn't it a convenient cover for anyone who wants something—or someone—gone?"

Tristan looks like he's going to be sick. Fletcher is shaking their head, and softly, they say, "Y'all's hometown is *awful*."

But Jess and I stare at each other, horror mingling with relief. How many times have I been warned that if I was bad, if I sinned, if I gave up what I shouldn't, I would be at risk of the Lord?

"Someone knows," I say, suddenly certain. "Someone is telling . . . well, let's be real. Someone is telling men who have to get out of a sticky situation what to do. And keeping it from us."

"And when they do . . . Tristan, is there a way for them to know when the girls are coming back?" Jess asks. She's so smart, always ten steps ahead of me. I want to hug her. Massively. Without her, I don't think I would've solved it on my own, especially addled with a half-dozen deaths that left no clues behind.

He frowns. Looks between Jess and me. "The ceremonial bowl. The one that you drink out of?"

"I didn't drink out of a bowl," I say, confusion furrowing my brow. But Jess looks at me sadly, and I remember—I didn't drink out of it. Pastor Samuel dipped his hand into it, red with blood, and pressed his palm to my chest. He made me a marked girl.

"Oh," I say, feeling weak. I grip the edge of a table. "*That* bowl."

"They're a pair. Enchanted. It should fill the eve before the girl is returned," Tristan says. "Just as ours fills when one of you is sent to me. So I know to come looking."

"I didn't do anything with a bowl," Jess says, half distracted.

"But you came looking for something. It's the same way anyone else comes, anyone who isn't a sacrifice. I still would've noticed, if I was paying any attention at all."

But he wasn't paying attention, and besides, everyone was so preoccupied with Leo.

Jess jumps up, comes over, takes her hands in mine. "We can end it, Leah," she says, eyes bright. "We can change all of it. Catch them at their own game. We can—"

"Leah."

I look at Tristan, now standing too.

"Yes?"

"If you go back . . ."

He doesn't finish the sentence. He doesn't have to. If I go back, they're going to be waiting for me. To kill me. Because it doesn't matter who offered the baby to the Lord—*someone* did, and that's enough for them to wait for me on the other side of the bank, to strike.

I shake my head. "We'll come up with a plan," I say. "We have to." Because there is no choice, not really. I have to go for Winston, to save the rest of the girls like me, if nothing else.

But Tristan is there in front of me. He doesn't seem to care about Fletcher or Jess when he picks up my hands in his, presses them to his lips. "You don't have to go," he says. "You were . . . frustrated. Tired, I know. Sad. You wanted a life where you didn't have to constantly be your brother's keeper—and I understand that. But why do you have to . . . ?"

He trails off, seeing the pitying look Jess gives me, hearing the sharp intake of my breath. Jess turns away and goes back to her seat by the fire. She doesn't want to be here to witness whatever happens next.

But Tristan is here, watching, waiting for me to answer. "Stay," he begs.

I let my hand skim over his cheekbone. Memorize his face. Gently touch his curls. Because once he knows the truth of it, once he knows what I am, what I've done . . . he won't care for me anymore. He won't want me, in whatever form he does. It doesn't matter that my memories didn't change his opinion of me. This will.

He turns his head. Kisses my palm.

"I think it's time for me to show you my song," I say, even though I know what it will mean. That it will change everything.

We pause long enough to go and get Ruth, who is there for both ceremonial purposes and at my request.

She joins us, pausing to kiss me on the forehead like a grandmother, and Fletcher brings Andrew for moral support. I suppose I should care about these people seeing the worst of me, but something has changed. I don't care. I can't care. This is just one more obstacle to get over, one last terrible thing.

It's not personal. It doesn't smart like it used to.

They follow me to the wood, to my piano. Tristan put his circlet on, but he doesn't bother with any other posturing. Jess shivers next to Fletcher, wrapped in one of their borrowed coats.

I take a moment. Look at the motley group assembled. Jess, who would come for me anywhere, who crossed the river and put her life on the line to drag me back. Ruth, the Keeper, who gave me purpose. Andrew, who I've only just gotten to know better, who is kind even when he doesn't have to be. Fletcher, who has taken care of me even when I've been difficult and terrible and awful.

And Tristan. Tristan, the Lord of the Wood, my worst nightmare. I drink him in: his mismatched eyes, his brown skin, the freckles that trace across his nose. The ring that glimmers on his hand as he keeps a fist pressed to his mouth, holding back whatever he wants to say. His circlet, marking him as what he is.

He could save me. He could destroy me. He will never look at me the same after he knows what I am, what I've done.

Tristan nods, letting me know it's time. I can get this over with, this one final thing, and then I'll be free. I already know I'll succeed—it's just a matter of pushing through.

"Ruth?" I ask, her name more of a croak—anxiety thickens in my throat. She pulls the folded cotton from her pocket and unwraps it on top of the piano, one of my memories shining like a pearl in the dim. Tristan sucks a breath through his teeth—I don't know what he remembers, what he expects.

I hesitate, looking over the scribbled, crossed-out, rewritten paper my lyrics are on. They're not enough. They never will be. I catch Jess's eye, cautious on the other side of the piano, and something in my heart starts to hurt. I rip up the sheet of lyrics, letting them fall to the forest floor. Nothing there is enough to hold all of it.

"Look at it, when you can," I say, nodding toward the memory, the one I asked Ruth to keep safe for me. The one I so wish she could take away. "And I'll play."

It's just notes, just agony, just emptiness. When I spread my fingers on the piano keys, nothing else matters. I let it all come rushing back.

They reach forward, into the memory, and I force my hands to keep moving as we all fall together.

Twenty-Five

I could say it started two years ago in the fall, after a basketball game, but that part doesn't matter. What matters is that frigid March day, the last grip of winter seeping in, when I forced Jess to drive me two towns over, where I spent half of my paycheck on pregnancy tests. I got them through the self-checkout and took them with Jess hunkered by the sink at a gas station halfway back to Winston.

"Leah?" she said, after too much silence.

"Fuck. Fuck fuck fuck *fuck fuck*."

She didn't tell anyone, just like she promised. But I went, later that week, to the silent church in the hour after night fell. I knelt and prayed, and prayed, and prayed. For this to go away, for some better choice to present itself. To be someone else—anyone else.

That's where I was when Pastor Samuel found me. He drew me into his office, promised me it was a safe space. And I believed him. The truth spilled out of me—I just wanted to *trust* some-one. An adult, who could tell me it would be okay, who would tell me what to do.

But his expression hardened. "Who's the father?" he asked. And when I got scared, when he yelled it over and over again, when he pulled the silver ring from my hand and threw it out of his window, told me I made a mockery of his God—I ran home. But it didn't matter, because Pastor Samuel had already called.

I was pulled out of school. Forbidden from seeing anyone. And my body changed in terrible ways, becoming something I didn't recognize. I woke, ate, cried, tried to do what I could to stay on top of schoolwork. Dad picked up more shifts, spent lon-ger and longer on the road. I used to think he hated me, was disgusted by me, but I'm not sure. Maybe he just couldn't bear to see his baby grow a baby, to see the physical reminders of my disgrace. Mom drove me to appointments and ultrasounds, made me take my vitamins. She cooed at the scans, at the alien thing growing inside me, but she didn't speak to me. With every pass-ing day, her disappointment became clearer and clearer: *You're a ruined thing.*

Trent didn't know, and no one bothered telling him. There was no point. I was not at school, barely out in town unless I was working shifts, and even then, I wore my baggiest clothes and temporarily quit for the last three months when it became impossible to hide, saying I had to focus on school for a bit.

I googled clinics, but how could I get there? I didn't have a car, and I couldn't ask Jess to go with me. Tried calling adoption clinics too, but Mom intercepted one of their callbacks and spent the whole week punishing me more. There were no options open to me, nothing I could do that I hadn't already done. No escape.

I got the message. I was only as valuable as the baby within me now. Leah Jones didn't matter anymore.

When the pain came in the middle of the night, when I woke to the terrible agony of it, I curled on my side and wept. I wished for death. I wished for something, *anything*, to come to save me.

No one came. Nothing. And the pain intensified, growing sharper. I dragged myself to the bathtub, tried to hold myself under as long as possible.

I let it go too long. I tried to remember the breathing I was taught, tried to keep still and quiet—maybe, if I was lucky, I thought, it would happen at home. Maybe I'd lose too much blood, maybe some terrible mechanism would go horribly wrong and they'd find me in the morning, in the bathtub, going cold.

Why has the thought of death been such a refuge to me? Because it's better, easier, than understanding all the ways I've fucked up, all the ways it's entirely my fault. Because I'm the charred remains of a girl who went too far, who burned too brightly until she was consumed.

That's where Mom found me. When she dragged me to the hospital, they offered to sedate me, to cut the baby out. But that wasn't enough—I had to suffer. I had to feel the full pain, the full consequences of my actions.

I couldn't stop screaming. Wouldn't.

There used to be this bit of knowledge, that mothers forget the pain of childbirth after it passes. They have to in order to want to have more, to keep us all going. It's this one cool evolutionary trick.

It's not true. I remember it all. I remember everything. Every awful tug of my insides, every cramp, every contraction that grew and grew in a massive crashing wave of pain, so full and agonizing that I forgot everything about myself: my name, my memories, my favorite color. I even remembered that I was supposed to want this, eventually, later in my life, when it wasn't a sign of ruination.

Forgetting would be a kindness. Numbness a salvation. And I did not get either.

I tend to avoid those memories, skirt around them like they're a back road I can divert around. But when I do reach for them, they're there in hideous clarity, and there's this: I remember him, cracking me open, breaking me from the inside. Slipping from my body in a wash of blood and coming into this world silently— so quietly that I was sure something was wrong.

But then someone patted his back. Suctioned his nose, his mouth. I stared up at the fluorescent lights, refusing to look down at the gore of my body, the blood and gristle, a cloying and awful smell in the air.

He started crying. Screamed into the room as if he hated to be here, hated to be alive, and I cried with him. When they put him on my chest, slick with blood and vernix, I couldn't keep the panic attack at bay.

Later, when I was something close to myself again, stitched together and clean of blood, Mom came in. I might've imagined it, but I swear her expression dimmed when she saw me. In her arms she held a bundle in blue blankets—I hadn't asked about the gender when he was inside of me, but she had. She knew him before I did, loved him before I did.

"Meet your baby brother," she said, leaning over close enough so I could see his face, but not so close that I could touch him. A mercy, I think. "Owen."

Later, recovered, on one of the awful days when everything hurt and I still didn't feel like myself, I looked up the meaning of his name. Ironic, isn't it? It means youthful. Well-born.

And that's all. That's all there is.

I don't hate him, not in the way I used to. I don't even really hate that he's here. But the truth is, I hate he's *mine*. That there's this thing that I grew against my will, that I never had the feeling I would sacrifice everything in the world for him even as the world told me I should. It was quite the opposite: that everyone was willing to sacrifice me.

New Year's Eve was the second time I offered Owen to the Lord of the Wood, even if I didn't know what would come of it.

But the first? Sitting in Pastor Samuel's office, his face red with rage, my breath hitching, hyperventilating as he shouted what a disappointment I was, as he clawed the purity ring off my finger and threw it through the window.

Take this away. Take this away. Somebody save me. Anybody. I would give it all up to be myself again.

I so badly want to believe that there's something out there, some divine power, that doesn't hate me.

Twenty-Six

We slip out of it, and my hands are still moving. Still playing. Muscle memory, even when my heart and brain are somewhere else.

The last chord rings in the silence of the forest. Ruth is wiping away tears and I can't look at her, can't allow myself to see her vulnerability and understand that it is sorrow. For *me.*

I am a mangled thing. I am soiled black with sin. I have broken the rules that were set out for me, trampled over the holiness of my body. There's that line from the play we read sophomore year, in the weeks before I found out: *You're pulling heaven down and raising up a whore.*

Me. I'm the terrible, black root of the rot that seeps through Winston. I'm the girl who went too far, tripped and kept on falling. There was no mercy to save me when I needed it most. And that is why I am cursed and broken; the pieces of me will never go back together right.

Except . . . Tristan comes closer, leaves crunching under his boots. I turn on the piano bench, sitting on the edge, waiting for him to rebuke me. I don't know what to do when he lowers himself, kneels on the ground in front of me. His eyes seek permission. I dip my head in a shallow nod.

Tristan rests his hands on my hips. "Who told you you were broken?" he murmurs, just loud enough so only I can hear.

I bite my lip. Turn my head so he can't see the tears spilling out. In the fairy-tales, the princes come to save the good girls, the pure girls. I spent most of my pregnancy cataloguing them, searching for some sign of salvation: the princess who is so pure she feels a pea under a stack of mattresses; puritanical Cinderella and her goodness, her desire to be nothing but a perfect, helpful girl; Snow White and her unflinching good character, even when she lives with men, even when she's in the perfect environment for ruination. I'm Red Riding Hood, lost to temptation, screaming forever in the belly of the wolf. The princes don't come for the ruined, the unchaste, the soiled girls—they only care for princesses. They don't come for girls like me.

I'm so, so tired of fighting to be seen as anything other than I am. I cannot become some bold, brash single girl when everyone one in Winston, everyone around me, sees only filth and shattered glass.

But his hand comes up, cups my chin. His fingers tickle the skin of my throat as he brings my head back so I look at him. So I can see that there's no trace of dishonesty when he says, "You are perfect. Whole. Leah, the things you think . . ."

There's a whole thing we've been taught about not seeking validation from a man, not letting someone tell us something about ourselves. But men have been telling me things all my life—that if I don't keep my legs closed, I'm going to end up desecrated; that I'm a slut, a whore, a broken thing. And it's not that Tristan is a boy, telling me something new. He's erasing the things that have been pressed into me like fingerprints.

Be a good girl. The only rule of Winston. And I wasn't—I broke it. I became something else, something my own mother couldn't handle, couldn't confront. I need someone, anyone, to tell me that I am more than the dead girl in that burnt-out house. Maybe when my back is turned, she'll get up, age backwards all the way through the disaster that was the last two years, flee Carver County and everything in it, run and run and run and never look back.

Maybe she'll make the decisions I wasn't strong enough to.

I lean into his hand. "But does it matter, if I don't believe it?"

"I will tell you every day for the rest of eternity," Tristan says, "if that will convince you."

I close my eyes. He catches the tear that falls from my cheek. I won't say it, and he already knows it: He doesn't get all the days of my life. The day after tomorrow, I have to go back to Winston and face my fate, and the rest of my life without him.

"Don't give me your kindness now," I beg. Not now that I'm leaving.

Tristan bites his lip, looks away. But he nods. Stands, and offers me a hand. "You've succeeded in your task," he says, more to the others than to me.

There is no celebration, no wild feast like the week of Leo's initiation. Instead, we spend the night in quiet planning. When dawn breaks, the first of our party must go.

There is the matter of Jess, and what happens to me after I leave this place. No one from Winston knows Jess is here, so she will be safe when she returns to the other side. There will be no mysterious figures waiting for her there.

The three of us walk through the wood toward Winston. More than once, I sense the ghost of Maria at my side, but every time she is close enough to appear, she vanishes when I turn.

Jess keeps her hand tight around mine during the walk. We don't speak, and Tristan doesn't ask anything else about our schemes, though I know he wants to. But when we come to the rushing water of the Yough, he draws her into a tight hug as if she spent the whole month with me and not just a few days.

"Take care of yourself," Tristan says. "You're welcome at my table any time."

I wonder if he'll say the same thing to me, when I leave. I think of his face when he pulled me up from underwater in the waterfall pool. I can't imagine him saying goodbye to me in such a cordial, friendly way—it's better to not say goodbye at all.

She nods, gripping him back. "I'm glad you're not a murderer," she says.

He snorts, releasing her. And then she turns to me.

The look on her face is unreadable when she opens her arm and pulls me into them. Jess, my best and dearest friend, the only one who knew the truth of it all and didn't hold it against me. Her grip is too tight, and mine is too—she's taller than me, and I bury my face in her shoulder. She holds me as if letting go would be the greatest sin of all.

"Be safe," I whisper against her: a plea, a promise, a prayer.

"I'll be waiting on the other side," she says back. It's not a goodbye.

I look up at her. There's the potential that this can all go very wrong, that this may be the last time she ever sees me alive. She leans in and kisses me on the cheek.

"You were never ruined to me," she says, and I can hear the pain in her voice. I should've spared her my song—perhaps that would have made this easier. But I think she needed to hear it just as much as I needed to sing it. The words that tore me open, blood and bones and gristle, must be the same ones she holds in her heart. Maybe every girl in Winston has them sewed upon their skin through years and years of growing up under the pressure of perfection.

Understanding rushes through me. It's not Tristan who can save me—no one can. I had to be the one to allow myself to open up, to let someone see me for something else. Jess has been here the whole time, waiting for me to realize it myself.

I wish I could say that I understand. Thank her. But she is stepping away, and there are words that we will say to each other later, words that will make sense. Maybe we're just not good at the words—she knows who I am. And now I see her for who she is.

That day on the riverbank feels so odd, so foreign. She didn't speak for me. She did so much more—she saved me, when I could not save myself.

"Promise you'll come for me?" she asks. But I know what she means: *Promise you'll come back.*

"I swear it," I say.

At this, Jess finally lets go. Tristan and I watch as she makes her way down the bank and steps hesitantly into the water. She is a good swimmer, I tell myself; she'll be fine. We've been in the Yough so many times. And no one else knows she's gone—there's no one on the other side waiting for her.

And we're right. Jess crosses over, steps onto the dry land of the other bank. She doesn't glance back at us as she raises a hand in goodbye. And then she's walking up the slope toward the road, the cemetery, the clapboard church. The place we've called home our whole lives. The place that destroyed us, that we may never escape from.

In the glimmer of dawn coming from the east, Tristan reaches out and takes my hand.

Twenty-Seven

We spend the day pretending that nothing is going to happen. Normalcy is a balm. I will soothe myself with routine, choke down the agony of leaving and replace it with duty.

I snatch a few hours of sleep, then wake to a hot breakfast on Fletcher's tray. They walk me to Ruth's, where I sing to the garden, and thank the memories of those who did not make it back, and do my best not to cry when she grasps my hand and tells me to take care of myself. I don't break; I don't bend nor push. Everything is fine. It will be fine.

There is no mention of Owen. I imagine Tristan will retrieve him tomorrow before we set off back to Winston.

But I push through. We have dinner together, a roast with potatoes and parsnips and carrots and good bread and butter, then dessert of sweet cherry pie. In the sitting room, Tristan and Fletcher take turns reading me stories from a book of folk-tales from the wood. They're not like our stories of princesses and kings and queens, but of Lords and trees and the spirit that resides in time.

I think about asking about those two deer I saw when I arrived into this realm, dead, their antlers twisted. But after living so many deaths in so little time, I want to keep myself here, in the realm of the living.

When the fire gutters low and the shadows are dark in the corners, I go to bed and try to will myself to sleep. To become something else.

It's my last night here, in this room that was once Tristan's. I stare at the ceiling and imagine what it was like to grow up here. To be so massively loved. I roll onto my side and look at the open wardrobe of Ruth's things, left to a girl she didn't know for no reason other than she wanted to make me feel comfortable.

So much care, so many sacrifices that are so easy that they aren't sacrifices at all. I wonder what it would feel like to be a part of something like that. To belong.

When I cannot find rest, I am hardly surprised. And then I am sitting, breaking through this haze of grief, and making my way quietly out the door.

I know the path to Tristan's room well—I take it nearly every day to raid his knitwear collection. But this is different. Tristan is *inside*, and I know it.

Whit sleeps at his door. I rub the great wolf's white head and whisper for him to let me in. He shifts, moving a few feet down the hall, gazing at me with his luminescent eyes. There's no whine in protest when I enter Tristan's room and let the door slip shut behind me.

He sleeps spread out along the bed, one hand knotted in the covers, the other resting on his bare chest. The window is cracked slightly, letting the cool air in. Tristan's boots are by the door; his circlet is back on its cushion. All of these are the trappings of what he is, the Lord of the Wood.

"Leah?"

I didn't notice him stirring, but he blinks at me blearily. I move like a ghost when he lifts the covers slightly, slipping in next to him. He is so warm, heat radiating through the covers. He turns onto his side so he can face me. I bury my cold feet against his warm calves, and he groans.

"You're *freezing.*"

"It's not my fault you don't have heaters."

"We have fireplaces," he growls, drawing me close up against him. I melt into his warmth.

I can't convince myself that I'm just here to steal his body heat—and neither can he. He is awake now, sleepy but present, and serious above all. He traces his fingertips over my cheek-bones. Runs a thumb over my lip.

"Why didn't you tell me?" he asks.

"About?"

"Owen."

I frown. I don't want to talk about it—but I do owe him answers. If the shift is coming, now that he's had more time to think about it, now that he sees me for who and what I am, I might as well get the heartbreak over with.

"I haven't told anybody," I say. "Jess only knows because she was there when I took the tests. Pastor Samuel knows because he overheard my prayers. And Mom and Dad only know because Samuel told them. So, I just. I don't know. It's like, if I don't say it, it's not true."

His fingers continue their maddening sweep back and forth, now skimming over my ear, down my throat, across my collarbone.

"You weren't . . . taken advantage of?"

I wince. "No," I say. Then, flushing red, "You saw the memory. Part of it, at least. I wanted it. I just . . . wasn't prepared. We were safe, in the ways we should've been, but something went wrong. I should've expected it." *I should've expected to be broken, impossible to piece back together.*

"You made one mistake," Tristan murmurs, swiping his thumb back over my throat. I shiver, feeling the goosebumps on my arms. "Not even a mistake—a choice."

"Mm. And it'll haunt me forever."

"It doesn't have to," Tristan says. He hesitates, like he's afraid of how I'll react. "You can leave Owen here. He'll grow up well.

Loved. He'll want for nothing."

I shake my head, fighting against the lump in my throat. "It's not that," I say. "They don't . . . if they were given the choice, they'd keep him. Not me. I don't mean as much to them. I don't know how to be the daughter they love anymore. I'm only a reminder of all the pain I've caused, all the things I've done wrong."

"Then *you* stay," Tristan says, his nose skimming my shoulder. "Stay here. With me."

Desire coils in my belly. I shift, moving under him as he rolls his weight up, hovers over me. His mismatched eyes are like coals of different heats, burning in the night.

"Wanting something . . . desire . . . lust . . . those are not inhuman things, Leah," he says. His eyes skim over me, and I feel exposed under his gaze. "In fact, I would say they're very, *very* human."

I lay my hand flat on his chest, fingers spread. If I shifted my hand up, locked on his shoulder, pulled him down . . . the thought is dangerous. Dangerous, and wanted.

"You are not a broken thing," Tristan says again.

I look up at him, feeling the last of my resolve melt. Maybe he's right. Maybe I'm not terrible because of this, because desire grows hotter in my veins. "Make me feel whole," I ask, and I nearly shiver at the dark look that comes across Tristan's face at my insistence.

His head dips, mouth going to the soft juncture of my neck and shoulder. I can't stop the sigh that escapes me as his lips trace lower, over my collarbone, my shoulder, then circles back to my neck. I shift my hands to his back, uncertain what to do with them—it's been so long since I've done anything with anyone, and even then, it was only a couple of times, fumbling in the back of Trent's car.

But this is not fumbling. Tristan is not ashamed, not afraid, as he pulls the nightgown up and over my head. As his mouth goes to my chest, my stomach, as his hands slide over my hips. As one of his hands slips between my thighs. I gasp at the contact and he pulls away, watching my face.

"Is this okay?" he asks.

I don't have words. I only pull his lips down to mine, consuming, as he continues his agonizing pattern.

And then his mouth is gone, and he is sliding down my body. I watch, terrified, entranced, as he kisses the scars Owen left behind, then my hipbone. His eyes are wicked and demanding as he slips lower, and then I feel his mouth on me.

Everything splinters. My thoughts are cluttered, chaotic, and I am lost to sensation. But this is what I know: I do not feel like a ruined girl in Tristan's bed. His mouth on me is honey-sweet. He is a knight against the worst thoughts I've ever had of myself all stacked together.

I knot my fingers in his hair, pulling him back to me as the world bursts apart in a blaze of light. I am not drowning, not submerged. I am so goddamn alive that I don't even remember what it felt like to be suffocating.

If this is what he can offer me, I don't know how I can bear to go back to Winston.

After, he tucks me up against him, his front to my back, as he kisses my shoulder and my neck. He expects nothing of me and I don't know how to react to that, but I don't have the brain space to care. I relax into him, pretend that the words he whispers to me are real and true.

Dawn is not that far away. And when it breaks, when the sun comes again, all of this will be over. And I will find myself again unmade.

Twenty-Eight

The banks of the Youghiogheny are cold and dark. Above us, stars are still visible, and probably will be for another hour or so. The path is speckled with little red and white flowers—trilliums, Tristan told me on the walk over. The flower of his domain. A mark of his power.

Tristan and I stand together, arms barely touching, and look at the shadows on the other side.

He woke me too early this morning to press a kiss to my shoulder, and then he let me sleep while he went to do his preparations for my return.

In my bedroom, the dress I arrived in waited. I shouldn't have been surprised to see it, shouldn't have felt so viscerally off guard. Ruth washed it and managed to get out the mud and dirt of the river, but the impression of the bloody handprint is still there, brown against the white fabric. But I was to leave this world as I came into it. Ashes to ashes. Dust to dust. Dress to dress.

I gritted my teeth and put it on.

When I came downstairs for a slice of bread and tea, Fletcher was already up despite the fact that it was barely the middle of the night. They braided my hair nice and tight and sat with me until Tristan returned with Ruth and Andrew, Owen bundled in his arms.

No one chided me when I turned my face away.

Now, Tristan still holds the bundle in his arms. He promised he would carry Owen through the woods, help take away some of the weight, if he could. In return, I carry his mask, the trappings of his Lordship. But the time has come for me to take it on. I open my arms, and Tristan gives me the bundle back and takes his mask.

"You don't have to go through with this," Tristan says for the hundredth time. But Jess is waiting on the other side. My whole life is there. I do. I *must*.

"You know every reason why I have to," I say.

Tristan nods. His face is shadowed, but I can still read the sorrow there. Suddenly, it's too much—I'm too afraid.

"Tristan," I say, my voice ragged. "I don't—I don't know what to believe in."

This softens him, turns him considerate. He sighs, looking out into the darkness of the trees. "The things you believe, the things you were taught . . . they don't align with the way you were treated. Be kind to yourself now. Worry about eternity later."

It's not an answer, but it's something. "What do you believe in?"

He leans forward, presses a kiss to my lips. I want to stay, more than I can confess, more than I can imagine saying out loud. "Come back here and I'll tell you. If you change your mind," he whispers into the inch of space between us, "turn around. Look back. I'll be here waiting for you."

I grip his arm with my free hand. If only it were so easy. But it's not. And we have a plan to finish.

He offers me a sip from the flask in his hand. It's the same tea that Maria drank, bitter and herby. That all of them did. I swallow it down, feeling the press of all those ghosts against my heart. For just a second, I can see Maria's ghost standing behind Tristan, waiting for me to make my next move.

I turn and face the other side. There are no sounds in the wood behind me, not even as Tristan lowers the deer skull mask to cover his face. I walk forward until I can feel the cold water seeping in through my shoes.

The shadows on the other side move forward to meet me. There are three of them—not that many, which is good. In other memories, I can recall as many as eight. But there's no reason to think I'll put up a fight. I've always been a docile thing, obedient, until I wasn't.

I knot my fingers in Owen's blanket and keep going. The river rushes around me, so cold that it knocks the wind out of me. But I move forward, and I watch the closest figure, one I think is Pastor Samuel, as he matches me step for step.

The water is at my thighs. My hips. My waist, up to my chest, to the point Owen should start screaming. It washes away all the things I did in the wood, all the things that happened to me before. I am whole and unbreakable in its grasp.

I take a deep breath, watching the shadowed form of Pastor Samuel as he hesitates, just a few feet away. I need to be ready. To be perfect.

I cannot look behind me.

When the water closes over my head, I know that death could be moments away. At least I became something other than the girl who always thought she was expendable.

The anticipation of drowning is dark on my tongue. I know, through seven deaths, what the river water tastes like. What it will feel like invading my mouth, my nose, my throat. What it will feel like as whatever makes me me slips out of me, fades to nothing.

I hope against hope not to give my body the eighth memory of death.

The hands are on my shoulders, pushing me down. They don't expect me to fight back, to expect it—and they don't think I'll let go of Owen. But I open my arms, releasing the pillow wrapped in

Owen's blanket, letting the current carry it away. When the cord comes around my neck, one of my hands is up, around my throat, protective. The other goes to my belt, fighting through my skirts in the water. My fingers wrap around the cold metal of Tristan's knife—too low. I slip off the handle and feel the bite of metal on my palm.

But it doesn't matter. Blood doesn't matter when I'm fighting for my life.

The cord wraps around me, my wrist caught up with my throat. But I can breathe, and when I break the surface, they're not expecting that. Not expecting the knife that I plunge into the side of the attacker in front of me, the one meant to hold me down; nor are they expecting the line of people dressed in animal skulls on the other side, all posed with weapons ready.

The howl of a wolf sounds, then splashing. The gnash of teeth, a scream behind me. Whit has launched himself into the river, gotten his big teeth into some fleshy part of the man that tried to strangle me from behind. The water froths pink with blood, canine snarling mixing with human profanity.

"You *bitch*," Samuel growls when he sees it, trying to grip my hair. Of course he's there, his image bleary and hazy in front of me, but it's him. Unmistakable. He struggles to grip my hair, to find purchase. But Fletcher braided it so tightly around my head that he can't pull it free.

I see her, beside me in the water, dress undisturbed by the

river. Maria. I watch for a split second as she wraps her hand over mine, guides the knife, and stabs him again.

I grit my teeth even though I know this is a bad idea. I'll let her have her revenge.

Samuel cries out, and he and the man behind me try to push me under. The first arrow makes the smallest sound as it flies from Tristan's bow and strikes the man behind me in the shoulder. He cries out and lets go, giving me the ability to make it out. I drag myself against the current, up on the other side.

Samuel is breathing hard, trying to get back to me, but he's hurt and the water is cold and I'm sure he's getting tired. Downriver, Jess is coming out of the woods, Owen wrapped safely in her arms from Ruth's handoff. I recognize the other man in the water as Mr. Benton, the one who leered at me when I was offered to the wood. Perhaps he knew this would be coming all along. And the third person on the bank, wide-eyed with his hands up, is Jake Benton. He's in my grade. I stare at him, pressing my bleeding hand to my soaked white dress, looking like a feral thing from the wood. Stricken, he stares back.

"Did you know they would do this?" I ask, unable to hide the rage in my voice. There's too much river water in me, and I spit it to one side, wiping my mouth, probably streaking it with blood. Everything hurts, but the betrayal hurts worse.

"They said they were coming to pray," Jake says, lips barely moving, like he's too numb to process what just happened. "A sunrise devotional."

I shake my head, moving past them. Mr. Benton and Samuel have dragged themselves back onto the shore. Jess shifts Owen into her other arm and approaches them, zooming in on the video she's recording on her phone, making sure to get their faces. Before anything else can happen, she sends it to me, backs it up in a safe place. It's a protection: Everyone will know that Samuel tried to drown me, that I acted out of self-defense.

"I'll kill you for this!" Mr. Benton shouts at my back. I flip him off. Truly, it would be better to give the signal, for Tristan to kill them both, for us to push their bodies in the river, but that's not the kind of retribution I came seeking. If they're going to go after the Lord of the Wood themselves, I'd rather they drown at their own hands and not mine.

I'm halfway to the church when Jess makes it to the road, Owen in her arms. She flings herself into her truck and locks the doors, just like we arranged. She's safe as can be, and I feel better with her contained.

She watches my back as I finish the path through the cemetery, passing the place where all those girls should've been buried.

The church smells of dust and pages, burnt candles and decaying flowers from Sunday's service. I march straight up the same aisle that I walked down a month before. Then, the eyes of the town were on me.

I don't have a problem with my faith, my God. I think I still believe in it—I don't think I can become unmoored, believing in nonexistence. But that's not the problem. It's the men like Pastor Samuel, like Mr. Benton, like all those men who came before, who sneered at me and took advantage of us and killed us when we became too inconvenient.

That's not the testament I believe in. That's not the rock I cling to. I make my way down the aisle, dripping river water the whole way, all the way to the altar. The bowl sits on the altar, half-full of clotted red liquid. I hesitate despite myself.

Tristan said the bowl would fill to announce when I was coming home. I thought it would fill with water—but no. It's full of blood. Perhaps I should've expected that.

I think of my own body in the wood, of Maria's ghost. It's our blood that fills this bowl, hungry for a new girl, a new sacrifice.

I take it in my hands. It's heavier than I expected, but not too heavy that I can't lift it high over my head and let it drop. Let it fall. Blood splatters, covering the stone floor, splashing the lectern and the pulpit, even spraying the first two rows of pews with ruby droplets. But the bowl does not survive the fall. When it hits the stone floor, it breaks in half.

"Leah Jones!"

I look up. It's Samuel, outlined in the open door. The sun rises, casting everything in eerie gold. I imagine I'm a horror, dripping with river water and covered in the blood that splashed from the basin, the ghost of his handprint a brown smudge on my chest.

But I don't care.

He starts toward me, undeterred by his stab wounds. I scrabble back, nearly slipping on the blood that slicks the stones.

If he gets to me—knowing what I know, I have no doubt he'll kill me. Perhaps it's the kind of retribution that needs to happen. If my love is sacrifice, then this is my last gift to the town I wanted so desperately to love me back.

Take me. Take me, and never again ruin another girl like you ruined me. I feel the slick handle of the knife, back in its holster, and draw it again. I will not go down without a fight. I will take Samuel down with me until both of our blood mixes with the gore by the altar, until we're both gnashed to nothing.

A second figure appears in the shaded entryway. Not Tristan, but a woman—her coiled red hair sticks out in pieces from the skeletal mask she wears. She sings something, just barely inaudible, and raises her hands from her sides.

Ruth.

She is the keeper of the ghosts, the memories, the echoes. She's the keeper of the girls like me who wanted so badly to make it back and drowned halfway across the river, lost to time, going down without a fight because they didn't know any better.

When the ghosts come, they do not hold back. They pour into the church, none of them masked in beauty and life. They're all dead, bloated things, all rotted and slick with gore, strangled and drowned. I see Maria, the one who unlocked it all; Susan and

Thea and Penny and Marjorie, and the ones whose names I never learned. At least a dozen of them stream up the aisle, silent as the grave, and wrap their skeletal, fish-eaten hands around Pastor Samuel. I force myself to listen as he screams, force myself to watch as they drag him away. I follow behind, tracking bloody footprints down the aisle, down the stairs of the church.

Ruth leads the way for the ghost girls, the murdered, the drowned, the forgotten. I don't know if Samuel is still alive by the time they reach the Yough, or Mr. Benton, but it doesn't matter for long. They disappear under the surface with the girls, leaving Jess sobbing with her face turned, Owen crying, and Jake Benton screaming in horror.

"Do something!" he begs me. Pleads. But I only stand there, still as a statue, until the river is again placid and lazy.

I wish there was something I could say to him about this place and it's legacy, and how we can't carry on like this. But I have no words left. I go to Jess, press a bloody kiss to her cheek, and take my baby from her arms.

"Is that your blood?" she asks, tears running down her cheeks. She wipes them away, tries to stop her hysterical breathing. I feel like I should be more stressed, like her. More reactive. But all I feel is a vast, terrible emptiness—and even worse, relief.

"No," I say. I hesitate, watching her face. "I have to do something. And then . . . can I meet you at your house?"

Jess nods. We both look across to that far bank, but nothing remains. Not even bones.

Twenty-Nine

When I knock on the door, there's a shuffling sound from inside the house, a call of "Who is it?," profanity as Mom bangs some body part on the coffee table. All of the sounds are so familiar that it makes my stomach ache. When she wrenches the door open, I'm certain I'm the last person she expects to see—let alone covered in blood, holding Owen, who has somehow managed to fall back asleep after the entire ordeal. Perhaps he prefers chaos above all else. Maybe he's a bit like me that way.

I see myself in her face. I think, when I grow older, I'll look more and more like her. The lines of my face will follow the patterns hers have already set. I'll gray in the same way, starting just above the ears, then on the crown of my head.

I remember, once, when I was a little girl. I couldn't sleep, crying about monsters in the closet, and she slipped into the narrow twin bed next to me. She pulled me to her chest, enveloping me with her body, a protection and a shelter. *I loved you before I ever knew you*, she used to tell me. *I loved you before you existed.*

She loved me so much. More than anything. More than anyone. I have lost it, been cast out of the castle, burned and shattered and soiled every good thing she ever saw in me. My mother. My mirror. My reflection. If she loved Owen like that too, before she knew him, before he existed, I wonder if it sucked away all the love she once felt for me.

But perhaps that's too harsh.

"L—Leah?" she says, shock clear on her face. Her shoulders sag, the fight going out of her. She looks older since the last time I saw her. I probably do too.

"Was I ever what you wanted me to be?" I ask.

"Why are you covered in blood?" she asks in return, waking up, moving back from the door, recoiling. After all this time, even when I've done what she'd ask of me, she *recoils* from me when it's even a bit unpleasant.

I bite down the anger—she grew up just as afraid of the Lord as I did, and can I fault her for that? Maybe. Because she threw me to the wolves when I needed her most, and I don't know if I'll ever be able to forgive her for that.

"Was I ever enough?" I ask, the sobs clawing from my throat before I can keep them down. My fingers hold Owen too tight, and he stirs, fussing against my chest. I wonder if he smells the blood, red and rich as the day it flowed out of me when he was born.

"You were my baby," Mom says, pressing a hand to her mouth. I wonder if she thinks I'm going to die—if she wants me to. Perhaps it would've been easier for her if I never came back. But all this blood isn't mine. Maybe that's a disappointment, too.

"Take him," I say, thrusting Owen out toward her. She doesn't even seem to think, acting on instinct as her arms open, as she cradles him. His fussing starts to go worse, hands and fists flying, wrecking the tight swaddle Tristan put him in this morning.

I turn away. For the first time, Owen cries out for me.

But I don't stop until I get to Jess's house. The door is open for me. She waits in her room, towel and clean clothes already set aside. She's still in her robe, hair wet from her own shower. I lock myself in her bathroom and strip off my wet, bloody clothes. Under the spray of the shower, where no one can hear me, where the water closes in on all sides, I allow myself to weep.

Oddly, unexpectedly, Trent McCoy is the first to visit me at Jess's. Though her mom isn't thrilled with housing me, she doesn't care enough to send me home. So, Jess and I are eating chips on the couch, watching as much *Below Deck* as we possibly can. Fletcher's right—it's terrible, but also wonderful, and more than anything, it's a welcome distraction.

We exchange a look. Both of us expect it to be my mother.

But it's not. Trent shifts his weight back and forth. In one hand, he has a bouquet of gaudy flowers, dyed Uniontown school colors for homecoming. I suck a breath through my teeth.

He hasn't talked to me since I came back to school. I think he knows, even though we never talked about it. That he put the pieces together.

"Leah?" he says, eyes searching my face. I remember when I thought he was the most beautiful boy in the world. "I just wanted to say that I'm sorry. For all the things that, um, you went through. And Jake just called me—I didn't know. I didn't know that, uh, they were going to do those things to you. If I had—"

"You don't have to defend yourself to me," I say, feeling the new flex of steel in my backbone.

He pushes the flowers toward me. "I should've figured it out, and maybe a part of me did, but uh. I didn't really . . . think too much about it. About most things. I didn't even know Owen was really yours until you were gone, and the rumors started, and then, uh, I realized that if he's yours, he's probably mine too. Unless there was someone else and—"

"There was no one else," I grit through my teeth. Not that it would matter. Behind me, Jess shifts on the couch, trying to get a better look at Trent around my body. "And you're not even on the birth certificate. You don't owe us anything. If that's what you're worried about."

I knew better than to go seeking him out, than to confront him, his family, our community with the truth of what happened. And now, looking back on it all, that was probably my best decision. That I got to face Tristan and the wood on my own terms.

For all I know, someone could've told Trent the secret of the LoW. Could've made him offer me, offer Owen, before the thought left me and caught. But none of that matters now, not really.

I lean against the door jamb, keeping my arms crossed. I don't hate Trent—I don't even think he used me. We had a thing, and now we don't, and it's as simple as that. I had to pay for it and he didn't.

But revenge still sings in my veins. When I close my eyes, I can still see the blood in the water, Whit's jaws clamping on Mr. Benton's flesh, the ghost's fingers digging in like claws when they dragged Samuel away.

"If I knew . . ." Trent says.

The words hang in the air between us. If he knew, then what? Then we'd be parents? We'd take Owen on, for real? I can't imagine it, the two of us drifting together, Trent getting some dead-end job to keep us alive, probably growing to hate each other. Or offering me to the wood himself. Or pretending that I was crazy, some girl out to trap him to keep him, all the hateful things we say about girls like me who end up with their choices taken away.

"It doesn't matter anymore," I say—and it doesn't. This whole conversation is just an exercise in poking at old bruises that don't hurt anymore. "Owen's not mine. My parents took him in, legally, and in all the ways that count. You don't have to worry about me, him, us."

"I'm sorry," he says, like he needs to get it all out. "That you were the one punished, when we both made a mistake."

But it wasn't a mistake. Not the act itself—we were safe as could be, but that didn't really matter, did it? The mistake was that every single choice I thought I had evaporated. Every support turned against me. And the fallout was exactly what I expected.

"Thanks, Trent," I manage. I don't take his flowers. I shut the door and turn my back to it, lean against the wood, slide down to the floor.

"That was . . . interesting," Jess says, watching me closely.

I hug my knees to my chest. Wrap my arms around them.

"I'm not mad about Trent," I say. "It's everything else. That I . . .
I wish Owen was someone else's. From someone else's body. I
wish unconditional love was unconditional. I wish I had snuck
away and done something about it when I had the chance."

Jess's smile is thin.

"Am I a bitch?" I ask.

"Yes," Jess says decisively, scooting next to me and draping
her arm over my shoulder. "And I love you for it."

Thirty

I can't stay with Jess forever, but it turns out okay. Kara Merritt, the artist a year older than us, who lives above the bookstore, needs someone to help keep her workshop clean and tidy. In return, she offers me her spare room. I split my time between there, school, picking up shifts at the gas station, and hanging at Jess's house. I try to keep up with school, and actually accept Jess's help when she offers it, but I don't know how much it all matters.

They never found the bodies of Pastor Samuel and Mr. Benton. Jake Benton doesn't spill, either—he tells police that they were doing a devotional in the river, got swept away. Everyone expects them to wash up at some point, but I don't know. I don't know if the ghosts left anything behind to find.

The first few weeks back at school are as weird as I would've expected but I go, to keep Jess off my back, to see if it's worth becoming something else. Someone else. As the leaves shift from orange to brown, fall in great heaps along the ground, as the first frost creeps closer, she talks excitedly about college applications. She puts Kara's address in so many info request inquiries that Kara starts using them to protect the furniture instead of newspapers.

I want to say things got better, or felt like they did. That people stopped whispering when I walked into the parties Jess dragged me to, that I didn't stop going to church even when the new pastor came, that I didn't feel the aching gnaw of emptiness growing in my chest. I want to say that I found something to believe in, reckoned with the faith I can't put down in a way that makes sense; or even that I found a way to be kind to myself. That I didn't spend inordinate amounts of time staring out of my bedroom window that overlooked the forest, searching for eyes, for bones, for a flash of Tristan's hair. Winter comes roaring with ice on its teeth and nothing changes. It only dulls, settles, as snow comes and melts and finally sticks.

But there are moments of reprieve. Kara is kind, and a good roommate, who makes me feel like at least some of this town doesn't hate me. Jess is steadfast as always, and it's the least I can do to read over her college admissions essays, offering critique when I can, and pretend I'm writing my own.

It's all a game of pretend, in a way. Pretending that I don't miss the wood and all within it. That I see any sort of future for myself. But I wake up, every day, and get dressed, and do the things I need to do. I push and push, willing the numbness to retract, for contentment to settle. I seek the small things that don't hurt. I don't think of drowning.

In the last week of November, I take a trip to the grocery store to pick up Kara's nondairy butter and a few packs of ramen for me. I keep my hood up, my head down, like I always do when I'm out in Winston these days. I'm halfway through the dairy aisle when I hear a familiar laugh, high and lilting, and it's like a knife to my chest.

I turn. Mom is leaning over the grocery cart, grabbing cream cheese for Thanksgiving. Owen is strapped into a baby seat, kicking his legs. He wears a puffer coat and a hat, and he looks so much bigger than the last time I saw him.

Breath whistles between my teeth. I drop the not-butter and the tub hits the floor with a thud. Mom looks over—and doesn't look away.

I don't look away either.

She loved me so much, once. Before she knew me. Before I existed. Maybe she loves me still, in a far-off way that can only hurt and hurt and hurt.

"Leah," she says wearily.

I wonder if she hated me as much as she loved me when I was born. If I came into the world screaming and I've been a disappointment ever since, if she wanted me to hurt as much as she did. But somehow I don't think that's true. I remember the tender moments, her scraping my hair into ponytails, giggling as we made cookies together; her hand in mine on the beach on the one and only vacation we took by the sea in the summer after Grammy died.

Maybe when she looks at Owen she sees all the ways that I went wrong, and the ways that she could be better.

I nod to her. She nods back. Strangers. So much of my DNA is in this grocery aisle but I turn away, drop the rest of my basket by the checkout, and keep on walking.

That's the first night that I think I can't bear it—that I can't do it. That this life might not be for me after all. Every day spent staring out the window at school, every party where someone calls me a whore under their breath, every odd, unreadable glance from Trent. It all adds up into one picture: Peace has returned to Winston, and I have no place in the community that exists now, even if I gave up everything to protect it.

On New Year's Eve, it's so cold that stepping outside feels like a meeting with death. I lock the door to Kara's walk-up behind me, then drop the keys through the mail slot of the bookstore. They'll get back to her eventually.

Other kids are out at parties or with their families, doing

normal things that people do to celebrate endings and beginnings. I am bundled from head to toe—it's not a long walk, but it's only going to get colder—braced against the wind. I take a detour through the cemetery to kneel at Grammy's headstone, to press my lips once against the frigid stone. The cold from the ground seeps through my skin, making my knees ache.

The river isn't frozen. Terrible as it is, it isn't quite cold enough for that yet. Cursing myself, I take off my heavy jacket, my scarf, my boots. Jess will come for them in the morning. For now, I am alone—she knew I needed to do it myself.

My legs are bare in the moonlight under the hem of my dress. I strip off my wool socks and stuff them in my boots, gasping at the cold mud of the river bank against my toes.

It'll be over soon.

The profanity that comes out of my mouth when my feet hit the water is fairly creative, but I push onward. Feet submerged, sure of myself, I turn around, walking backwards deeper and deeper into the river.

I don't know if this is going to work the way I hope it will, but it should, and I pray that it does—I want to come out on the other side clean and whole, made anew.

"I'm looking back," I say to the frosted trees, the old church, the cemetery. "I'm turning around."

The water is icy, cold enough to knock the wind right out of me when I duck my head under. But I come up, eyes closed, hands pressed to my face, and spit out the water. I push my hair back and look over my shoulder.

He couldn't have known I was coming, but the how doesn't matter. When I look at the far bank, Tristan waits for me on the other side.

I push myself forward, out of the freezing river, up on the bank. He's there immediately, unpinning his cape and wrapping it around my shoulders, trying to rub warmth back into my skin.

"You're a fool," he says delightedly, pulling me close against him. It's still cold on this side, but it doesn't have the same bite.

"You came for me."

"I would always come for you," he promises. "I waited for you."

I slide my fingers past his heavy coat, under his shirt. He shivers when my frozen fingers press against his skin, but his smile crushes any fear I have of him rebuking me.

"How did you know?" I ask.

He does not answer, but his eyes glimmer with something I dare not speak into existence. He knew. Of course he knew.

"Let's get you home and warm," he says, but he makes no move, like he's unable to take his eyes away from my face. I can't blame him—I'm drinking him in the same way, memorizing the planes of his face after months apart. Searching for differences, anchoring myself in the fact that he is exactly the same as I remember.

"Did you bring shoes?" I ask. "I didn't."

He laughs, and then his lips are on mine, warm and beseeching and begging all at once. I kiss him back, warmth running through my veins. "I'll carry you," he says against my skin.

"It's far," I murmur back.

He kisses my forehead, pulls away so he can look at me. "Until the end of time. To the end of the earth. I will carry you as far as I go, across this world and back."

Warmth blooms in my chest. I press my hand against his skin, feeling his heartbeat thud against my fingers. "It's not *that* far."

He swings me up into his arms and the laugh that bubbles out of me is unlike any I've felt before, carefree and open.

Tristan smirks, leaning in to steal one more kiss. "I'll take the long way."

Acknowledgements

First, a confession: I never intended to write this book. When I was putting my option materials together, this was the absolute last thing on my mind—and then a chain of events kicked off in the US, and it was impossible not to pour that anger into something that hurt.

I can never thank my editor, Lauren Knowles, enough for her patience, kindness, and sincerity while working on this project. Lauren understood the book from the very first draft, and I am eternally grateful for her insight. I would not have managed this project without the guidance of my agents, Uwe Stender and Amelia Appel, who continuously support me (even when I turn up with surprise projects that are *nothing* like what we previously discussed—sorry!!). Thank you to the entirety of Team Triada for all of the support and guidance, especially to Brent Taylor for wrangling rights.

The team at Page Street YA has been incredible to work with over the last few years and I genuinely cannot believe that this is our fourth book together. Lauren Cepero is a publicity miracle worker, and I owe literally all commercial success to her hard work. Many thanks to the whole team: Will Kiester, Lizzy Mason, Hayley Gundlach, Shannon Dolley and Cas Jones. I am forever indebted to Tristan Elwell for creating such a beautiful cover illustration, and to Rosie Stewart for designing the cover and book.

Across the pond, the team at Titan Books has also been amazing from day one. Michael Beale, you are a force to be reckoned with, and your insightful, intelligent commentary brightens my day. To George, Nick, Viv, Paul, Ian, and the rest of the team: you're all legends.

My family has loved and supported me through it all, and they remain much better than the families I write about. Much love to my parents, Vic and Jane; my sister, Lex, and her husband James; and to Dana and Tony; Kim and Craig; Susan; Lindaly and Win Sr; Jeanna, Michael, Mikey, and Mickaylin; Win, Crystal, Kayliegh, Ava, and Gracie; and all family; Grandma Peg; Stacey, Doug, Jacob, and Squid; Jeff, Britt, Chris, and Taylor; Morgan, Ronnie, Nora, and Jackson; and all others. My love and thanks also goes to Shirley, Ken, Andy, Judith, Katie, Josie, Anna, Maisie, Archie, Christopher, and all of the Moss, McKenzie, Mutchell, and Bird families for taking me in, supporting me, and being overall wonderful. MAC, I still have not written a book appropriate for you to read—but there is still time, and maybe someday you'll be old enough for this one (though I will beg you not to read it, love you, thanks). My love and thanks to my wonderful, supportive friends: Becca, Kat, Rebekah, Erin, Lara, Mike, Kali, Katina, Joe V., Jess H., Rachel, Michael, and Kish.

This book would not exist without Tasha Suri and Shakira Toussaint, who listened to me ramble and offered advice and encouragement when I was too afraid to commit to a book concept that scared me so, so much. Thanks to my writing friends, who are so damn talented, and impress me always: Kelsey R., Alechia D., Courtney G., Allison S., Chloe G., and Alex B. My love and thanks to the London crowd, who have to deal with me and my various breakdowns: Daphne, Kat, Saara, Karin, Cherae, Samantha, Sarah, Emma, and Maddy—even though I don't see y'all all the time, it always is a delight when I do. Special thanks to the ever-supportive team at RHUL for insightful discussion and guidance. My love, adoration, and thanks goes out to Caitlin, Katie, Debbie, Davi, Bec, Ellie, Romie, Yas, Tiffany, Imi, Lauren, Akash, Jane, Hannah, Nel, and Atiya, who make day-to-day life so much fun.

Thank you to all of the booksellers, bloggers, bookstagrammers, booktubers, and booktokers who supported my work along the way. I am constantly awestruck by the love and dedication readers put into reviews, videos, and content, and I am honored that anyone reads my books, let alone takes the time to talk about them.

Thanks to Sir Gordon, who continues to be the loudest cat in Buckinghamshire. And last of all, thank you to my husband, Matt (please note, reader, that we are not married at the time in which I am writing this, but we *will* be married when this is published, so . . . husband it is). Thank you for supporting and encouraging me, and for dealing with my enormous and ever-growing book collection. You are, without a doubt, the weirdest and best person I have ever met, and I am very lucky to love you.

About the Author

Tori Bovalino (she/her) is the author of *The Devil Makes Three* and *Not Good for Maidens*, and edited the Indie-bestselling anthology, *The Gathering Dark*. She is originally from Pittsburgh, Pennsylvania and now lives in the UK with her partner and their very loud cat. Tori loves scary stories, obscure academic book facts, and impractical, oversized sweaters. She can be found on Instagram as @toribovalino.

OTHER BOOKS
BY TORI BOVALINO
FOR PAGE STREET
PUBLISHING

An Anthology of Folk Horror

The
Gathering
Dark

Edited by Tori Bovalino

not good for maidens

tori bovalino

THE DEVIL
MAKES
THREE

TORI BOVALINO